Albert Marrin

AMERICA AND VIETNAM

The Elephant and the Tiger

VIKING

VIKING
Published by the Penguin Group
Penguin Books USA Inc.,
375 Hudson Street, New York, New York 10014, U.S.A.
Penguin Books Ltd, 27 Wrights Lane, London W8 5TZ, England
Penguin Books Australia Ltd, Ringwood, Victoria, Australia
Penguin Books Canada Ltd, 10 Alcorn Avenue, Toronto, Ontario, Canada M4V 3B2
Penguin Books (N.Z.) Ltd, 182–190 Wairau Road, Auckland 10, New Zealand
Penguin Books Ltd, Registered Offices: Harmondsworth, Middlesex, England

First published in 1992 by Viking Penguin,
a division of Penguin Books USA Inc.

3 5 7 9 10 8 6 4 2

Grateful acknowledgment is made to the following
for permission to reprint copyrighted material:
Alkatraz Corner Music: from "I-Feel-Like-I'm-Fixin'-to-Die-Rag,"
words and music by Joe McDonald. © 1965 Alkatraz Corner
Music. Used by permission.
Appleseed Music, Inc.: from "I Ain't Marchin' Anymore"
by Phil Ochs. © copyright 1964 by Appleseed Music, Inc.
All rights reserved. Used by permission.

Library of Congress Cataloging-in-Publication Data
Marrin, Albert. America in Vietnam: the elephant and the tiger/
by Albert Marrin. p. cm. Summary: Examines the political history,
military events, social impact, and long-term effects of the Vietnam War.
ISBN 0-670-84063-7
1. Vietnamese Conflict, 1961–1975—United States—Juvenile literature.
[1. Vietnamese Conflict, 1961–1975.] I. Title. DS558.M36 1992
959.704'3373—dc20.   91-28795   CIP   AC

Printed in U.S.A.
Set in 11 pt. Bembo

C O N T E N T S

We will be as the elephant and the tiger. When the
elephant is strong and rested near his base we will retreat.
And if the tiger ever pauses, the elephant will impale him
on his mighty tusks. But the tiger will not pause, and the
elephant will die of exhaustion and loss of blood.

—Ho Chi Minh, 1946

Once on the tiger's back, we cannot
be sure of picking the place to dismount.

—George Ball, Undersecretary
of State under LBJ.

*For the POWs, MIAs, and all the
others who deserved better*

AUTHOR'S NOTE

I HAVE WAITED A LONG TIME TO WRITE THIS BOOK. During the Vietnam War—or at least until I became a college teacher in 1968—I taught social studies in a junior high school in New York City. Because I was too old for the draft, there was never any chance that I would be called into the armed forces.

Of course I knew what was happening over there; I saw it every night on television and read about it in the newspapers. Only later did critics of the media reveal how poor the coverage had been at certain times. In any case, the war was, to me, at once distant and very close. It was distant, because I was working hard and studying at Columbia University for an advanced degree in history; close, because it constantly intruded.

At Columbia, I witnessed the student takeover of university buildings and the police "bust" that ended it violently. I heard the cries for revolution and equality. I saw Viet Cong flags on campus and watched the janitor scrubbing anti-

American slogans off the walls of the journalism building.

My own students were often touched by the war, touching me in turn. These were kids who could not afford a college education and the draft deferment that went along with it. Their older brothers went off to Vietnam, and a number of them followed. Occasionally, one of those boys came home in an aluminum box.

When I began writing books, I focused on military history, an area of special interest to me. But Vietnam was a subject I carefully avoided. I felt that the war was still too close to deal with in a book for young people. Vietnam was the longest, and in many ways the most bitter, conflict in American history. It spanned the terms of five presidents, each committed to a part of the world he scarcely understood for stakes higher than his nation could afford to pay. The war—morally, politically, militarily—was so complex that I needed time to sort out the issues in my own mind.

Finally, in 1989, I began to read hundreds of books, articles, and personal accounts by those who had been through it. I interviewed men who had served in Vietnam. And the deeper I delved into the subject, the more I found myself reliving those times. Strangely enough, they now became more real to me than they had been when I lived through them.

It was rough going. The issues were not cut-and-dried matters of good versus evil. Each side had a case which had to be acknowledged. Each side suffered and caused suffering.

Being surprised became a normal part of a day's work. I knew that war is by nature brutal, but I was unprepared for the brutality revealed by my research. Viet Cong terrorism, to give just one example, was shocking. But did this mean our enemy was innately cruel? There is a popular—and unfortunate—notion that Orientals are insensitive, placing less value on human life than Westerners do. But the facts showed that this is a racist myth. Our enemies were people like ourselves, sharing with us the bright and dark sides of human nature. They loved their wives and children and friends. They were just as upset by harm coming to their loved ones as we are. But, as with all peoples, they were able to suppress their humanity for a cause they saw as just and noble and sacred. Similarly, the Americans who committed atrocities, as at My Lai, saw their actions as fit replies to enemy terrorism.

In short, writing about Vietnam has been a learning experience for the author. He can only hope that the reader will find the subject equally enlightening.

LAND OF THE DISTANT SOUTH

Although we have been at times strong
at times weak,
We have at no time lacked heroes.

—*The poet Nguyen Trai, 1428*

ONCE UPON A TIME THE DRAGON LORD OF LAC SET out to explore the lands bordering the Great Salt Water. During his wanderings he saw many strange things and met many strange peoples, but none stranger than the fairy princess Au Co. Fascinated by her beauty, he wooed her, won her, and took her as his wife.

They lived happily until, in time, Au Co gave birth to a sack containing one hundred white eggs. After one week, the eggs hatched into one hundred fine, sturdy sons. Yet the Lord of Lac was deeply troubled. "I am a dragon, you are a fairy," he told his wife sternly. "We cannot remain together." And so, on the day they parted, they shared their sons equally between them. He took his fifty sons to the Kingdom of the Waters; their brothers followed Au Co into the mountains near the present city of Hanoi, where they founded Vietnam. Their descendants still call themselves *Tien Rong*—"Children of Dragons and Fairies."

The story of the Dragon and the Fairy is a legend. But

like most legends, it contains a kernel of truth. Historians believe that the Great Salt Water was actually the South China Sea, and that the Kingdom of the Waters was the area around Canton, a seaport in southern China. In ancient times, the inhabitants of this area were mainly non-Chinese, wanderers from the plains of Mongolia, beyond the Great Wall of China to the far northwest. They called themselves *Viet* after their Chinese name *Yüeh,* or "southerners."

Five centuries before the birth of Christ, the Viet people were attacked by invaders and fled farther south, settling in the mountains near the village of Hanoi. In 208 B.C. they were overrun by a rebel Chinese general, whose army continued down the coast, halting near the present city of Da Nang. The general then declared himself king of Nam Viet—the Land of the Distant South. Later, for reasons that are unclear, the names were reversed and Vietnam was born.

The kingdom of Vietnam existed for less than a century. In 111 B.C. it was conquered by China and remained a province of the Celestial Empire for the next thousand years. China was then the most advanced country on earth, responsible for such engineering feats as the Great Wall, the only man-made object visible from space, and the invention of paper, printing, and gunpowder. It was ruled from the Forbidden City in Beijing by the emperor, known to his millions of subjects as the Son of Heaven, a living god.

In the centuries after the conquest, the Chinese made many improvements in their new province. They built roads and canals and began to develop Haiphong, the seaport that still serves Hanoi. They taught their subjects how to cultivate rice, farm with iron plows, and build dikes to control river flooding. Schools were set up, enabling the Vietnamese to develop a written language. Chinese priests introduced Buddhism, one of the world's great religions.

The Vietnamese appreciated these things, being a practical

people. But they did not like their conquerors or the Chinese military camps and the taxes collected for their upkeep. These feelings went so deep that they became ingrained in the Vietnamese character. Independence became a sacred word to them. Conquerors might come and go, but the people would always yearn to live on their own and in their own way. Nothing that follows in this book makes sense unless we recognize this, *the* basic fact of Vietnamese history.

The Chinese learned this fact through painful experience. In the year A.D. 40 they executed a Vietnamese nobleman for treason. Rather than weep, his wife, Trung Trac, and her sister Trung Nhi[1] started a rebellion that swept across the land. They were joined by Phung Thi Chinh, who, though pregnant, always led her troops into battle. Surrounded during one encounter, she gave birth as Chinese arrows darkened the sky overhead. She then tied the infant to her back, took a sword in each hand, and cut a bloody path through the enemy ranks. Despite his early defeats, however, the Son of Heaven vowed to hold Vietnam at all costs. He sent new armies, which defeated the rebels in several pitched battles. Their rebellion crushed, the Trung sisters and Phung Thi Chinh committed suicide by drowning.

One rebellion was crushed, but the spirit of rebellion still burned within the people. It burst out again in A.D. 248, once more led by a woman. Trieu Au was a peasant with a genius for war. "My wish is to ride the tempest, tame the waves, kill the sharks," she shouted to her followers. "I want to drive the enemy away and save our people." The Chinese must have seen Trieu Au as part human and part goddess, for their paintings show her dressed in magnificent golden armor riding an elephant. As she charges into battle, her

3

---

[1]In Chinese, Japanese, and Vietnamese the family name comes first. It is polite and correct practice to refer to Vietnamese people by the last part of their given name (ie. Nhi, Trac). We shall follow this custom throughout the text and in the index.

breasts, ten feet long, fly over her shoulders! But within a year she, too, was defeated and committed suicide rather than surrender.

The Vietnamese finally drove out the Chinese in 939, after a war lasting thirty years. Their methods were simple and would change little through the centuries that followed. Their weapon was patience, outwaiting the enemy while inflicting enough damage to make him lose heart. General Tran Hung Dao explained the plan three hundred years later. "When the enemy is away from home for a long time and produces no victories, and families learn of their dead, then the enemy population becomes dissatisfied. Time is always in our favor. Our climate, mountains, and jungles discourage the enemy."[2] Future invaders would have spared themselves much pain had they taken General Tran seriously.

The Chinese armies left, but large numbers of Chinese people remained in Vietnam. City dwellers for the most part, they made their living from business and trade. Except for a brief return of Chinese rule from 1407 to 1427, Vietnam was to remain independent for nine hundred years. Yet the memory of Chinese occupation remains vivid to the present day. The Vietnamese have always distrusted their neighbor to the north.

Independent at last, the Vietnamese became empire builders in their own right. About the year 1000, as Viking sailors found their way to the New World, the Vietnamese began their *Nam Tien,* or "March to the South." This was not a massive advance, but a slow, steady movement lasting centuries. Bands of soldier-settlers would conquer fertile lands and farm them for several generations. Then, as the population increased, some would leave and continue the march. By the time of the American Revolution, the March to the South was complete. Vietnam's emperors built their capital

4

---

[2] Quoted in Robert Pisor, *The End of the Line: The Siege of Khe Sanh,* p. 147.

at Hue on the banks of the Perfume River. From Hue's cit-adel, a fortress-palace modeled on Beijing's Forbidden City, they ruled an S-shaped territory 850 miles long bordering the South China Sea.

Vietnam, like America, became a "melting pot" where different groups blended into one. As the soldier-settlers advanced, they intermarried with the peoples they conquered along the way. These peoples were related to the Khmer, or Cambodians, to the west, the Malay to the south, and the Filipinos from the islands to the east. Gradually, there emerged the Vietnamese as we know them today.

Their language, like Chinese, is tonal—that is, the same word may be pronounced several ways, each having a different meaning. Depending on the tone, the word *ma*, for example, means "ghost," "cheek," "but," "grave," "horse," or "rice seedling." Small wonder that Westerners have always found it difficult to learn Vietnamese.

Early visitors saw much to admire in the Vietnamese people. They are short—scarcely more than five feet tall—and slender, with jet-black hair and broad faces. A traveler named Louis de Grammont wrote in the 1860s:

> They are capable of loyalty and gratefulness. They are some-
> times generous, full of respect for justice and veneration for
> the aged. They do not lack gaiety, though basically they are of
> an apathetic temper. They are less refined than the Chinese
> but have more moral strength. . . . They are unimpressed by
> fits of rage but can be captivated by friendliness.[3]

Their country is part of Southeast Asia, the area between India and China which includes Burma, Thailand, Malaysia, Laos, Cambodia, and Vietnam. The last three are also known

5

---

[3] Quoted in Joseph Buttinger, *The Smaller Dragon: A Political History of Vietnam*, pp. 419–420.

as Indochina, so called when they were colonized by France. Indochina's climate is controlled by seasonal winds called monsoons. From May to October, the summer monsoon blows across the Indian Ocean, bringing drenching rains, high temperatures, and suffocating humidity. The air becomes so thick and clammy that it seems to be glued to your skin. From November to April, the winter monsoon blows from the cool uplands of Central Asia. This is the dry season, with little rain and temperatures hovering around eighty-five degrees Fahrenheit.

Vietnam has been compared to two rice baskets balanced on either end of a bamboo carrying-pole. It is a good comparison. The "rice baskets" are the deltas of the Red River in the north and the Mekong River in the south. A delta is a plain formed by soil deposited near a river's mouth as it flows into the sea. Delta lands are ideal for farming, being flat, well watered, and fertile. The "bamboo pole" is the Annamite Chain, a mountain range with peaks as high as 8,500 feet. The mountains are steep and rugged; they, and the valleys in between, are covered with dense tropical forests. More than half of Vietnam is jungle, where monkeys chatter and fierce rats run wild. Tigers and elephants can still be found in certain areas. Jungle trails and rice paddies swarm with leeches. Thirty-one types of snake are found in Vietnam, all but two poisonous. The green bamboo viper, for example, is the size of an American garter snake. A harmless-looking creature, its bite will paralyze a healthy man in two minutes and kill him in five. The types of insects are too numerous to count, though visitors say they are all horrid.

6

The growing of rice, the basic food of the Vietnamese, was easier or harder, depending on where you lived. It was easy in the delta of the Mekong, one of the world's longest rivers. Flowing southward from the Tibetan highlands, the Mekong gently makes its way in long, graceful loops; it seldom overflows its banks to ruin crops planted in the fields on either side. Smaller streams teem with fish, and children learned to catch them easily with their bare hands. The peasants knew how to make nature work for them in countless ways. A favorite trick was to force a young frog through a hole drilled in a coconut. The main hole was then plugged up and several narrow breathing holes cut in the sides. The frog fed on the coconut meat, growing fatter by the day. When it filled the inside of the coconut, the peasant cracked the shell open for a tasty meal.

Life was harder in the delta of the Red River. Rising in the mountains of western China, it is swift, angry, menacing. In order to prevent flooding, the northern peasants had to enclose its banks with earthen dikes. Sixty feet wide in places, these dikes stretch for sixteen hundred miles and represent centuries of backbreaking labor by countless peasants. If ever the dikes should burst, thousands of square miles would be flooded, causing mass starvation.

Most Vietnamese lived, not in cities, but in thousands of small villages. Surrounded by tall bamboo hedges, each village stood in the midst of its rice fields, an island closed to outsiders. Villagers lived simply. Each family had a small hut furnished with straw mats on the floor, a bed made of rough wooden boards, and a few cooking pots. A mirror placed on the front door frightened away evil spirits with their own images.

Although the huts were separate, their inhabitants were bound to each other not as individuals but as part of two communities that controlled their lives. First came the family. Old-time Vietnamese never asked such questions as "Who am I?" and "What shall I do when I grow up?" From the moment you knew anything, you knew your place in the world. Your name immediately gave your position in the family. A firstborn child was called Number Two, because the child was second to the father. The secondborn was Number

7

Three, and so on down the line. To avoid confusion between the various numbers, each child received a nickname. Having a squint, for example, might make you Nguyen Number Four Squinty-Eyes; Nguyen is a common family name, like Smith in the United States. Once you had a nickname, it stayed with you for life.

Youngsters quickly learned what was expected of them. Reading and writing, though important for the emperor's officials, or mandarins, were of little use to peasant children. They needed practical knowledge, which was best taught in the home. Fathers taught sons to plant rice and look after farm animals. A six-year-old would care for the water buffalo that pulled the plow; he'd jump on its back for fun, balancing on the powerful muscles as it sloshed through the paddy mud. Mothers taught daughters the thousand and one things needed to care for a family and a home. Everyone learned good manners and how to get along with others. When you met another person, you did not offer to shake hands; that was rude. You clasped your hands together in front of you and bowed. When a boy wanted to speak to a girl, he spoke to her mother first. If mama approved, he could walk out with the girl but not hold her hand in public. Yet boys, even grown men, walked about holding hands; hand-holding was a sign of friendship, nothing more.

The Vietnamese respected their elders, both living and dead. This was filial piety, the idea that children must honor their parents in all things. It made no difference if parents were wrong; they deserved respect because of who they were, not because of what they did. Talking back to a parent, let alone disobeying, brought shame in the eyes of the community. One who lacked filial piety lost face, was unworthy of trust and friendship.

Equally important was worshiping one's ancestors. Just as children owed their lives to their parents, the family owed

8

its existence to its ancestors. Each home had an altar where prayers were said for the ancestors and incense burned in their memory. In a way, they never really died. They were still present—in spirit—watching over their descendants, smiling at their good fortune and weeping at their troubles. Buried in the rice fields that fed the family, they were the family's link to the land and to future generations. Leaving the land was the true death for the Vietnamese. If a person had to leave, relatives went into mourning, for he was leaving his soul behind. The worst thing was for an entire family to move away, leaving no one to care for the ancestors' graves.

The second community was the village. Villagers knew that their survival depended on cooperation with others. Someone who was independent, who demanded only his rights, endangered everyone. The Vietnamese knew nothing of "freedom of speech" or "speaking your mind." One who spoke freely was like the fellow who shot arrows without aiming: words, like arrows, can wound others, harming the entire community. Living peacefully meant swallowing anger, hiding bad feelings for the sake of peace. Children, for example, had no contact sports, such as tag, since these might cause arguments and fistfights. Adults always tried to avoid arguing with neighbors. If there was a disagreement, it was settled politely, with soft words and broad smiles, by the village council. Each village was governed by a council of the oldest, most respected men. Besides settling disputes, the council made sure that roads and dikes were repaired. In hard times, it collected food and clothing for the needy. Everyone gave what they could, since there was no telling when they would need a favor in turn.

The Vietnamese were devoted to their ancient ways. An industrious people, they lived satisfying, self-respecting lives. They knew little, and cared less, about the outside world. The old ways were the best ways, they believed. As long as

9

the emperor left them alone and taxes remained low, they were satisfied.

Yet they were about to be thrust into the modern world against their wishes. Enemies stronger and more skilled than any they had ever known were on the way. When they arrived, the Land of the Distant South would be changed. Changed violently and forever.

Europeans had been interested in Asia for centuries. Long before Columbus sailed for the New World, Arab traders had sold Asian spices, jewels, and silks in Europe. Venetian Marco Polo returned from East Asia in the fourteenth century with tales of lands of fantastic beauty and wealth. By the early 1800s Europeans had claimed part of that wealth, setting up colonies throughout the Far East. Great Britain ruled India, Burma, and Malaya. Spain owned the Philippine Islands. Dutchmen held the East Indies, also known as the Spice Islands, and Indonesia. European powers seized portions of China. Such takeovers were easy, thanks to the Europeans' iron warships, long-range guns, and powerful explosives.

Colonies served both God and greed. Christian missionaries saw them as places for doing holy deeds. It was a religious duty, they claimed, to save the souls of "heathen" natives, bringing them to the "true faith" and eternal life in heaven. Merchants, however, saw colonies in less spiritual terms. They were open treasure chests waiting to be plundered. Moreover, Asia's huge population was a ready market for European manufactured goods. Labor was cheap and natural resources plentiful.

French Catholic missionaries arrived in Vietnam in the early 1600s. At first, the emperors welcomed their useful knowledge; not only did the missionaries preach the word of God, they were able doctors, mathematicians, and scientists.

They even taught the Vietnamese to write in the Roman alphabet, which was easier to learn than the Chinese system.

Yet the missionaries quickly outwore their welcome. Their real work, of course, was converting people to Catholicism, a faith very different from Buddhism. Bonzes, or Buddhist priests, were offended by the outsiders' efforts to win over their followers. Worse, missionaries taught that one's first loyalty was to God, not the community or the emperor. That was too much, since it threatened the entire social order. The emperors struck back, persecuting missionaries on and off for the next two centuries. Missionaries were forbidden to preach, jailed, and driven out of the country. A few were killed. In 1851, the Emperor Tu Duc ordered French priests to be sewn into sacks and thrown into the sea; Vietnamese Catholic priests would be cut in half. Missionary leaders, fearing for their lives, appealed to the French government.

Their pleas were heard in Paris. Frenchmen liked to boast about their *mission civilisatrice,* their "civilizing mission." If, as they said, their country was the most civilized on earth, it must raise others to its level. Never mind that others might not want to be "raised." They were like silly children who refused to bathe or brush their teeth, Frenchmen said. Papa France would conquer these "child peoples" for their own good. He would uplift them, forcing them to be clean and decent, religious and moral. And, of course, papa was entitled to some reward for his kindness. His merchants would develop Vietnam's resources, enriching both themselves and their beloved homeland.

In August 1858, a French fleet anchored off Da Nang. After a brief bombardment, marines landed and easily captured the seaport. Yet nature was harder to defeat than a handful of poorly armed Vietnamese soldiers. The summer monsoon lasted longer than usual that year, and rain turned the invaders' camp into a swamp. Soldiers, dressed in heavy woolen uniforms, collapsed in the suffocating heat and humidity. The commanders, seeing their army melting away, decided to leave before it was too late. In February 1859, they sailed south to capture Saigon, the chief town of the Mekong delta. Reinforcements soon arrived and began to push into the countryside; by 1863 the French controlled six Vietnamese provinces. Success, however, only encouraged French greed. In August 1883, their forces turned northward to occupy Hanoi and the towns of the Red River delta.

So ended nine centuries of Vietnamese independence. True, the emperor still sat on his gorgeous throne, but he was kept there for show. The invaders smiled at him, bowed to him, showed him every respect. Yet their very politeness was an insult. Everyone knew that the actual ruler was the governor-general appointed by Paris. Vietnam as a nation disappeared; in fact, speaking its name became a crime. For nearly a century after the conquest, encyclopedias mentioned no such country as Vietnam. Maps showed no such place. Since the French had also conquered Laos and Cambodia, the entire area was called French Indochina.

The civilizing mission proved to be nothing but empty words. The French record in Indochina was one of shame, brutality, and exploitation. Colons—French settlers—were tough, narrow-minded people out to make their fortunes. Their aim was simple: take everything, give nothing. And since government was of, by, and for the French, they could do as they pleased. They were the law in Vietnam, and God help anyone who stood in their way!

The French raised taxes, then took the land of those unable to pay. A peasant would do anything to keep his land, his family's link to its ancestors. He would sell his possessions, including his water buffalo, harnessing himself and his sons to the plow. If he was desperate, he would sell his daughters, since there was always a demand for pretty young prostitutes in the towns. For millions, however, even that sacrifice was not enough. Crushed by taxes, they lost their land, which the government sold at bargain prices. The land was bought either by colons or by wealthy Vietnamese who cooperated with them. Such people were, in effect, no longer Vietnamese. They spoke French, copied French dress and manners, and sent their children to school in France.

Landless peasants provided cheap labor for the French-owned plantations. By the early 1900s, Vietnam had become one of the world's leading producers of rubber and rice. But the peasants enjoyed none of the benefits of their labor. Life on the rubber plantations was nasty, brutal, and short; indeed, one out of every twenty rubber workers died of disease and starvation. The plantations of the Michelin Company, Europe's largest manufacturer of rubber tires, were hellholes. On one Michelin plantation twelve thousand out of forty-five thousand workers died within a few years. Rice farmers suffered nearly as much. Their efforts had made Vietnam the world's third largest grower of rice. Still the farmers went hungry, even in good years, since most of the crop was sold overseas to enrich their masters.

The same was true of Vietnam's mineral wealth. When the French arrived, they found large deposits of coal, tin, and zinc. To encourage mining, the government built a modern transportation system. Roads and railroads opened the country's interior. Iron bridges spanned its rivers. Docks for oceangoing vessels sprang up at its seaports.

These projects were paid for by the Vietnamese with their money, their labor, and their lives. Thousands of peasants were rounded up and herded into barracks where they slept jammed together on long wooden shelves. Each morning they were marched to the workplace by armed guards. There they worked long hours under the broiling sun. They worked until they dropped, for sickness was no excuse for taking it easy.

13

Eighty thousand men, for example, were sent to build a three-hundred-mile stretch of railroad near Hanoi. Of these, twenty-five thousand died on the job. In addition, uncounted thousands were crippled, to be tossed aside like so many broken teacups. Those who managed to return to their villages were broken men, unable to care for themselves or their families.

The money to pay for these projects was squeezed out of the Vietnamese by the government monopolies. Every ounce of salt produced in Vietnam had to be sold to the government at a low price. The government then resold it at up to eight times its original cost. This was a serious matter, for, without refrigeration, food could not be preserved unless it was salted. Time and again, fishermen, unable to afford salt, wept as their catches rotted in the sun. To make matters worse, each village had to buy a certain amount of whiskey from the government. If it did not, the village leaders were fined.

The most hateful monopoly dealt in opium. Opium is made from a type of poppy that grows throughout the Golden Triangle, an area where the borders of Thailand, Burma, and Laos meet. Today, raw opium, the plant's juices formed into a thick paste, is chemically changed into different drugs. Morphine and codeine are valuable painkillers; heroin is a deadly narcotic. For centuries people had smoked opium to put them into a trance and make them feel as if all was right with the world. It wasn't. Opium is highly addictive, and once people became hooked, it ruined their lives. Opium addiction is a disease as deadly as any plague.

14

The Vietnamese emperors had banned opium; anyone caught selling it was immediately put to death. The French knew the dangers of opium; however, they preferred profits to human lives, just like today's drug lords. A government monopoly was formed to sell the drug in Vietnam. Each year the monopoly sent tons of raw opium from the Golden Triangle to its Saigon factories to be prepared for market. Profits soared, along with the people's misery. Families were destroyed. Peasants became addicts and lost their land. Miners squandered their wages in opium dens, places where the drug was smoked in pipes. By 1918 the monopoly had 1,515 licensed opium dens, plus 3,098 opium shops where the drug could be bought for home use. In most years, the monopoly spent more on importing raw opium than the government did on all of Vietnam's schools, hospitals, and libraries. It was a shameful record, matched only by that of the British, who controlled the opium trade in India and China.

The French knew how to take care of themselves. Growing homesick, they tried to re-create at least the feeling of their own country in Southeast Asia. Hanoi took on the appearance of a French city, with wide streets, a theater, and a university. But Saigon was their masterpiece, their "Paris of the Orient." Its main streets, once dirt roads, became wide, paved boulevards lined with tamarind trees to shade the sidewalks. Its public buildings, among them the opera house and city hall, imitated those in Paris. Visiting troupes performed the latest plays and musicals from the Paris stage. Bookstores offered the latest reading material; restaurants served delicious meals. All the finest foods were available, direct from France: pickled snails, preserved meats, wines, champagne, brandy. Bakeries sold flaky croissants and the long, crusty bread so dear to Frenchmen. There was even a Street of Flowers, as in Paris, lined with flower stalls from end to end.

Colons had a life-style enjoyed only by the very rich back home. They were not supposed to work hard, since that would have put them on a level with the lowly Vietnamese. Each day they took a siesta promptly at noon. Frenchmen went home for a long nap, returning to work at three o'clock; Frenchwomen were not supposed to work at all. Wages were

15

so low that anyone could afford Vietnamese servants. A typical businessman's family had a cook, a nanny to look after the children, and a woman to serve meals, clean up, and do the laundry. There were always barefoot "boys" eager to help the businessman across a muddy street; for a few coins he could hop on a boy's back and be carried to the other side without soiling his shoes. Instead of walking, tourists saw the sights from sedan chairs carried by teams of sweating porters.

Frenchmen despised the very people who made their lifestyle possible. They spoke to the Vietnamese as they would to children, with the familiar *tu,* never the polite *Monsieur* or *Madame*—sir or lady—as one would to an adult. Nothing showed their contempt more than a game played by those going out for a night's entertainment. They would climb into separate rickshaws, small two-wheeled cabs pulled by one man, and race each other to a restaurant or theater. The rickshaw men often collapsed, and might then be paid less than the agreed amount or not be paid at all. Any protest brought a slap in the face, which closed the matter, since a Frenchman's word was automatically accepted in the courts.

The feelings of the Vietnamese meant nothing to their masters. As Phan Chu Trinh, a former mandarin, told the governor-general in 1905, "In your [French] papers, in your books, in your plans, in your private conversations, there is displayed . . . the profound contempt with which you overwhelm us. In your eyes, we are savages, dumb brutes, incapable of distinguishing between good and evil . . . and it is sadness and shame that fills our hearts when we contemplate our humiliation."[4]

The Vietnamese repaid contempt with hatred. France was seen as a nation of greedy oppressors. Frenchmen were so different from Vietnamese that they hardly seemed human.

---

[4] Quoted in Stanley Karnow, *Vietnam: A History*, p. 112.

Known as "long noses," they made the Vietnamese laugh at their misshapen faces; their strange body odor turned Vietnamese stomachs. With their long arms and hairy bodies, the French "monkey men" belonged in trees, not among civilized people. Their behavior, especially their shouting and temper tantrums, made them look foolish. In Vietnamese eyes, losing one's temper showed poor upbringing, a reflection on one's parents and ancestors.

Every decade after the conquest saw at least one serious rebellion in Vietnam. The Scholars' Revolt, from 1885 to 1888, was led by mandarins from the emperor's court. Though poorly armed, the rebels held off the French in the northern mountains for three years. In 1907, rebels planned to seize power after poisoning French army commanders in Hanoi. A Catholic priest learned of the plot and reported it to the authorities in the nick of time.

The French were constantly on the alert for rebels. The *Sûreté*, or secret police, used Vietnamese to spy on their fellow countrymen. Although a few were paid for their work, most were ordinary lawbreakers released on the condition that they served as spies. The Sûreté acted on their information, arresting suspects or shooting them while supposedly attempting to escape. If a rebel did escape, his parents were taken hostage and threatened with prison or death unless he surrendered—that is, handed himself over to the executioner. Vietnamese who chose national independence over filial piety were tortured by guilt. Some went insane, even committed suicide.

Rebels were never spared. If there was trouble in an area, French troops were sent to "pacify" it. Pacification was actually a license for troops to kill, loot, and destroy as they pleased. Arriving at a village, they surrounded it and closed in without warning. Villagers were driven from their homes at bayonet point and held for questioning. Known rebels of-

17

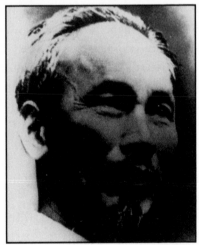

Vietnamese rebels jailed by the French around 1907, above. By day, their feet were locked in stocks; though they were released at night, the wooden halters made it easy for guards to drag them around by the neck. Such treatment turned the French prisons into "schools for revolutionaries." Ho Chi Minh, at right, would lead that revolution.

ten had an arm cut off as a warning to others. Men, their hands tied behind their backs, were forced to their knees and beheaded; photographs of troops standing among the bodies were made into postcards to be sent to loved ones back home in France. Villages also learned about "collective responsibility"; that is, everyone suffered even if only one person had aided a rebel. The village leaders were executed, the villagers' property stolen, and the village itself burned to the ground. On several occasions, all villagers were shot by firing squad, including the children.

Thousands were imprisoned each year. Although the French built three times as many jails as schools, there was always a shortage of cells. To prevent escapes, scores of prisoners were lined up and their feet locked in stocks. They ate this way, slept this way, and were unlocked once á day to use the toilet; you either controlled yourself or sat in your own filth. Hard-core prisoners were kept in tiny cells known as "stone coffins." Yet prison had an unexpected result. It was a school for rebels, a place where they could meet, share their feelings, and learn from one another. Le Duc Tho, who we shall meet toward the end of our story, described his experiences in a poem entitled "Cell of Hatred":

> In my cell—so alone—
> To whom can I pour out my fierce hatred?
> My gaze is barred by a bolted door
> High walls shut out the sun's rays
> Wretched existence!
> My bowl and my straw pallet stink
> The only shirt, the only pair of trousers, are in rags
> My feet are bound in rings of steel. . . .
> Mosquitoes and fleas make me pass sleepless nights
>   Body aching, I lie down, rise again—
>   Wrath seizes me, faced with that evil fate

19

That hounds me unceasingly to cast me back
  into the cells!
Rice mixed with paddy mud and pebbles
Putrid vegetables, rotten fish,
Buffalo's sinew soaked in coarse salt.
The black hair of youth turns white quickly.
The intestines wither, the complexion pales.
Shut away for weeks without washing,
Lice and fleas swarm, filth mingles with sweat.
What words can tell of all that?
This suffering—only those who have known it
  can comprehend it.
Why must I endure this torture?
Rage grips me against those barbaric imperialists,
So many years their heels have crushed our country.
A thousand, thousand oppressions, a thousand,
  thousand tests.
Resolutely we must . . . break these chains
To build a life without misery
A society free at last. . . .[5]

A visitor to Vietnam early in this century might have pitied its people. Prisoners in their own land, they existed only to serve foreign masters. As far as the French were concerned, this was just and natural, and would remain so forever. The only "rights" the Vietnamese had were to work for their masters, keep quiet, and serve them loyally unto death. But although the people seemed to have lost everything, much still remained. They still had their yearning for independence and their hatred of invaders. These emotions burned within them, waiting to be roused by the right leader. By one who would call himself "He Who Enlightens."

---

[5] Le Duc Tho, "Cell of Hatred," *The New York Times*, February 3, 1973.

HE WHO ENLIGHTENS

I am a revolutionary. I was born at a time when my country was already a slave state. From the days of my youth I have fought to free it. That is my one merit.

—Ho Chi Minh

THE MOST IMPORTANT PERSON IN THE MODERN HISTORY of Vietnam was born May 19, 1890, in Kim-Lien village, Nghe An province, in the northern part of the country. His name at birth was Nguyen That Thanh, or Nguyen Who Will Be Victorious. During his years as a revolutionary, he often changed names to stay ahead of the Sûreté, using no fewer than seventy-six aliases. For a long time he called himself Nguyen Ai Quoc—Nguyen the Patriot—and Nguyen O Phap—Nguyen Who Hates the French. But his favorite alias was Ho Chi Minh—He Who Enlightens. Under that name he became the hero of his people and famous the world over.

Ho claimed that he was born a revolutionary, which was no exaggeration. His earliest memories were of resistance against the French. Nghe An was the last province to fall under their control, and that only after savage fighting. Ho's father, Nguyen Sinh Huy, had left a good job in the government rather than serve the invaders; he refused even to learn their "corrupting" language. Huy fought in the Scholars' Revolt, joining a secret society to spread anti-French ideas after its defeat. Ho's elder brother, Khiem, denounced the invaders openly, though he never fought against them. His sister, Thanh, spent much of her adult life in prison for stealing French guns and giving them to resistance fighters. "Other women bring forth children," said the judge who sentenced her, "but you bring forth rifles."

Ho, the baby of the family, continued the tradition. Hatred of the invader was as much a part of his growing up as ancestor worship. As a child of nine, he carried messages for his father's secret society. As a teenager, he heard gruesome accounts of the French civilizing mission, accounts which haunted him for the rest of his days.

After completing elementary school in his village, Ho attended high school in a neighboring town. Little is known about his life there, other than that he was expelled. School officials blamed poor grades; Ho later said it was for spreading propaganda among his schoolmates. He attended another school in the old imperial capital of Hue, but left without a diploma. He then became a teacher in a small fishing village, only to quit when he found that the work was not for him. But what was for him? He could not say. All he knew was that he was unhappy in a land ruled by "monkey men." So, in 1911, at the age of twenty-one, he signed on aboard a French steamship as a kitchen helper. Perhaps seeing the world would help him find his mission in life.

For the next two years, Ho visited seaports in Europe and Africa. After trips to San Francisco and Boston, he settled in Brooklyn, New York, supporting himself as a laborer on construction sites. On his days off, he would walk across the Brooklyn Bridge into Manhattan. Manhattan fascinated him. The tall buildings, the bustle, the traffic—he had never imagined that such things were possible. And the people—it was as if all of humanity had gathered on this tiny island. He was amazed to learn that the inhabitants of Chinatown enjoyed the same rights as any American citizen. He was equally amazed at the doings of the Ku Klux Klan, bands of racist thugs that killed blacks who asked for equality with whites.

In 1914 he moved to London, England, arriving just weeks after the start of World War I. We know little of his life at this time, except that he took no part in the British effort against Germany. By day he did odd jobs in a school; at night he worked in the kitchens of a fancy hotel. In time, the quiet, gentle Vietnamese was promoted to the pastry department, where he became an expert baker. By 1917, having grown tired of London, he moved to Paris. But the one thing he never tired of was fine food. Throughout his life, first as a rebel chief and then as president of North Vietnam, he enjoyed cooking for friends.

Ho soon realized that not all Frenchmen were like the ones he had seen back home. The French worker seemed to be an ordinary person, like himself. Poor and hungry, fearing for his country's survival, he led a life of misery. Ho could talk to him man to man, without feeling that he was looked down upon as a member of an inferior race. Surely, he thought, such people had more in common with oppressed Vietnamese than with their oppressors, the colons. Didn't they understand this?

Finding the answer was not easy, since Ho was also busy making a living. Wartime Paris was a harsh place. Although he earned a few francs a week by retouching photographs, that barely met his needs. He ate little and moved often; he would take a room and leave before the rent came due. Yet he was never lonely. When World War I began, the French government brought 100,000 Vietnamese to work in the armaments factories. Ho made friends with hundreds of these

23

men, spending many hours discussing their lives and problems. He also joined the Socialist party, where he found Frenchmen who opposed colonialism and wanted some government control of business for the benefit of society as a whole.

The defeat of Germany brought the Western leaders to a peace conference at Versailles, near Paris. Early in 1919, as the conference opened, Ho and his Vietnamese friends tried to appeal to the leaders' sense of justice. They drew up a "List of Claims for the Vietnamese People," politely asking for such things as equality among Vietnamese and French. Then they rented Ho a dress suit and sent him off to present the petition in person. Such powerful men, however, had "more urgent" matters to discuss, and he was sent away without the courtesy of an interview.

Ho returned to Paris a changed man. The leaders' refusal convinced him that appeals to reason were useless. Now he believed that only through force could the claims of justice be heard. True, generations of Vietnamese revolutionaries had resorted to force and failed. Yet Ho could see no alternative. There must be a way of overthrowing the French, and he must find it.

The solution to Ho's problem came from the East—from Russia. A revolution had broken out in Russia in 1917. Led by Nikolai Lenin, the revolutionaries overthrew the government and created the Soviet Union. Lenin and his followers were Communists, followers of Karl Marx, a German economist who died in 1883. In books like *Das Kapital* ("*Capital*") and the *Communist Manifesto*, Marx said that society was divided into classes always in conflict with one another. Wealthy businessmen, or capitalists, forced the workers, or the proletariat, to work at low wages under inhuman conditions. Marx predicted that as the capitalists grew richer, the workers would grow more miserable until they revolted.

The revolution might fail time and again, but would eventually succeed, because the "laws of history" were on its side. The proletariat would then crush the capitalists and rule unopposed. Under their rule, called the "dictatorship of the proletariat," all factories and mines, railroads and farms, banks and stores would be taken over by the community— hence *communism*, the holding of property in common for the good of all. People would still hold jobs, but would receive whatever goods and services they needed, rather than money. Marx believed that communism would sweep the earth, causing nations to disappear and enabling humanity to live forever in peace and plenty. Time would prove him wrong on every count.

Lenin turned the Soviet Union into a base for spreading communism worldwide. A major target was Asia, whose peoples seemed ripe for revolution. Beginning in 1919, Soviet agents were sent to contact local patriots and convert them to communism. Moscow issued pamphlets, just as missionaries issued Bibles, in native languages; but instead of teaching Scripture, the pamphlets denounced colonialism in Marxist terms. Moscow even started a "missionary college," the University of the Toilers of the East, to train revolutionaries for the task ahead.

Early in 1920, Ho read Lenin's "Thesis on the National and Colonial Questions." It was a revelation, like finding God amid darkness and doubt. Lenin described the oppression of the colonial peoples and explained how communism would set them free. He did this so clearly that Ho became an instant convert to communism.

Ho was happy for the first time in years. All his questions had been answered, all his doubts laid to rest, as if by a miracle. The joy of that moment always remained vivid. "What emotion, enthusiasm, clear-sightedness and confidence [Lenin's pamphlet] instilled in me! I was overjoyed," he wrote

25

forty years later. "Though sitting alone in my room, I shouted aloud as if addressing large crowds: 'Dead martyrs, compatriots! This is what we need, this is our path to our liberation!'"[1]

Ho gave every ounce of his energy to the Communist cause. Small and frail, suffering from tuberculosis, he lived only for his newfound faith. In October 1920, he became a founding member of the French Communist party. He wrote articles for its newspapers and spread its message among homeward-bound Vietnamese. He soon became known as one of the party's best workers, an opinion shared by the Sûreté; they began tracking his movements until, in 1923, he vanished as if swallowed by the earth.

Actually, Ho had moved up in the world—to Moscow. There he met Lenin and his closest aides, whom he liked and who apparently liked him. But Ho had been called to Moscow for political, not social, reasons. For the next two years, he attended the University of the Toilers of the East. He never spoke about the school, but we know from others what its course of study was like. Students concentrated on three subjects: Marxist theory, "agitprop," and subversion. Agitprop, short for agitation and propaganda, teaches how to turn people into Communists while turning them against their government. Subversion deals with undermining the government's authority. This can be done in various ways, including corrupting its officials, destroying the loyalty of its armed forces, and organizing secret resistance groups for spying, sabotage, terrorism, and assassination. These methods, though illegal in all countries, were considered proper in furthering the Communist cause.

Ho was equally silent about the Soviet dictatorship. By the time of his death in 1924, Lenin had built one of the most

---

[1]Ho Chi Minh, *Ho Chi Minh On Revolution: Selected Writings, 1920–1966*, p. 24.

frightful tyrannies in human history. His successor, Joseph Stalin, raised that tyranny to a new height. Stalin became the greatest mass murderer of all time. Under him, civil liberties vanished in the Soviet Union. Churches were closed and priests shot in batches. Private property was seized by the government. Political parties, except for the Communist party, were abolished and their leaders executed. Opposing communism brought quick death with a bullet, or slow death in Siberian slave labor camps. Ho does not seem to have been bothered by any of this. Certain that communism was the wave of the future, he was prepared to use any means to ensure its victory. If millions must be sacrificed in its name, then so be it. Future generations would only praise the Communists' "courage" for doing what was "necessary."

In 1925, Ho became a missionary for Communist world revolution. Upon completing his studies, he traveled to Canton as a secret agent. Canton was the center of Communist activity in the Far East. Already a young Chinese named Mao Tse-tung was building party strength among Canton's workers. Hundreds of Vietnamese patriots, driven from their homeland, sought safety in the sprawling city. Ho's task was to aid the Chinese Communists and win the loyalty of his fellow Vietnamese.

Ho formed several Revolutionary Youth Associations for Vietnamese fugitives. Using methods learned in Moscow, he trained thirty agitators every three months. Nearly all returned to Vietnam with orders to form secret party groups, lead student demonstrations, and form Communist-led unions. One of Ho's best agents was the son of a former mandarin from the emperor's court. His name was Pham Van Dong, and he is now prime minister of the Socialist Republic of Vietnam.

Not every student proved to be so trustworthy. Patriots often had their own ideas about how to get rid of the French and rebuild their country. Although eager to learn about rev-

27

olution, they had no desire to become Communists or obey their orders. Such people were dangerous to Ho's plans, and he dealt with them ruthlessly. Ho was a master of the double-cross. After their return to Vietnam, he passed their names to the Sûreté, which was only too glad to "welcome" them. Ho once betrayed a patriot for a large sum of money, which he donated to the Associations. At a funeral service for one of the men he betrayed, Ho told a friend, "He was a great patriot and we mourn him. All those who do not follow the line which I have laid down will be broken."[2] Ho did not hesitate to sacrifice anyone who stood in his way. Individual lives, even those of people he respected, meant nothing compared to the Communist cause.

Ho's Revolutionary Youth Associations were destroyed in a Chinese government crackdown on Communists. During the spring of 1927, thousands of Communists were executed in the streets of Canton and other cities. These killings began a civil war that would last until Mao Tse-tung's victory twenty-two years later.

Ho escaped the Chinese government's assassins and made his way to Moscow. No sooner did he arrive there than he was sent on secret missions throughout Europe. We know that he stayed for a time in Belgium, Switzerland, and Italy; he also lived undercover in Germany, where Adolf Hitler had begun his rise to power. Returning to Asia, he shaved his head, put on yellow robes, and traveled around Thailand disguised as a Buddhist priest. His life became a never-ending round of false names, coded messages, secret contacts, and grubby hotels. Small wonder that he learned several foreign languages. In addition to Vietnamese, he spoke perfect English, French, Russian, Thai, some German, and at least two Chinese dialects. "I've become a professional revolutionary,"

28

---

[2]Quoted in David Halberstam, *Ho*, p. 71.

he told a companion. "I travel through many countries, but I see nothing. I am always on strict orders, and my itinerary is always carefully prescribed."

In 1930, Ho visited the British colony of Hong Kong. There, on February 3, he met the heads of Communist groups from all over Vietnam in the bleachers of a soccer stadium. An all-star game was in progress and loud cheering and booing filled the air. This was exactly what Ho wanted. With the noise masking their discussions, they formed the Vietnamese Communist party. The party's aims were simple: End French rule, make Vietnam independent, and set up a Communist dictatorship.

The Communists led their first major demonstration in Vietnam on September 12, 1930. The crowd of peasants stretched for miles along the road leading to the city of Vinh. Men carried banners protesting French injustices. Women marched in the column, holding small children by the hand. Communist organizers led in chanting anti-French slogans.

As the crowd neared Vinh, French fighter planes appeared overhead. The planes swept in low, engines whining and machine guns chattering. Marchers fled in panic, leaving behind more than two hundred dead and hundreds injured. That night planes attacked people who were burying their relatives, killing another fifteen. "An awkward error which had a bad effect," a French official noted. A "bad effect" indeed! By shooting the marchers, the French turned many others against the government. That was a valuable lesson, and the Communists learned it well. If they stood to gain, they would not hesitate to provoke the enemy into firing on innocent people.

Nevertheless, the road ahead seemed long. French rule was as firm as ever. Try as they might, Vietnamese patriots, Communists or otherwise, seemed to be banging their heads against a wall—that is, until everything suddenly went

29

topsy-turvy. The year was 1940, and nothing would ever be the same again, either for Vietnam or the world.

Adolf Hitler had taken power in Germany seven years earlier, bent upon conquering the world and exterminating its "inferior races." Hitler's friend, Italian dictator Benito Mussolini, wanted to carve out an empire in Africa. Their Asian ally, Japan, had already been fighting in China on and off since 1931. It was a savage war in which millions of civilians were tortured, enslaved, and killed by the Japanese "dwarf bandits." Despite losing all its seaports, China held on, aided by imported supplies carried on the Haiphong-K'un-ming Railroad. Japan was determined to cut that lifeline, no easy task as long as France remained a world power.

Things changed when Hitler unleashed World War II. On June 16, 1940, his army marched into Paris after a six-week campaign. Japan, seeing its chance, demanded the right to station forces in French Indochina. The French governor-general replied with an act of cowardice unworthy of a brave people. Although he commanded 50,000 troops, he let the Japanese take over without a fight. The French were not expelled from Indochina, but were allowed to rule it as Japanese puppets. Their government officials stayed at their posts. Their Sûreté still hunted patriots. Their army continued its "pacifying" expeditions. Their colons gave Japan a monopoly on Vietnam's rice, rubber, and minerals. Frenchmen were so cooperative that Japan never kept more than 35,000 troops in Indochina.

30
The occupation made a deep impression on the Vietnamese. Of course they resented the Japanese, as they did all foreigners. But by lording it over the French, the men of the Rising Sun showed that Europeans were not supermen. They were only men. They could be defeated—and by Asians like the Vietnamese. No one knew exactly how it would

happen or when. Yet one thing was certain: France was finished in Vietnam.

Ho Chi Minh realized this at once. For years he had served the Communist party on missions in Europe and Asia. Now, at long last, his chance had come. In February 1941, he returned to his homeland for the first time in thirty years. Accompanied by a few close aides, he slipped across the Chinese border and set up headquarters in a hillside cave. A mountain cast its shadow on his new home; this he named Karl Marx. A nearby stream was called Lenin.

Ho at fifty looked more like a respected elder than a rebel chieftain. A lean, frail man, he had a high forehead, black hair, and a wispy beard. Never one for fine clothes, he dressed simply, as a man of the people. His favorite outfit was rubber sandals, a cotton shirt, and baggy pants held up by string. The revolution meant everything to him and was the only reason for his existence. In serving it, he had sacrificed his personal happiness. "I am all alone," he told a visitor. "No family, nothing . . . I did have a wife once."[3] Her name has never been revealed in the West, and it is unknown whether the couple had any children. Ho probably would have made a good father; he enjoyed being with children, giving them candy and giggling when they pulled his beard.

Ho worked far into the night, every night, pecking out orders on a portable typewriter. To keep awake, he drank endless cups of strong tea and smoked countless cigarettes; his favorite was Philip Morris, an American brand so strong it was said to taste like dried buffalo dung rolled in a death certificate. By day, he roamed the countryside to meet the peasants. A kindly man when he wanted to be, he would sit cross-legged on the ground and invite them to join him. To put them at ease, he handed out cigarettes and asked to be

31

---

[3] Quoted in Halberstam, *Ho*, p. 16.

called Bac Ho—"Uncle Ho." Politely, gently, like a member of the family, he asked about the peasants' problems, carefully weaving his own message into the conversation. By the time he left the village, he could count on their support.

That support was shaped into a powerful revolutionary force. In May 1941, Uncle Ho created the Viet Nam Doc Lap Dong Minh, or League for Vietnamese Independence. The league would quickly become famous under its shorter name: Viet Minh.

The Viet Minh was a type of Communist organization known as a "front." A front served two purposes. First, it united people of different backgrounds and beliefs against a common enemy. For example, within the Viet Minh were sections for women, students, teachers, writers, musicians, peasants, and factory workers. Although members might disagree on many things, they agreed on the most important issue of all: national independence. Second, a front served to mask its leaders' true nature and purpose. The Viet Minh was a Communist tool, led by Communists for Communist aims. The reason for the disguise is quite simple. Ho knew that few Vietnamese understood communism and that many who did disliked it. Making the Viet Minh openly Communist, he said, would drive people away. Thus, its program spoke grandly of patriotism and justice, but was silent about communism. Ho downplayed communism for all except his trusted followers, who controlled the Viet Minh from behind the scenes; indeed, the Viet Minh never admitted to being Communists.

32   Uncle Ho was a *Vietnamese* Communist, not a *Communist* Vietnamese. There is an important difference here. Being a Communist Vietnamese would have meant patriotism came first. Ho certainly loved his country, but patriotism was no longer his chief concern. It had become a means to an end, a way of uniting people against the French. His chief loyalty,

however, was to communism; he called it the "magic bag" from which all blessings flowed. Once the French were gone, he would show his true colors. Vietnam would be remade into a Communist dictatorship. If other patriots objected, then too bad for them. He would handle them Stalin's way—with bullets.

Ho's agents spread his patriotic message far and wide. As people joined the Viet Minh, they were formed into military units. These units were led by Vo Nguyen Giap, one of Ho's most trusted lieutenants. Born in 1912, he was so handsome that Ho teased, "Vo Nguyen Giap is . . . beautiful like a girl." Although outwardly calm and cheerful, there was more to Giap than met the eye. Those who knew him gave him the nickname Nue Lua—"Volcano Under the Snow."

If Ho was the brain and spirit of the Viet Minh, Giap was its sword. Like his chief, Giap was born into a family of revolutionaries. In 1887, his father had led one of the last rebel bands to surrender to the French. The surrender took place at a village near the Laotian border. That village is called Dien Bien Phu, a name Giap would make famous sixty-seven years later.

Giap began his career not as a soldier, but as a high-school history teacher. Yet his mind always seemed to be on war. In his spare time he read every book he could find on military history. He worshiped Napoleon Bonaparte, possibly the greatest general who ever lived. Students found it easy to throw "the general," Giap, off the day's lesson. They had only to mention Napoleon and he would get carried away with descriptions of his battles. Giap's other heroes were Sun Tzu, an ancient Chinese general, and T. E. Lawrence, the legendary "Lawrence of Arabia," a British commander during World War I. Giap memorized long passages from the writings of both men. Sun Tzu's book, *The Art of War*, is the earliest known work on the subject. Lawrence's *Seven*

33

Pillars of Wisdom is a classic on the art of guerrilla warfare. Giap also admired Mao Tse-tung, who was fighting both the Chinese government and the Japanese invaders.

Giap paid a heavy price for becoming a Communist. Before joining Ho's staff, he had married a woman named Minh Thai. In the same month that Ho founded the Viet Minh, the Sûreté arrested Giap's wife, their daughter, and his sister-in-law. Both women were tortured to death; the child died in prison, no doubt from neglect. Giap swore vengeance upon the French. One day they would suffer as his loved ones had suffered.

Giap believed that day lay far in the future. The war would be protracted, lasting years, possibly decades. That had to be, he said, since the enemy had too many advantages. The French and Japanese had modern weapons, the Viet Minh only knives, spears, and old rifles. Still, as Giap's heroes had shown, the strongest enemy was only human, with human weaknesses. He was like a giant boulder under a leaky water faucet. Drip. Drip. Drip. Drip. Billions of tiny drops fell on the boulder over the years. Sooner or later they found its weakness, broke it to pieces, and turned these to sand. Similarly, a general could learn his enemy's weaknesses and use them against him.

Giap knew his enemy's weaknesses. The enemy was trained to fight big battles in the open. The French would try to draw out the Viet Minh, tempting it into actions it had no hope of winning. Giap refused to fight on these terms. He would trick the enemy, making them believe lies and distrust facts. When weak, he would pretend to be strong; when strong, pretend weakness. He would fight guerrilla style, using small units to strike swiftly and escape before the enemy could react. If outnumbered, it was all right to run away. After all, soldiers who died heroically were still dead, useless in the next battle. But if Giap saw an ad-

34

vantage to be gained, he would strike with everything he had. He'd go for blood. He'd kill the enemy's soldiers, destroy their bases, and take their weapons.

At such times men's lives were "cheap" and could be used up as needed. "Every minute, hundreds of thousands of people die on this earth," Giap explained. "The life or death of a hundred, a thousand, tens of thousands of human beings, even our own compatriots, means little." When asked if he ever had a moment's pity for all those he sent to certain death, Giap answered, "Never. Not a single moment."[4] Only the cause mattered. Given enough time, and enough blood, he could wear down the strongest enemy.

Fighting, however, was only one aspect of war. Giap recalled a saying of Napoleon's: "You can do anything with bayonets except sit on them." By this, Napoleon meant that force had its limits. Weapons alone do not win wars; soldiers do. Unless the soldiers believe in their cause, their weapons are little more than expensive junk.

Giap wanted his men not only to fight, but to give their lives freely, gladly, joyfully. He had good human material to work with. Viet Minh soldiers were usually peasants, men of marvelous stamina gained in a lifetime of physical work. Upon joining the Viet Minh, they were put into three-man teams known as "bands of brothers." A soldier's brothers were his army family. As with his real family, he must look after them and they must care for him. They shared their food, protected each other in battle, and tended each other's wounds. Each night they discussed whatever came to mind, sharing their innermost thoughts. If one seemed to be wavering, his comrades soothed him or reported him to their superiors.

Uncle Ho had taught these superiors, or cadres, all he knew

35

----

[4] Quoted in Karnow, *Vietnam: A History*, p. 141; Morley Safer, *Flashbacks: On Returning to Vietnam*, p. 18.

about propaganda. They in turn used his lessons to build morale in several ways. Songs and slogans were written to raise men's spirits. Storytelling sessions were devoted to Vietnam's ancient heroes, who died for their country. Recruits were asked to describe their sufferings under the foreigner, proving that all Viet Minh shared the same experiences. Each soldier came to see himself as a special person. He was a volunteer in a crusade for independence and justice. He fought for a cause he believed in, one that gave life meaning and for which he would gladly give his life.

Giap planned each operation down to the tiniest detail. This was especially important if men were seeing action for the first time. First-timers must always win, Giap believed; otherwise they would lose faith in themselves. If an outpost was to be attacked, the troops rehearsed on a mock-up of the target. Each man knew why the attack was necessary and his role in it. Before an ambush took place, officers studied the site carefully. Surprise was usually complete. The attackers struck quickly and vanished into the jungle before help arrived. Left behind were a few French dead, minus their weapons.

Each victory became a stepping-stone to the next. And as the Viet Minh grew bolder, the French increased their pacification efforts. French methods had not changed since the conquest, only now they were backed by the Japanese. As long as Frenchmen did the dirty work, the Japanese saw no reason to interfere. The only problem was that each burned village, each dead peasant, hurt the French more than the Viet Minh. Cruelty had a ripple effect, fueling the hatred of the victims' relatives, friends, and fellow villagers. Thus, every French "success" meant more recruits for the Viet Minh.

Nature seemed to favor the Viet Minh. In 1945, heavy rains broke the Red River dikes at several points, ruining the rice crop and bringing starvation. The French did little to help the people, the Japanese nothing; in fact, rice was shipped to Japan from the stricken areas. Two million people died in northern Vietnam. Dr. Tran Duy Hung of Hanoi likened the countryside to a vast, open grave:

> Peasants came in from the nearby provinces on foot, leaning on each other, carrying their children in baskets. They dug in garbage piles, looking for anything at all, banana skins, orange peels, discarded greens. They even ate rats. But they couldn't get enough to keep alive. They tried to beg, but everyone else was hungry, and they would drop dead in the streets. Every morning, when I opened my door, I found five or six corpses on the step. We organized teams of youths to load the bodies on oxcarts and take them to mass graves outside the city.[5]

Ho knew how to take advantage of the famine. His agents whipped up the peasants' hatred and led them in raids on Japanese granaries. Since those who took part in raids became outlaws in Japanese eyes, and therefore were marked for death, they had no choice but to join the Viet Minh.

Outside events finally brought matters to a head. The United States was drawn into World War II in part because of Indochina. President Franklin D. Roosevelt was deeply troubled by world events. By the summer of 1941, Hitler seemed unbeatable. His armies dominated western Europe and were racing across the plains of Russia toward Moscow. The President feared that the same would happen in Asia if Japan was allowed to continue its aggression.

Japan's takeover of Indochina stirred Roosevelt to action. To show his displeasure, he halted the sale of American oil, gasoline, machinery, and scrap iron to Japan. Tokyo's warlords, however, did not apologize; if anything, his action made them wild for revenge. Since only America could

37

---

[5] Quoted in Karnow, *Vietnam: A History*, p. 145.

check their ambitions in Asia, its power had to be broken as quickly as possible. On December 7, 1941, Japanese forces attacked Pearl Harbor in the Hawaiian Islands, crippling the U.S. Pacific Fleet. During the next six months, they overran American bases on Guam and Wake Island, captured the Philippines, defeated the British at Hong Kong and Singapore, and took the oil-rich Dutch East Indies.

In attacking Pearl Harbor, Japan set the stage for its own downfall. America, then the world's leading industrial nation, threw its resources into the war effort. Slowly at first, then with growing speed, American forces counterattacked across the Pacific. Japan's island fortresses fell one by one, bringing American power closer to Tokyo.

By the spring of 1945, World War II was nearing its end, with Allied invasion troops closing in on Germany. In April, Hitler committed suicide rather than be captured. On August 6, the Japanese city of Hiroshima was incinerated by "Thin Man," the first atomic bomb. On August 9, a second atomic bomb, "Fat Man," leveled Nagasaki. On August 14, one of the most terrible wars in human history came to an end.

These events gave Ho Chi Minh his big chance. Japanese troops were ordered by Tokyo to remain in their barracks until disarmed by the Allies. Better yet, five months before the surrender, Japan had taken over direct control of Vietnam. In a surprise move, French troops had been disarmed and put into prison camps. Now nothing stood in the way of the Viet Minh. On August 19, it occupied Hanoi without firing a shot. Citizens lined the streets, tossing flowers and cheering as their liberators marched through the city. It was the same in Hue, Da Nang, and Saigon. By August 25, eleven days after Japan's surrender, the Viet Minh held power everywhere.

Ho lost no time in declaring independence for the newly proclaimed Democratic Republic of Vietnam (DRVN). On September 2, he stepped onto the balcony of Hanoi's French theater. A half million people stood below, heads turned upward, waiting. Slowly he unfolded a paper and started to read into a microphone: "All men are created equal; they are endowed by their Creator with certain unalienable Rights; among these are Life, Liberty, and the pursuit of Happiness."

Suddenly Ho lowered the paper. His voice rising with emotion, he asked the crowd, "Do you hear me distinctly, fellow countrymen?"

"Yes!" they roared. "We hear you!"

Ho explained that his words came from the American Declaration of Independence. They were fine words, but they were not only for Americans. They belonged to all peoples. "All of the peoples of the earth are equal from birth, all the peoples have a right to live, to be happy and free. . . . Those are undeniable truths."[6]

Again the crowd roared in approval. Its enthusiasm amazed one of Ho's guests. Standing an arm's length from Ho, next to Vo Nguyen Giap, was an American major, Archimedes Patti, celebrating the birth of a nation that would one day be his country's bitterest foe. But for now they were allies.

President Roosevelt had wanted to aid all enemies of Japan, including Communists. On his orders, American advisers and weapons were flown into China by way of India. Although most went to the Chinese government, Mao Tsetung's rebels also received a share. Americans turned their attention to Indochina as well. Ho had gone out of his way to be helpful to them. Viet Minh patrols rescued American airmen downed in raids near Saigon. Viet Minh spies collected information on the Japanese. In 1944, the Office of Strategic Services (OSS), a "dirty tricks" unit specializing in guerrilla warfare, parachuted agents into Viet Minh territory. Their mission was to arm the Viet Minh and conduct joint

[6]Ho, *Ho Chi Minh On Revolution*, p. 141.

operations against the Japanese. Major Patti was one of the OSS officers.[7]

Ho looked to America for more than guns, valuable though these were. His real concern was not Japan's defeat, but preventing a French return afterward. The Soviets would be too busy rebuilding their ruined cities to support a small Southeast Asian country. The Western European countries cared nothing about Vietnam. Mao Tse-tung was saving every gun and bullet for another round of civil war. Only the United States was strong enough to deal with France.

Ho tried to use OSS agents as goodwill messengers to their leaders in Washington. He welcomed them with open arms and sweet words. He entertained them. He praised their country and pledged it eternal friendship. He even told Major Patti that the Vietnamese loved America. The OSS men responded in kind. "He was an awfully sweet old guy," an officer told a reporter ten years later. "If I had to pick out one quality about the little old man sitting on his hill in the jungle, it was his gentleness."[8]

Was this an act? That is a big question. For if Ho was sincere, then Washington's later actions were both foolish and unnecessary; indeed, next to the Civil War, they produced the worst tragedy in our nation's history. Unfortunately, we shall never learn the whole story, for Ho never revealed his innermost thoughts—at least not to Westerners. There are, however, hints of his insincerity from the very beginning. Remember, hints are not proofs. Nevertheless, they point in a certain direction.

In his dealings with Americans, Ho avoided the subject of communism. If cornered, however, he replied in one of two ways. First, he lied. State Department official Kenneth Lan-

---

[7]The OSS later became the Central Intelligence Agency, or CIA.
[8]Quotations in Michael Maclear, *The Ten Thousand Day War: Vietnam, 1945–1975*, p. 16; Robert Shaplen, "The Enigma of Ho Chi Minh," *The Reporter*, January, 1955.

don recalled, "He handed me . . . the . . . line that he wasn't a Communist. . . . That he'd been branded a Communist, but he really wasn't really." Or he admitted the truth, claiming it was of no importance whatsoever. Ho told Major Patti that "he was not a Communist in the American sense; he owed only his training to Moscow and, for that, he had repaid Moscow with fifteen years of party work. He considered himself a free agent." Actually, Ho said, he felt closer to America than to the Soviet Union. But this, too, was a lie. In 1945, in a private conversation, he snapped: "They [the Americans] are only interested in replacing the French. They want to reorganize our economy in order to control it. They are capitalists to the core. All that counts for them is business."[9]

This did not prevent Ho from using American aid for his own ends. Smiling his sweet smile, he asked OSS men to pose for pictures with himself and Viet Minh guerrillas. Ho's propaganda teams then showed the pictures to the peasants. Mrs. Le Thi Anh, a southern resistance leader, remembered how team members came to her village. "Do you want independence?" they asked, holding up the pictures. "We have to go with the victorious Allies. And Ho is the person who has the Allies' blessing."[10] Peasants may have known little about the outside world, but they did know that the United States was the strongest nation on earth. And if America supported Ho, then he alone deserved their loyalty.

There is no telling what would have happened had Franklin Roosevelt lived. Roosevelt disliked the French, whose colonies he considered business ventures run by well-dressed pirates. All their talk about a civilizing mission in Indochina was claptrap. "France has had the country . . . for nearly one hundred

41

---

[9] Quotations in Harry Maurer, *Strange Ground: Americans in Vietnam, 1945–1975: An Oral History*, p. 40; Thomas D. Boettcher, *Vietnam: The Valor and the Sorrow*, p. 75; Karnow, *Vietnam: A History*, p. 138.
[10] Quoted in Al Santoli, *To Bear Any Burden: The Vietnam War and Its Aftermath in the Words of Americans and Southeast Asians*, p. 34.

years," he told a White House guest, "and the people are worse off than they were at the beginning. . . . The people are entitled to something better than that."[11] That meant preventing France's return to Indochina after the war. Roosevelt wanted to put the area under United Nations control, with the aim of making it independent as quickly as possible. Unfortunately, he died in April 1945, and his plans died with him.

Late in the summer of 1945, the Allies began to take over Vietnam from the Japanese. Two hundred thousand Chinese government troops swarmed across its northern border. Hungry and ragged, many without boots, they looted villages along the way. Arriving in Hanoi, they broke into private homes to steal food, clothing, and bedding; they even tore tiles off the roofs and water pipes out of the walls for sale back home in China. Some fellows, who had never seen bars of soap, mistook them for food.

British forces occupied southern Vietnam. These troops had a double mission. Not only were they to disarm the Japanese, they were to help the French in any way they could. Helping the French seemed the sensible thing to do, for both countries had colonial empires. London feared that France's loss of Indochina would encourage patriots in its own territories, notably India, where Mahatma Gandhi led the movement for independence. It wanted France to reclaim Indochina, and the quicker the better.

The British freed all French prisoners and returned their weapons. The French then moved to overthrow Viet Minh authority in the south. Striking without warning, they seized every important building in Saigon. No Vietnamese patriot, Communist or otherwise, was safe from their vengeance. Hundreds were beaten, arrested, or shot while the British

42

---

[11] Quoted in James William Gibson, *The Perfect War: Technowar in Vietnam*, p. 45.

looked on, doing nothing. To add insult to injury, the British rearmed Japanese troops to "keep order" while Frenchmen went on their bloody rampage.

Ho's only choice was to make a deal with one enemy to get rid of another. On March 6, 1946, he agreed to allow 15,000 French troops to come north on condition that the Chinese return to their own country. The French promised in return to remove their troops within five years and recognize Vietnam as a free country within their empire.

Not all Viet Minh leaders approved of the agreement. It was a sell-out, they insisted, and they criticized Ho for allowing himself to fall into a trap. The Vietnamese people demanded independence as a human right, not as a French gift. And they demanded it now.

Ho listened to them patiently, until he could listen no more. "You fools!" he shouted at one meeting. "Don't you realize what it means if the Chinese remain? Don't you remember your history? The last time the Chinese came, they stayed a thousand years! The French are foreigners. They are weak. Colonialism is dying. . . . But if the Chinese stay now, they will never go. As for me, I prefer to sniff French shit for five years than eat Chinese shit for the rest of my life."[12] Coarse words, to be sure, but they had the ring of truth. After heated debate, the leaders went along with Ho's agreement.

The French, however, were acting in bad faith. They had no intention of surrendering the jewel of their empire to Viet Minh "peasants." On June 1, they separated the southern and northern parts of Vietnam, creating two countries. The southern part, with its vast plantations, became the State of Vietnam under the former emperor, Bao Dai. Known as the "playboy emperor," he had been taken to Paris as a child and raised as a Frenchman. Bao Dai had three loves: pretty women,

43

---

[12] Quoted in Karnow, *Vietnam: A History*, p. 153.

fattening foods, and fast horses. Governing was a bore and best left to others—that is, to Frenchmen. His State of Vietnam was merely the old French colony under another name.

The French had other plans for Ho's DRVN. During the fall of 1946, ships sailed from France loaded with combat troops. These included units of the French Foreign Legion, some of the toughest men who ever carried a gun. Hundreds of Legionnaires were French traitors who had served Hitler during the war; Paris had promised them full pardon in return for five years' service with the Foreign Legion in Indochina. Others were not Frenchmen at all, but oddballs, misfits, and criminals from every corner of the globe. Among them were former Nazi soldiers fleeing punishment for war crimes. In the evenings, before turning in, they would gather on deck to recall old times and sing their old marching songs. There were also units from France's African colonies: Algerians, desert tribesmen from Morocco, soldiers from Senegal and Upper Volta.

Each day brought war closer to Vietnam. A trigger-happy Legionnaire might shoot into a group of peasants carrying Viet Minh flags. That night a French jeep might be blown up on a Hanoi street, or a sentry found with his throat slit. Small incidents became big incidents, until they exploded into open warfare. On November 23, 1946, the French demanded that the Viet Minh leave Haiphong. To underline their demand, warships lobbed shells into the city, killing six thousand people. French troops then overran Haiphong and moved against Hanoi.

Ho abandoned Hanoi, pulling his troops back into the countryside. But before leaving, he issued a call to arms: "All Vietnamese must stand up to fight the French colonialists. . . . Those who have rifles must use their rifles; those who have swords will use their swords; those who have no sword will use spades, hoes, and sticks. Everyone must endeavor to oppose the colonialists and save his country."[13] The first Vietnam war had begun. It would last eight years.

Vo Nguyen Giap dug into his bag of tricks. Unable to match enemy firepower, he started an endless round of ambushes, hit-and-run raids, and sabotage operations. French commanders found it impossible to fight except on Giap's terms; and after three years of this, they gave up trying. Rather than chase the elusive Viet Minh, they decided to hold only key areas. Cities and important towns became strongholds defended by thousands of troops who seldom ventured beyond their forward outposts. Bridges, roads, and railway lines were guarded by smaller units. French army engineers built forts and pillboxes, concrete shelters with room for ten men and three machine guns. Forts and pillboxes were surrounded by trenches and coils of barbed wire. Thus the French army imprisoned itself, allowing the Viet Minh to move about the countryside freely.

This was exactly what Uncle Ho wanted, for it gave him a free hand with the people. Ho realized that this was not a war of armies or machines. These were important, of course, but they would not decide its outcome. This was a people's war, a struggle for the hearts and minds of ordinary men and women. The Viet Minh claimed to be the people's army; it lived among the people, drawing its strength from them. It might lose a piece of ground, but that meant nothing in the long run. The people alone mattered. As long as the Viet Minh kept their loyalty, it was unbeatable. It could take terrible losses, retreat to lick its wounds, and return stronger than ever.

Ho's orders were simple: the Viet Minh should do everything to win over the people. It must teach the illiterate to

45

---

[13] Quoted in Jean Lacouture, *Ho Chi Minh: A Political Biography*, p. 170.

read and bring medicine to the sick. It must help the peasants with their crops, working alongside them in the fields. Above all, it must respect them as human beings. Soldiers were to address civilians as members of their own families: *me* ("mother"), *bac* ("uncle"), *anh* ("elder brother"), and so on according to their age.

Anyone who stood between the Viet Minh and the people was to be killed without hesitation. Hundreds of non-Communist leaders were sent "crab fishing" by Viet Minh murder squads—that is, they were tied together in bunches and thrown into a river, slowly drowning as they floated down to the sea. Patriots who fought the French but refused Viet Minh control had two enemies. On several occasions, the Viet Minh betrayed non-Communist resistance fighters to the French.

The turning point came in 1949. In October, Mao Tse-tung swept to victory in China. At last the Viet Minh had a powerful friend nearby. Mao recognized the DRVN as Vietnam's only government and offered it aid. Years of hard fighting still lay ahead, but the outcome was certain. Ho already had the loyalty of millions; now he would have weapons for a real war. Mao sent loads of rifles, machine guns, and light cannon down secret trails in Laos. Viet Minh soldiers trained at Chinese army schools as engineers, radio operators, and artillerymen. Chinese advisers joined Viet Minh combat units.

France also found a friend. Americans had hoped for peace after World War II. Instead, they heard Soviet leaders declare that the future belonged to communism. The Soviets promised that one day Communist "freedom fighters," aided by Moscow, would set up "people's democracies" everywhere.

These boasts could not be ignored. By 1949, China had turned Communist and the European nations of East Germany, Poland, Romania, Hungary, and Czechoslovakia were ruled by local Communists backed by Soviet troops. The following year, Communist North Korea invaded South Korea, an American ally. American forces were sent, only to have a million Chinese troops intervene just when victory was in sight. After heavy fighting, a truce was signed. Yet the price had been high—more than 33,000 Americans dead and over 100,000 wounded.

Panic swept the United States. Wherever Americans turned, they saw communism on the march. A "cold war" had begun, a political rather than military struggle where the enemy could be anywhere—even in the U.S. government itself. Something had to be done, the nation's leaders believed, or democracy was doomed. In 1950, Senator Joseph McCarthy began a congressional witch-hunt to uncover Communists in the federal government and the army. Meanwhile, President Harry S. Truman had drawn the line in foreign policy: the United States would pledge its resources to resist communism everywhere around the globe.

A week after the Korean War began, Truman promised to support the French in Vietnam. This seemed the right thing to do at the time, for there was more at stake than French pride. Communist expansion had to be stopped, even if this meant supporting a colonial power.

American aid grew until it covered 78 percent of France's war expenses. Yet money could not buy victory. The more troops the French sent, the longer the casualty lists became. By 1953, their dead and wounded numbered 90,000, and there was no end in sight. The French people gradually tired of the war, calling it *la sale guerre,* "the dirty war." Anti-war demonstrations led to riots and police brutality. French Communists stoned hospital trains that carried wounded returning from Vietnam. Communist dockworkers refused to load vessels bound for the Far East, or to unload coffins of the dead shipped home for burial. *La sale guerre* was tearing the country apart.

47

General Henri Navarre, the commander in Vietnam, knew that time was running out. If France was to win, he had to act boldly. He would offer Giap a tempting target and, when Giap reached for it, smash the Viet Minh in an all-out battle. The target was to be a remote mountain valley in northwestern Vietnam. Only ten miles from the Laotian border, the valley lay within easy reach of Viet Minh supply lines from China. The valley takes its name from the village of Dien Bien Phu.

In November 1953, French paratroopers dropped into Dien Bien Phu. Here they dug trenches, strung barbed wire, and built dugouts roofed with sandbags. In the surrounding hills were outposts manned by Legionnaires, mostly Germans, and linked to the main base. The key to the whole position, however, was a small airstrip. Navarre knew that Giap would cut the roads, and that his supplies would have to come by air. That was no problem, he believed. Although France had only a hundred warplanes in all of Indochina, the Viet Minh had none. Moreover, the Viet Minh had no heavy guns, and even if they did, it would be impossible to get them through the rugged hills. Giap would have to rely on manpower alone, which the French could blast at will. Navarre was so confident that he could see only victory. "I can see it clearly," he said, "like light at the end of a tunnel."

Uncle Ho knew better. Studying his maps, he saw that Dien Bien Phu was a death trap—for the French. The truce in Korea had enabled Mao Tse-tung to supply whatever Ho needed for the final campaign. Chinese aid included 600 trucks filled with supplies, plus heavy artillery, heavy machine guns, and antiaircraft guns. Many of these weapons had been taken from the Americans in Korea.

Giap set out to do the "impossible." One hundred thousand *dan cong*, "civilian laborers," were sent to build a mountain road from the Chinese border. The work was difficult,

General Vo Nguyen Giap (above, in
white suit) reviews the people's army in
1952. During the course of the first
Vietnam War, Giap turned a small
guerilla army into a force powerful
enough to defeat the French on their
own terms. At right, French soldiers run
for cover during the Viet Minh's nonstop bombardment of Dien Bien Phu.

since they had only picks and shovels, but they kept going. As the road progressed, their comrades dragged "steel elephants," heavy guns, up steep hillsides. Day by day, inch by inch, they trudged toward Dien Bien Phu. To encourage them, agitprop teams chanted a slogan: "Everything for the Front! Everything for Victory!" People did, indeed, sacrifice everything. One crew, for example, was hauling a gun when the rope snapped. A man immediately threw himself under the wheels rather than have the weapon roll over a cliff. He died instantly.

Giap was now racing a deadline. The great powers—the United States, Great Britain, the Soviet Union, China— feared that world events were spinning out of control. To avoid catastrophe, a conference was called to settle various problems, including Vietnam. The conference was to meet in Geneva, Switzerland, in the spring of 1954; on May 8 it would begin discussing a cease-fire in Vietnam. All eyes suddenly focused on Dien Bien Phu, for whoever held it when the conference began could negotiate from a position of strength. Giap had to take it before the conference opened. The French had to hold it at any price.

Navarre's troops were in a dangerous position. The Viet Minh outclassed them in every way at Dien Bien Phu. In manpower, they held more than a four-to-one advantage: 49,000 Viet Minh troops to 10,800 French. In artillery, the Viet Minh outnumbered them at least five to one: 200 heavy guns to 40. While the French guns stood in the open, the Viet Minh's were hidden in hillside caves. The only way to destroy them was with a direct hit. But if enemy fire came too close, the crews could easily pull the guns back into the caves.

On March 13, 1954, Giap gave the signal to attack. His guns roared, hurling tons of explosives into the valley below. Their fire was so accurate that they knocked out the airstrip in the first minutes of combat. Burning fuel and ammunition sent up clouds of thick black smoke. Planes became masses of charred, twisted metal. The base's aerial lifeline was cut; from then on it had to be supplied by parachute drops. Yet the day had only begun. The barrage lifted, opening the way for the Viet Minh infantry. Attacking in human waves, they wiped out the first of Dien Bien Phu's eight outposts.

Day one was a disaster for the French. In the days that followed, things grew steadily worse. Dien Bien Phu was hammered in round-the-clock bombardments. One by one the outposts were overrun by infantry assaults. At night, the Viet Minh advanced toward the base by digging lines of trenches. They even drove a mine shaft under one outpost, blowing it sky-high with dynamite.

The Viet Minh kept up the pressure despite terrific losses. An Algerian sergeant saw their determination up close. He had been captured and was being led back to enemy lines through a minefield. Mangled bodies of Viet Minh soldiers lay thick on the ground. The Algerian was told to use the bodies as stepping stones; at least there were no mines under *them*. He was about to step on one supposed corpse when its eyes opened, staring at him in stark terror. The soldier was alive, but as good as dead, for his chest was torn open. "You can step on him," an officer exclaimed. "He has done his duty for the People's Army."[14]

The French fought bravely, but it was no use. Supplies dropped by parachute usually drifted into Viet Minh positions; heavy antiaircraft fire prevented pilots from coming close to the base. Food and ammunition began to run out. Medical supplies were so scarce that wounds became infected. The underground hospital filled with feverish, moaning men lying naked on stretchers, covered with their own

51

---

[14]Quoted in Boettcher, *Vietnam: The Valor and the Sorrow*, pp. 135–136.

vomit and filth. Finally, on May 7, Day fifty-six of the battle, the last French position fell. Giap had met his deadline with a day to spare. He had won a great victory, but no peace.

The day after the surrender, U.S. Marine drill sergeants at Quantico, Virginia, lined up their men and announced: "Dien Bien Phu just fell. Your rifles had better be clean."

TWO VIETNAMS
BETWEEN THE WARS

---

*Our Vietnam is one, our nation is one. You must
remember, though the rivers may run dry and the
mountains erode, the nation will always be one.*

—Ho Chi Minh

THE FALL OF DIEN BIEN PHU MOVED THE ACTION
from the battlefield to the conference room. This was strange
ground for Uncle Ho's representatives, and things did not
go smoothly for them at Geneva. Having won a decisive victory, they expected to make peace on their own terms. The
conference, they insisted, must unify Vietnam and recognize
its independence without delay.

Yet that was easier said than done. President Dwight D.
Eisenhower saw Vietnam as the first "domino" in a row that
contained all the nations of Southeast Asia. If the Communists won in Vietnam, according to the domino theory, the
other nations would topple. Rather than see this happen, Eisenhower hinted that he might send troops to Vietnam. This
was no idle threat. Americans had taken an active role at
Dien Bien Phu. Civilian pilots, hired by the CIA, flew many
of the resupply missions to the base. As the French position
crumbled, a carrier task force was alerted for possible air
strikes against the Viet Minh. There was even a plan to drop

atomic bombs on Viet Minh troop concentrations. Code-named "Vulture," the plan called for using up to six bombs, each three times more powerful than the one that destroyed Hiroshima. The President, however, failed to win congressional approval and no action was taken.

The Geneva conference was meant to ease tensions, not provoke World War III. After all, the Soviets had their own arsenal of atomic bombs. Rather than risk American intervention, the Soviets and Chinese persuaded Ho's men to accept a compromise. On July 21, 1954, two documents were made public. The first was a cease-fire, signed by both sides, in which Vietnam was divided along the 17th Parallel. French forces were to regroup south, Viet Minh forces north, of this Demilitarized Zone (DMZ). Civilians who wished to move from one zone to the other could freely do so for ten months. An International Control Commission made up of Canada, India, and Poland would supervise the cease-fire and report any violations.

The second document, or Final Declaration, called for free elections within two years to decide on reunification. The Final Declaration was neither signed nor voted on by the conference members. This strange behavior has puzzled historians ever since. Some believe that it was a polite way of saying that Vietnam was to be divided permanently; otherwise, allowing civilians to cross the DMZ would make no sense at all. Just as there was an East and West Germany and a North and South Korea, there would be a North and South Vietnam.

The United States kept its distance from the Geneva agreements. Signing them, it was felt, meant accepting and supporting a Communist conquest, something the nation could never do. The American representative simply "took note" of the agreements, promising that his government would "refrain from the threat or use of force to disturb [them]." In addition, he warned that the United States would look upon any violations with "grave concern." Translation: Washington would not be bound by an agreement it did not like. It would see how things worked out, hoping for the best but preparing for the worst. If the Communists threatened South Vietnam, it could do as it thought best without having broken a treaty.

South Vietnam made no promises at all. In June 1954, France granted it full independence. Emperor Bao Dai and his prime minister, Ngo Dinh Diem, opposed reunification elections from the outset. As an independent state, South Vietnam could accept or reject any treaty, they said. By rejecting the Final Declaration, it was not legally or morally bound by its provisions. Besides, elections meant suicide for South Vietnam. Ho Chi Minh could win any free election with 80 percent of the vote, according to experts. Yet elections were a one-way street; once elected, no Communist government had ever been "unelected." Ho might take power democratically, but he would never be bound by the will of the people. Only the Communist party, he believed, knew what was good for the nation. Those who opposed it were fools or criminals and would be treated accordingly.

Nobody was happy with the Geneva agreements. France had lost its best colony. The Viet Minh had to give up hard-won territory. The United States and South Vietnam feared for the future. Having ended one war, Geneva planted the seeds of a far more terrible struggle.

One summer's day in 1954, Viet Minh soldiers boarded ships at a South Vietnamese seaport. They were among the 100,000 men being sent north in keeping with the Geneva agreements. Waving good-bye to their families, they held up two fingers for the victory sign and for the two years they would be gone. As the ship pulled away from shore, French troops sitting on the dock burst into laughter. Leaning backward, they took off their boots and wiggled their toes and hands in the air. Their message was plain: the Viet Minh had been tricked. They would be in North Vietnam not for two years, but for twenty. The departing Viet Minh smiled. Two years! Two years! The Geneva agreement said so, and they believed.

Had Ho and his aides been at dockside, they might have laughed along with the Frenchmen. The joke was on their own faithful soldiers. We know that they never expected reunification elections to be held. But that did not matter— for the time being. They would use the two years to rebuild North Vietnam and prepare for the coming struggle.

Ho understood the importance of having firm ties to South Vietnam. Although most southern-born Viet Minh left for the North, several thousand hard-core troops stayed behind. Some lived undercover in the populated areas to build secret organizations. Most, however, lived deep in the jungles along the Cambodian border, avoiding contact with outsiders. They were the embryo of an army waiting to be born. An unusual number of "funerals" were held in South Vietnam during 1954. Opening a coffin, however, might give you the shock of your life; for instead of a body, you might find guns and ammunition wrapped in plastic. They were to be kept in the ground until Hanoi gave the order to fight.

Since that might not be for years, Ho turned to the younger generation. Soldiers bound for the North were encouraged to marry local girls and get them pregnant before leaving. The girls would have their children, thereby linking them to the Viet Minh. In addition, hundreds of children between the ages of seven and fifteen were kidnapped from their families and taken north. Some of these youngsters, as North Vietnamese soldiers, would fight their way into Saigon twenty years later. Uncle Ho always took the "long view."[1]

Southern children might be persuaded to attend secret

---

[1] Santoli, *To Bear Any Burden*, pp. 55, 59.

Viet Minh schools. Among them was Truong Mealy, who became a spy in Saigon. Mealy was ten when his schooling began. His teachers never called themselves Communists, only patriots committed to reuniting their beloved country. They taught him all sorts of "useful" things. He learned, for example, how to lie to his mother so he could go on training missions lasting several days at a time. "From the very beginning we were taught the art of deception," he recalled. "Telling lies is part of winning the victory. . . . We say: The victory will justify everything." His books included one about brave children, like the hero who thrust his head into the barrel of an enemy cannon to block it during an attack. The boy died happily, a true patriot. Above all, Mealy learned to look upon Ho as a god. He and his teacher would stand with their eyes fixed on Ho's picture, giving thanks for the blessings he had brought the people.[2]

Life with Uncle Ho, however, was anything but blessed. Under him, North Vietnam became a dictatorship run by the Communist party. True, there was a constitution that guaranteed freedom of the press, speech, and other civil liberties. But none of these freedoms were ever put into effect. They remained words on paper, masking the reality of Communist rule.

All political parties except the Communists were abolished and their leaders jailed or killed, as were hundreds of non-Communist members of the Viet Minh. The Communist party controlled the government and was in turn controlled by a handful of leaders chosen in phony elections. Free elections were fine for South Vietnam, as long as the "right" people were chosen. But they had no place in the North. The party named all candidates and saw that they won by huge majorities; Communists once received 99.8 percent of

57

---

[2] *Ibid.*, p. 59ff.

the vote. People voted not because they liked a candidate, but because a stamped voting card was also a ration card, without which you could not buy food. Ho Chi Minh was president, Pham Van Dong prime minister, and Vo Nguyen Giap minister of defense. These titles, too, were meaningless, since Ho kept power in his own hands.

Citizens became the property of the Communist party. Their only "liberty" was that of obeying its commands with a show of enthusiasm. The secret police watched everyone, peered into everything. Nothing was too petty to escape notice. Ordinary people could not move about freely, since travel was strictly regulated. Before setting out, even for a neighboring village, you had to tell the police who you wanted to visit and why. If they approved, you were issued a pass, which must be shown to bus drivers, innkeepers, and guards posted at crossroads. Anything suspicious had to be reported to the police at once. And God help you if you could not explain your actions! There was no one to appeal to if you were wronged by the police. Courts and judges served the party, not the law; in any case, law was whatever the Communist party decided.

All means of expression were kept under tight control. The idea was to shape people's thoughts by controlling the information they received. Newspapers and magazines printed only what the party considered the truth. Owning a radio became a privilege; in order to buy one, you needed a letter from your local party boss. Most people, especially those living outside the cities, got their information from loudspeakers. Thousands of these devices blanketed the country. There was no way to turn them off, and they blared at full power. Several times each day, they broadcast news and music. News items came straight from Radio Moscow or Radio Beijing. Music was . . . well, practical. No song could be printed or sung in public without official approval.

58

Songs dealt with patriotism and work, not love and mushy sentiment. Western popular music was considered "degenerate" and never played in North Vietnam.

Thought control began in school and continued throughout one's life. Before being allowed near a classroom, teachers had to pass tests in both communism and their subject areas. Yet these were really the same, for all subjects were given a Communist slant. For instance, mathematical problems might give a machine gun's rate of fire, asking how many bullets it could shoot at a "colonialist aggressor" airplane in a given time.

Once a privilege not everyone could enjoy, education was now offered free to all children. And the first lesson all youngsters were taught was to put duty to communism above everything else. Private concerns, such as falling in love, interfered with work and must therefore be postponed. Le Thanh, an engineer who escaped to the West, recalled his school days: "We had no private lives to speak of. Although we were teenagers, we didn't have any girlfriends. I told myself that I should live as a real Communist lives, the pure life of a revolutionary. We tried not even to think about girls. We would feel guilty if we caught ourselves singing some romantic song. At that time the Party had a slogan called 'Ba Khoan'—'The Three Delays': 'If you don't have a child, delay having one. If you aren't married, delay getting married. If you aren't in love, delay love.' So we delayed love."[3]

Private businesses had no place in North Vietnam. Ho began by seizing stores, factories, mines, railways, and banks. The state fixed prices, wages, and working conditions. While workers were assured of stable food prices and free medical attention, they were powerless. The unions, which once served their members, now served the government. Strikes

59

---

[3] Quoted in David Chanoff and Doan Van Toai, *Portrait of the Enemy*, p. 61.

were outlawed. Poor quality work was punished by a term in a forced labor camp. On certain holidays, such as Uncle Ho's birthday, unions volunteered their members for extra work at no pay. Those who did well were named "heroes of labor."

Late in 1954, Ho turned his attention to the countryside. Squads of trained cadres were sent to the villages to stir up peasant anger against the landlords. Not every landlord, of course, had been a "thief and bloodsucker," but that was not the issue. Landlords were the largest group of property owners and therefore had to be eliminated. The party's orders were not to bother about innocence or guilt: "Better to kill ten innocents than let one reactionary escape."[4] A reactionary was anyone who disagreed with the Communists.

When the peasants' anger reached its boiling point, landlords were put on trial for their lives. They were not allowed to defend themselves, only to confess their "crimes" and plead for mercy. "Evidence" against them was given by neighbors, who either hated them or feared the Communists. Worse, children were forced to denounce their parents in order to stay alive. Hoang Van Chi, a Viet Minh soldier, recalled what happened in his village. "If the eldest [child] is a girl with younger brothers and sisters, she is told: 'If you do not denounce your father, you will be classified as a landlord, too. But if you publicly denounce your father and say that he raped you, you can stay home to take care of your brothers and sisters.' To save the rest of her family, she was obliged to go along."[5]

The more landlords killed, the more blood Hanoi demanded. Each district had its quota of landlords to be executed. If the quota was not met, the cadres were held responsible. Cadres,

---

[4] Santoli, *To Bear Any Burden*, p. 46.
[5] *Ibid.*, p. 45.

desperate to save themselves, labeled peasants as landlords when there were no longer any real landlords to kill. This in turn triggered serious revolts. The largest revolt occurred in 1956, only a few miles from Ho's birthplace, and a whole army division was needed to restore order. Like the French earlier, it did so with extreme cruelty. Ho finally called off the campaign and apologized for its "excesses." Still, that was cold comfort for the 50,000 victims and their families.

In the meantime, Ngo Dinh Diem had taken power in the South. Born in 1901, Diem belonged to one of Vietnam's wealthiest Catholic families. Acquaintances—he had no friends—found him stubborn and bigoted, always demanding his own way. No lover of democracy, he believed that only superior men, such as himself, were qualified to rule. Yet he was anti-Communist, and that excused many sins as far as Americans were concerned. Communism, for Diem, was not simply wrong. It was a crime against God that he could not tolerate and remain a Christian.

Washington decided to help Diem turn South Vietnam into a strong nation. It began with his fellow Catholics in the North. While the southern Viet Minh were sailing north, northern Catholics were heading south. To encourage them, CIA agents spread the word that "the Virgin Mary is going south" to escape persecution. Catholics, however, needed little encouragement; they could see the persecution with their own eyes. Catholics, many of whom had favored the French, became targets for Viet Minh revenge. Desperate to leave, entire villages packed their belongings and made for the coast. Eventually, 860,000 people were brought south by U.S. Navy vessels.

American aid began to flow into South Vietnam. Engineers helped repair war damage and improve the transportation system. Experts in criminology reorganized the police

61

A Catholic priest flees North Vietnam with his congregation in 1954, at left. Below, President Diem meets with Buddhist monks. Denied religious freedom by the pro-Catholic Diem, Buddhists in South Vietnam rebelled against his policies.

and trained them in the latest methods. The bulk of the aid, however, went to the military. The Army of Vietnam (ARVN) received weapons, along with instructors to teach their use. These instructors, only a handful at the beginning, would grow to thousands within a decade.

Diem's power grew steadily. In 1955, he asked the people if they wanted to get rid of Emperor Bao Dai and replace him with a president. Bao Dai was unpopular, and there was every reason to believe that voters would support Diem. Unfortunately, he, like his foes in Hanoi, believed that the best election was a rigged election. Diem's goon squads, paid with American dollars, stood beside the ballot boxes to "help" citizens make up their minds. Diem won with 98.2 percent of the vote. His vote in Saigon was larger than the number of registered voters, proof that the election was a fake.

Having won the presidency, Diem turned South Vietnam into a dictatorship. Reunification elections were blocked. The national assembly was packed with Diem supporters, corrupt men more interested in making money than in their country's welfare. Only those loyal to Diem received government jobs. His younger brother, Ngo Dinh Nhu, headed the secret police. Nhu's wife, Le Xuan ("Beautiful Spring"), became the nation's moral governor. Known as the "Dragon Lady," she had strong opinions about right and wrong. It was right for the rich to get richer; she enjoyed the latest Paris fashions and wore large diamond rings. It was wrong for citizens to behave "improperly." At her insistence, divorce was abolished, abortion outlawed, beauty contests and boxing matches banned, and dancing forbidden even in private homes.

63

Anyone who objected was labeled a criminal or a Communist. In fact, few of Diem's opponents were Communist party members, but patriots who could not bear to see him ruin their country. That made no difference to brother Nhu's police. Thousands were arrested, beaten, and held for years without trial. As a result, millions of others, who would have supported a democratic leader, turned against their president.

The Viet Minh received Diem's special attention. Anyone who had resisted the French was seen as a threat to his rule. The homes of former Viet Minh soldiers were raided and their families tortured to reveal their whereabouts. Men were hunted down and shot. Prisoners were crowded into "tiger cages," cement pits roofed with iron bars. Tiger cages were tiny torture chambers where prisoners nearly drowned in the rain and broiled in the sun. Life in them was so unbearable that inmates went mad with thirst, drinking their own urine.

The story of the Vietnam War is not one of good versus evil. Though different in their beliefs, the governments of North and South Vietnam were very much alike in their methods. Nevertheless, Washington saw Diem as the lesser evil. Although his country was no democracy, it might become one with American help; the North could never become a democracy under Communist rule. In any case, supporting Diem seemed better than having the dominoes fall throughout Southeast Asia.

In January 1959, Ho met with his advisers to discuss the situation in the South. After careful consideration, they decided to unify the two Vietnams by force. An army detachment, Unit 559, was formed to extend the old Laotian supply trail southward through eastern Cambodia and into South Vietnam. Never mind that Laos and Cambodia were neutral under the Geneva agreements; the trail mattered more than any scrap of paper. Begun in secrecy, the Ho Chi Minh Trail, as it came to be known, would play a key role in the coming war. In 1959 alone, at least 5,000 southern-born Viet Minh used it to return to their homeland. Their mission was not to fight; there would be plenty of that later.

For the time being, they were to lay low, re-form their guer-rilla bands, and expand their contacts in the countryside. Many returned to their villages to see their children, now five, for the first time. The village was good cover, and they easily blended into the population.

Hanoi took its next step toward the end of 1960. In De-cember, it created the National Liberation Front of South Vietnam (NLF). The moment Diem heard the name, he dubbed it the Viet Cong—Vietnamese Communists. His term stuck, and we shall use it from now on.

The Viet Cong, as its official name indicates, was a front. Like the Viet Minh, it had several goals. One was to give the impression, particularly in the Western democracies, that the coming struggle was a civil war in the South, not an invasion from the North. Another aim was to rally Diem's opponents under a single banner. Viet Cong propaganda stressed unity. Its flag—half red, half blue, with a gold star in the center—symbolized national unity and justice. Its program avoided Communist slogans in favor of democratic principles. It promised all the right things: high wages, low taxes, land to the peasants, respect for private property, women's rights, an end to illegal arrests, peace with other nations. Enemies were to be forgiven and the two Vietnams unified "by peaceful means" after Diem's defeat.

The Viet Cong, however, was not an independent orga-nization. Southerners never controlled it, even though it bore their name. It was a puppet, with only a privileged few knowing the identity of the puppet master. Every important position was held by a Communist appointed by Hanoi. Hanoi made all the decisions, gave all the orders, pulled all the strings.

Few saw through the fraud at the beginning. Among those who did was the father of Truong Nhu Tang, a founder of the NLF and its minister of justice. Although no Communist,

Tang was prepared to work with the party for the common good. He joined the NLF because he believed that Uncle Ho was above all a patriot. He knew nothing of the dictatorship Ho had set up in the North. But his father knew a great deal. "In return for your service," the old man warned, "the Communists will not even give you a part of what you have now. Worse, they will betray you and persecute you all of your life."[6] Tang would not listen. And, like so many other naive people, he learned the truth only when it was too late.

Hanoi ordered the Viet Cong to expand without delay. Its expansion plan had four parts: propaganda, taking over villages, terrorism, and military action. Each part was linked to the others, pieces of a vast jigsaw puzzle. Although important in itself, each part depended on the others to form the whole picture—that is, the final victory.

Viet Cong propaganda was handled by agitprop teams made up of highly talented people. Team members sharpened their skills in scores of hidden jungle camps. Professional actors taught speakers to regulate their voices, keep eye contact with the audience, and use hand gestures to drive home a point. Performers learned to dance, sing, and put on skits with the Viet Cong message. Not only did these deal with serious matters, they were also quite amusing. Filled with jokes and pranks, they used laughter to undermine respect for Diem. A favorite prank was to dress monkeys in pants and shirts, paint their faces to look like Diem, write slogans on the backs of their shirts, and release them in a crowded place. The monkeys would start leaping around and chattering. Passersby roared with laughter at their antics and those of the police, who tried to catch the monkeys to tear off their clothes. Shooting them would have been like killing Diem, and therefore treason.

Taking over a village was no laughing matter. It began

---

[6] Santoli, *To Bear Any Burden*, p. 77.

with an agitprop team coming to help the peasants in some small way; a health worker bandaged cuts, or laborers dug a ditch, or a blacksmith repaired a broken plow. Its work done, the team left the village, only to return in a day or two. There were more favors, and a few questions were asked: "Don't Diem's officials steal our taxes?" "Aren't we entitled to a better life?" People nodded their heads in agreement. In time, the team asked for a favor in return. For instance, it would be nice if the village council let them hold a meeting to discuss important matters. At the meeting, speakers explained the Viet Cong program and what it meant for ordinary people. The meeting ended with a skit, or a song, or a team member teaching a slogan. It might be Uncle Ho's slogan, "*Khong gi quy hon duc lap tu do*"—"Nothing is more precious than independence and liberty." Or "*Muon doc lap phai do mau!*"—"For freedom you have to spend your blood!" Or simply, "*Vietnam, muon nam!*"—"Long live Vietnam!"

Eventually, a few team members stayed behind when their comrades left. Since they knew everyone by then, it was easy to organize associations for farmers, women, and young people. Association members helped one another in their work, as good neighbors should; they also enabled the Viet Cong to keep an eye on the people at all times. Eventually the agitprop team returned to ask for food or recruits for Viet Cong fighting units. After all, the leader explained, they served the people and deserved their help.

ARVN troops, hearing that Viet Cong were nearby, visited the village. Viet Cong were seldom found, for they looked like everyone else. In searching for them, the troops spoke rudely to the villagers, perhaps beat a few with their rifle butts. When they left, the Viet Cong easily convinced the villagers that the ARVN would be back with guns blazing. They must defend their homes, and the Viet Cong knew just what to do.

67

Village defenses, though simple, were highly effective. Roads near the village were cut with ditches to block motor vehicles. The surrounding tree lines held camouflaged foxholes and trenches. Pungi stakes, bamboo sticks with razorsharp points, were set in the mud of the rice paddies or in the high grass on either side of paths. A pungi could easily slice through the sole of an army boot; the Viet Cong liked to smear them with human excrement and let the bacteria do the rest. The wound became infected, putting the victim out of action for weeks; many died of blood poisoning.

A village in Ben Tre province south of Saigon defended itself with bees. In this area, there is a type of wild bee with a potent sting. Villagers would plug up the entrance to a hive with sticky paper, attach a string to the paper, and place the hive alongside a path. When government troops approached, they would disturb the string, pulling away the paper. That did it! Swarms of bees would cover the troops from head to foot. Men would leap into the air, slapping themselves, rolling on the ground, diving into paddies—anything to escape the insects. The villagers were so encouraged by this that they began to raise bees especially for their defenses. After a short time, they had so many hives that government troops took long detours to avoid the village.

Viet Cong efforts were always supported by terror. *Terror* is defined as the deliberate use of murder, torture, and fear, mainly against the defenseless, to gain a political objective. For the Viet Cong, terrorism was "education by violence," teaching that they would do anything to cripple Diem's government. Those who served Saigon went in constant fear of their lives. Civil servants, tax collectors, and policemen were stalked by roving assassination squads. Yet one did not have to be seen as evil to be marked for death. The worst and the best were chosen: the worst because removing them showed the Viet Cong's "love" for the people, the best in order to remove the people's natural leaders. Among the best were village leaders, doctors, nurses, public health officers, teachers, and social workers.

Although executions took different forms, the Viet Cong tried to carry them out publicly as lessons to others. A victim might be shot outside a church, with a note explaining why pinned to his shirt. Or a bus might be stopped on a highway and a policeman in civilian clothes taken off at gunpoint. As passengers looked on silently, a Viet Cong would read the death sentence while another beheaded the victim with a machete. A particularly vicious method was disemboweling: slashing open a victim's belly and allowing the guts to spill onto the ground. An estimated 4,118 South Vietnamese were assassinated by the Viet Cong up to 1962. During that same period, 4,436 were kidnapped and never seen again. There were probably a lot more, but the Viet Cong did not report the numbers to Saigon, much less invite Western newsmen to watch them in action.

Terrorism's other purpose was to isolate the people from the government. Any activity sponsored by Saigon was banned by the Viet Cong. Take, for example, traveling along a public road. The Viet Cong mined roads used by peasants to carry their produce to market. Likewise, hospitals, clinics, and ambulances were blown up or machine-gunned in hit-and-run raids.

The Viet Cong tried its best to close the public schools. In doing so, it intentionally harmed children, which Diem's thugs never did. Once, some Viet Cong entered a school near Hue, where the teacher was discussing Vietnamese history. They shot him in front of the class, explaining that he was giving government propaganda. As a warning to others not to listen to government lies, they hammered pencils into several children's ears.[7] Another team stopped a school bus

69

---

[7] Tim Page, *Nam: The Vietnam Experience, 1965–1975*, p. 25.

to tell the driver the children must not go to school again. The driver gave the message to the parents, who did not believe they were serious. But they were *very* serious. A few days later, they stopped the bus again, took off a little girl, and cut off her fingers. The school closed. Viet Cong also threw grenades into schools and ambushed a bus carrying twenty girls, members of a government youth group, killing nine. Miss Vo Thi Lo, a schoolteacher, was kidnapped; villagers found her three days later with her throat cut. In each case the lesson was obvious: "We are teaching you not to cooperate with the government."[8]

Terrorism provided a daily reminder that Saigon could not protect the people. This was important for two reasons. First, it kept citizens in fear. A Viet Cong threat had to be taken seriously, since its agents could strike anyone whenever it pleased. Second, it kept the Viet Cong's own followers in line. The Viet Cong used a "double hostage" system in which a fighter's relatives suffered if he deserted, or he suffered if they failed to support the cause in any way. Mrs. Xom Lang, for example, was taken from her home and beheaded in a rice field because her husband had deserted his unit. The Viet Cong claimed responsibility, explaining why it was "necessary."[9]

Nothing could save a Viet Cong deserter. Without exception, deserters' punishment was cruel and fatal. A young woman named Thuy was typical. Thuy was married to an ARVN soldier when the Viet Cong caught up with her. Let Nguyen Van Thich, her killer, tell what happened next:

> Thuy was living near the electric company in Soc Trang City. Around midnight one night we broke into her house.

---

[8]Douglas Pike, *Viet Cong: The Organization and Techniques of the National Liberation Front of South Vietnam*, p. 244; Pike, *The Viet Cong Strategy of Terror*, pp. 29, 94ff.
[9]Pike, *The Viet Cong Strategy of Terror*, p. 111.

Her husband . . . wasn't at home. She was sleeping and was obviously pregnant, near term. But I couldn't afford any indecisiveness. I had orders to kill her. So I woke her up. . . . Once we got her out into the open I told her, 'You have harmed the Liberation Movement a lot. The people have sentenced you to death and I have been given the job of executing you. . . . If I spare you, I will be killed myself.' . . . We took her over to the road and stabbed her in the chest. She slumped down without a moan. . . . I regret that I killed her while she was pregnant. I should have waited for her delivery.[10]

The largest single act of terrorism occurred at Dak Song, a village that had refused to cooperate with the Viet Cong. Located seventy-five miles northeast of Saigon, Dak Song was home to 2,000 people. On the night of December 5, 1967, a Viet Cong force attacked with Soviet-made flamethrowers. The villagers were unarmed and helpless, since their few defenders were cut off in a camp nearby. Spraying fire as they went, the raiders burned everything—trees, fences, gardens, farm animals, houses, and people. When they ran out of flamethrower fuel, they rounded up survivors and shot them in the head. Those who saw Dak Song the next day could scarcely believe their eyes. An American adviser described the scene:

As we approached the place I thought I saw charred cordwood piled up the way you pile up logs neatly beside the road. When we got closer I could see that it was the burned bodies of several dozen babies. The odor of burned flesh . . . reached us outside [the village] and of course got stronger at the center. . . . I saw a small boy and a smaller girl, probably his sister, sort of melted together in a charred embrace. I saw a mother burned black still holding two children, also burned black.

---

[10]Chanoff and Doan, *Portrait of the Enemy*, p. 170.

Villagers found themselves caught in the middle of the conflict between the Army of Vietnam (ARVN) and the Viet Cong. Above, the wife of a Viet Cong cowers in fear with her children as an ARVN patrol enters her village. Below, a survivor of the VC terrorist attack on Dak Song weeps among the ruins.

Everything was burned and charred. The worst was the wail of the survivors who were picking through the smoldering ruins. One man kept screaming and screaming at the top of his lungs.

The toll: 252 dead, mostly women and children; 200 kidnapped, never to be seen again; and 500 missing and presumed dead. One man lost 13 members of his family. Dak Song had been taught a lesson it would never forget.[11]

Military action completed the Viet Cong program. The Viet Cong had two types of fighting units. Local Force units consisted of poorly trained peasants armed with old rifles, spears, crossbows, machetes, and clubs. Farmers by day, they went into action at night, setting booby traps, killing individual ARVN, and making general nuisances of themselves.

Main Force units were full-time guerrillas who operated from camps hidden in jungles, mountains, and the swamps of the Mekong delta. In addition to living quarters, these camps had hospitals for the wounded and workshops for repairing weapons. Even so, this was no life for weaklings. Each soldier, in order to move quickly, had few possessions other than his weapon. A pair of black cotton pajamas, underpants, hat, canteen, hammock, and a mosquito net were all he owned; sandals were cut from rubber tires and held in place by strips of inner tube. Food was always scarce, so he had to get by on a diet of rice and vegetables. Meat was a luxury, and no animal was safe near his camp. Elephants, tigers, wild dogs, frogs, monkeys, and cats went into the camp cooking pots. Rats were a delicacy in the Mekong delta, minced and mixed with spices. Main Force Viet Cong regularly left camp to ambush ARVN patrols, overrun outposts,

73

---

[11]Pike, *The Viet Cong Strategy of Terror*, p. 108; "The Massacre of Dak Son," *Time*, December 15, 1967.

attack airfields, and destroy bridges, tunnels, and rail lines.

Viet Cong units usually included women; indeed, up to 50 percent of certain units were women. Not only did they serve as nurses and cooks, they fought as equals alongside their menfolk. At least one woman commanded a Main Force unit. Ut Tich was her name, and she was the mother of six children. Upon joining the Viet Cong, she left her children in the care of neighbors. An expert at attacking ARVN troop barracks, in one battle she shot down a helicopter, killing thirty-five enemy soldiers.

The ARVN was no match for such foes. Its troubles began at the top, with its leaders. President Diem chose commanders for their loyalty to himself, not their fighting skill. High-ranking officers came from wealthy land-owning or merchant families who had supported the French. The army was merely another business to them, not a way of serving a cause in which they believed. Commanders sold promotions, hired out their troops as laborers, taxed the peasants illegally, and took bribes. With fortunes to be made, fighting was the farthest thing from their minds. They played it safe, stayed close to base, and avoided battle whenever possible. Their children never gave a thought to battle; papa either bought them out of the draft or sent them to school in Europe.

It was different with the ARVN enlisted man. Usually a peasant, he was drafted into a seemingly endless prison term filled with misery and danger. His pay, $15 a month, was about as little as one could get in South Vietnam: Saigon taxi drivers earned $40 a month. Even so, he never received his full wages. Before anything—money, food, equipment—came to him, it had to pass through his officers' hands. And they were sure to take their share. Commanders also charged enlisted men for food and medical attention even if they were wounded in the line of duty. A soldier's family often followed him from post to post, living in filthy tent cities nearby. Yet they were out of luck if anything happened to him. If he was killed and an officer stole his pension, they had nothing. No wonder he had no fighting spirit: he had nothing to fight *for*.

As the Viet Cong neared its first birthday, it was clear that Ngo Dinh Diem could not survive. His army was steadily losing ground. His enemies controlled much of the country-side. Millions of people hated the sound of his name. It was only a matter of time—a short time, at that—before Uncle Ho held his victory parade in Saigon. Or so it seemed, until John F. Kennedy became President of the United States on January 20, 1961.

Young, handsome, and rich, "Jack" Kennedy prided himself on being the first American President born in the twentieth century. Kennedy's inaugural address was a call to action. A new generation had come into its own, he said, one that must live up to its obligations as its forefathers had done: "Let every nation know, whether it wishes us well or ill, that we shall pay any price, bear any burden, meet any hardship, support any friend, oppose any foe to assure the survival and success of liberty." And who would do all this paying, bearing, meeting, supporting, opposing, and assuring? Kennedy was blunt. "My fellow Americans, ask not what your country can do for you—ask what you can do for your country." Americans must be willing to sacrifice for the sake of their country and the peace of the world.

These were more than mere words. They were a warning to Communist leaders. Two weeks earlier, Soviet Premier Nikita Khrushchev had given a speech of his own. For eight hours nonstop, he denounced the West, vowing to support "wars of national liberation" in Asia, Africa, and Latin America. In short, governments friendly to the West would be overthrown by Communist or Communist-aided revolutionaries. Kennedy and his advisers decided that Moscow was about to challenge the United States across the globe. That challenge could not be allowed to succeed.

Kennedy backed his words with a show of force. On April 17, he allowed Cuban exiles to land at the Bay of Pigs in Cuba. The invasion, aimed at toppling Communist dictator Fidel Castro, failed miserably. Two months later, Kennedy met Khrushchev face-to-face in Vienna, Austria. The Soviet leader, a chubby little fellow with a loud voice, ranted, raved, and shook his fist in the President's face. Pausing for breath, he repeated his promise about wars of national liberation—"sacred wars" he called them. Worse, he threatened to make trouble over Berlin, divided between the Allies since World War II. And he backed up his words with action, building the Berlin Wall in August to prevent East Germans from escaping to the West.

The President was shaken by these events. Each Communist challenge undermined respect for America in the world. Foreign leaders were beginning to doubt that the United States would use force to defend its interests. And that was dangerous, for one false move might send atomic missiles on their way. The President had to show that the nation would stand firm. But how, and where? He knew: "Vietnam is the place."

Kennedy raised the stakes in South Vietnam. When he took office, 875 American advisers were with Ngo Dinh Diem's forces. That number climbed to 3,164 by the end of 1961. Among the advisers were U.S. Army Special Forces, or Green Berets, experts in jungle warfare. Heavy weapons—artillery, tanks, armored personnel carriers—arrived weekly. Fighter-bombers lined the airstrips. Although these were older, propeller-driven models, they were deadly against ground targets. The buildup frightened the Viet Cong, who had never faced warplanes in large numbers. It also frightened one of Kennedy's advisers. Undersecretary of State George Ball warned that America was heading for a full-scale war. "George," the President snapped, "you're just crazier than hell. That's not going to happen."[12] He could not imagine things getting *that* bad.

Ball, unfortunately, was right. By the end of 1963, there were 16,263 Americans serving in South Vietnam. Not only did they train Diem's forces, they joined in operations against the Viet Cong. Americans planned attacks, piloted ARVN troop helicopters, and led air strikes against enemy positions. There seemed to be no other way, given the ARVN's incompetence. Inevitably, advisers lost their lives: 32 died from 1961 through 1962. Slowly but surely, American blood and credibility were being committed to a war on the other side of the globe. And the deeper the commitment, the harder it became to leave without victory. Vietnam was becoming a trap.

Still, no amount of aid would make the ARVN fight better. This was shown near Ap Bac, a village in the Mekong delta forty miles south of Saigon. On January 2, 1963, a 2,500–man force surrounded 250 Viet Cong. Besides a ten-to-one advantage in numbers, the ARVN had American advisers, helicopters, armored personnel carriers, artillery, and large numbers of automatic weapons—the works. The Viet Cong commander expected the worst. "Better to fight and die than run and be slaughtered," he wrote in his diary, which was found later. Yet he was pleasantly surprised by the South Vietnamese commander. The fellow was a coward pure and simple. The Americans begged and pleaded, but he refused to fight. Result: 165 ARVN dead, 5 helicopters downed, 3 American helicopter pilots killed. The Viet Cong escaped, losing 12 men.

It was South Vietnam's Buddhists, however, who finally turned Washington against Diem. Buddhists had many grievances against the president. Although they were a majority, with nearly 90 percent of the population, they were discrim-

---

[12]Quoted in Kim Willenson: *The Bad War: An Oral History of the Vietnam War*, p. 52.

inated against in favor of the Catholic minority. Catholic villages received a larger share of government aid. Nearly all province chiefs and army generals were Catholics.

On May 8, 1963, the government forbade the flying of Buddhist religious flags during a celebration in Hue. When crowds took to the streets in protest, military police opened fire, killing nine and injuring fourteen. Buddhist protest increased during the weeks that followed, along with government brutality.

Matters came to a head on a busy street in downtown Saigon. On June 11, an elderly monk sat down in the gutter. Thich Quang Duc was his name, and he had served Buddha for nearly all of his seventy-three years. He sat upright, peaceful and serene, surrounded by brother monks dressed in orange robes. After a brief prayer, a monk poured a can of gasoline over him. Instantly, Thich Quang Duc struck a match, killing himself in a swirl of flame and smoke.

This event, shocking as it may be to Westerners, had a long tradition in Vietnam and China. For centuries, monks and nuns had burned themselves to death, sometimes to honor Buddha as a final offering after a lifetime of service, at other times to protest a government action. Thich Quang Duc's burning was a staged event to arouse opposition to Diem and win American sympathy. American reporters had been invited to attend hours earlier. As the gasoline was poured, a monk called over a microphone in Vietnamese and English: "A Buddhist monk burns himself to death. A Buddhist priest becomes a martyr."

Thich Quang Duc's sacrifice had its intended effect. Six more monks and a nun followed his example, inspiring further demonstrations. Ngo Dinh Nhu answered by sending in his bullyboys. Buddhist temples were raided by club-swinging thugs, who beat and arrested hundreds of priests and nuns. Madame Nhu, a genius at making things worse, called the burnings "barbecues." They were funny to her. "Let them burn," she said, a grin on her face, "and we shall clap our hands."[13]

Nobody was clapping in America. People were stunned by the pictures of a burning man on their television screens. They found it horrible, nauseating, that Washington should be supporting a "murderer" like Diem. If he was the best leader it could find, perhaps, they wondered, we should leave South Vietnam to its fate. Diem's generals heard the message loud and clear. Fearing a cutoff of American aid, they began to plot a coup d'état, an overthrow of the Diem government.

President Kennedy favored a change of government—by force, if necessary. South Vietnam, he insisted, was too important to lose because of one man's bigotry and lust for power. Although Kennedy did not publicly call for a coup, he hinted in a televised interview that it might be a good thing. Privately, he indicated that America would support those who overthrew Diem. Thus, by encouraging the plotters, he shared responsibility for their actions.

Kennedy may actually have aided them directly. It is unclear to historians if he knew of the activities of CIA agent Lucien Conein. A master of "dirty tricks," Conein was Ambassador Henry Cabot Lodge's contact with the plotters, and Lodge reported directly to the White House. Conein gave the plotters detailed plans of Nhu's secret headquarters. Now and then he worked at their command post, keeping in touch with the embassy by means of a special radio. He even told the plotters that, once the coup began, they must not hesitate, but follow it through to the end. They did. On November 2, Diem and his brother Nhu were murdered by rebel soldiers.

Saigon went wild with joy. Crowds smashed statues of the hated dictator. Opponents, many weakened by years of torture, were released from his jails. Ambassador Lodge shared

79

---

[13] Quoted in Karnow, *Vietnam: A History*, p. 281.

the enthusiasm. A few days after the coup, he congratulated the plotters and sent a message to Kennedy: "The prospects now are for a shorter war."

The coup actually had the opposite effect. Instead of shortening the war, it began a free-for-all among the plotters. During the next two years, there were ten changes of government, as generals staged coups against one another. Their names are not important for our story; they did nothing to help the South Vietnamese people.

Two generals finally took power and held it for ten years. Army General Nguyen Van Thieu, the senior man, had fought in the French army during the war against the Viet Minh. Thieu's intelligence and cunning were matched only by his corruptness and superstition. He once bought a house for his mother, only to learn from a fortune-teller that it rested on the neck of an earth dragon; he had the house demolished and rebuilt in a safer place. Thieu became president of the Republic of Vietnam. His vice president was Air Marshal Nguyen Cao Ky, another French supporter. A daring pilot, Ky enjoyed going about in a black flying suit with a purple silk scarf tied around his neck. His flying skill, however, was outweighed by his political stupidity. Ky admired Adolf Hitler, one of history's most evil men, and said so: "I have only one hero—Hitler. We need four or five Hitlers in Vietnam."[14]

President Kennedy never knew of Diem's successors. Exactly three weeks after the coup, he was gunned down in Dallas, Texas. While the nation mourned, there were those who felt that his assassination was a punishment for the murder of Diem. That was unfair, for Kennedy did not want any harm to come to Diem. Still, some saw the hand of a just God in Kennedy's death. Among them was his successor, Lyndon B. Johnson.

●

---

[14]Quoted in Boettcher, *Vietnam: The Valor and the Sorrow*, p. 316.

"LBJ" was a complicated person—kind and cruel, generous and selfish, gentle and coarse. Growing up had not been easy for him. Raised in the poverty of the Texas hill country, he believed his mission in life was to help those who could not help themselves. As President, he gave America the "Great Society," a series of programs to aid the unfortunate: Project Head Start, the Job Corps, the War on Poverty, medical care for the elderly (Medicare) and the poor (Medicaid), and the Neighborhood Youth Corps for unemployed teenagers. It was an impressive record, and he had reason to be proud of it. Had there been no Vietnam War, he might have been remembered as one of our greatest presidents.

Johnson was not a man of war. As a senator, he had opposed the use of American forces to rescue the French at Dien Bien Phu. He called President Kennedy's death "a retribution for the assassination of Diem" and took it as a personal warning from God.[15] A war over South Vietnam was the last thing LBJ wanted.

The President had little interest, and less experience, in foreign affairs. He saw himself as a crusader for social justice at home, not an international statesman out to remake the world. Still, he could hardly ignore South Vietnam. America had promised to resist communism throughout the world. Three presidents—Truman, Eisenhower, and Kennedy—had supported South Vietnamese independence. Moreover, LBJ took the domino theory personally, applying it not only to Southeast Asia, but to life in general. Life had taught him that giving in to a bully only makes him bolder. "If you let a bully come into your front yard one day," he said, "the next day he'll be up on your porch and the day after that he'll rape your wife in your own bed."[16] The only way to stop a bully, or an aggressor nation, was to be tough from

81

[15]David Halberstam, *The Best and the Brightest*, p. 292.
[16]Doris Kearns, *Lyndon Johnson and the American Dream*, p. 258.

President John F. Kennedy, above, determined to keep South Vietnam out of Communist control, began the escalation of American aid. His successor, President Lyndon B. Johnson, below, continued Kennedy's policy, sending America's first combat forces.

the start. Besides, failing to take a strong anti-Communist stand abroad would ruin his efforts at home. Critics would call him a coward and wreck his Great Society programs.

Coward! That word sent chills up Johnson's spine. His greatest fear was being called "an unmanly man, a man without a spine."[17] For the sake of world peace, for America's downtrodden, for his own self-respect, LBJ dared not back down in Vietnam. Thus, by wishing to do good, he gradually moved America into the longest war in its history. That is the tragedy of both Lyndon Johnson and the nation he loved.

LBJ hoped to make Hanoi abandon the Viet Cong without war. He began by increasing aid to the South; by the end of 1964, there were 23,310 American advisers in Vietnam. In addition, he tried to show the North how costly its actions could be if it did not listen to "reason." This involved helping the ARVN with Operations Plan 34A, a series of secret attacks on North Vietnamese targets. Although illegal under international law, these attacks were no more so than Hanoi-ordered terrorism in the South; they were, in fact, meant to bring terrorism to an end.

On dark, moonless nights, ARVN naval commandos landed in North Vietnam to assassinate local Communist officials, kidnap people for questioning, and mine roads. Swift gunboats, directed by American officers, shelled northern naval bases along the Gulf of Tonkin. U.S. Navy destroyers faked attacks, suddenly darting toward the coast at top speed. Granted, they were in international waters and had every right to be there. Their purpose, however, was anything but peaceful. It was to trigger alerts to record the defenders' radar signals, vital information in the event of war.

On the night of July 31, 1964, South Vietnamese gunboats attacked two North Vietnamese islands in the Gulf of Ton-

83

---

[17] *Ibid.*, p. 253.

kin. The next day, August 1, the destroyer U.S.S. *Maddox* appeared nearby in international waters. The North Vietnamese, believing that the gunboats and the destroyer were acting together, sent three torpedo boats after the *Maddox.* After a short, sharp fight, the *Maddox* sank one torpedo boat and drove off the others. LBJ personally ordered another destroyer, the U.S.S. *C. Turner Joy*, to join the *Maddox* without delay.

In the early hours of August 4, the destroyers flashed a message that they were under attack. A radar operator aboard the *Maddox* reported seeing North Vietnamese torpedo boats on his screen; lookouts counted twenty-two torpedoes fired at the ships. Firing their guns in all directions, the destroyers zigzagged to avoid the torpedoes speeding toward them. But no sooner did the gunfire stop than their captains began to have doubts. No one, it turned out, had actually seen an enemy vessel. Buffeted by high winds and thunderstorms, the ships' radar had apparently gone haywire. Moreover, Commander James B. Stockdale, flying overhead in his fighter plane clear of the surface haze and spray, saw nothing except the American destroyers.[18] There was no second attack, and LBJ knew it. "Hell," he growled, "those dumb stupid sailors were just shooting at flying fish."[19]

Johnson, however, was thinking of the future. He wanted both to appear strong in the eyes of the American people and to gain a free hand for widening the war if necessary. The second "attack" was just what he needed. On August 5, fighters rose from the decks of the carriers U.S.S. *Ticonderoga* and *Constellation* to bomb the North Vietnamese port of Vinh; Jim Stockdale led the first wave to the target. Two days later, August 7, Congress gave LBJ its wholehearted support.

That support is known as the Gulf of Tonkin Resolution.

---

[18]Willenson, *The Bad War*, p. 29ff.
[19]Quoted in Karnow, *Vietnam: A History*, p. 374.

By a House vote of 416–0 and a Senate vote of 88–2, Congress authorized the President to take "all necessary measures to repel any armed attack against the forces of the United States and to prevent further aggression." It approved "all necessary steps, including the use of armed force" in answering friendly nations' calls for assistance. In effect, Congress had given its approval for LBJ to make war if, when, where, and how he chose. He said the resolution was "like Grandma's nightshirt—it covered everything." And he was right.

Nevertheless, LBJ had been too clever by far. By not mentioning Plan 34A or naval officers' doubts about the second attack, he deliberately misled Congress, and with it the entire nation. A fight that grew out of American and South Vietnamese actions against the North was made into a North Vietnamese violation of freedom of the seas. That deception would cost him dearly in the years ahead.

For the time being, LBJ's show of strength won the confidence of the American voter. In the election year 1964, he presented himself as the "peace candidate" against his opponent, Arizona Senator Barry Goldwater, who wanted to hit North Vietnam much harder. LBJ urged caution. No one, he said, need fear "escalation," a wider war, with him in the White House. He would not lose Vietnam, but neither would he "send American boys nine or ten thousand miles from home to do what Asian boys ought to be doing themselves." Voters believed him, and he easily won reelection in November. What they did not know was that, behind the scenes, his aides were planning to bomb North Vietnam if it did not back down.

85

These plans remained secret until Hanoi tested LBJ's resolve early in 1965. On February 7, Viet Cong raiders attacked the American air base at Pleiku in the Central Highlands, killing 8 men, wounding 126, and destroying 20 aircraft. Within twelve hours, Johnson sent navy bombers to a Viet Cong camp just north of the DMZ. On February 11, the Viet Cong struck American barracks in the coastal town of Qui Nohn; 19 died and 13 were wounded. Again Johnson ordered reprisals.

Those reprisals, however, were only for openers. By then LBJ had decided that he must increase the pressure on North Vietnam. On March 1, he gave the go-ahead for Operation Rolling Thunder. At dawn the next day, carrier-based planes bombed North Vietnamese bridges, roads, oil storage tanks, and harbor facilities. As they neared their targets, LBJ addressed the nation: "I regret the necessities of war have compelled us to bomb North Vietnam. We have carefully limited those raids. They have been directed at concrete and steel and not at human life."

The second Vietnam War—the war of the elephant and the tiger—had begun.

ROLLING THUNDER

Well, you know, what is our history? There's nothing else in our history except struggle. Struggle against foreign invaders, always more powerful than ourselves; struggle against nature. . . . And the result of this after two thousand odd years is that it has created a very stable nervous system in our people. We never panic. And whenever a new situation arises, our people say, "Ah well, there it goes again."

—*Pham Van Dong, 1965*

LYNDON JOHNSON HAD NEARLY AS MANY DIFFICUL-ties with his own generals as with his North Vietnamese enemies. Professional soldiers thought his policies foolish and had no respect for him as a leader. He was, they felt, simply a politician playing war games with live people. From their student days at the service academies, they had learned that wars are fought to be won. And the best way to win is to hit the enemy with everything you have. Maximum force must be aimed at the heart of the enemy's war-making ability: his armed forces, factories, food supplies, and transportation system. Force must be used swiftly, to win as quickly as possible with the smallest loss of life—American lives certainly, but enemy lives as well. This was how Ulysses S. Grant had fought the Civil War, and it was the strategy of American planners in both world wars. It was, in fact, called "the American way of war."

The Joint Chiefs of Staff, the commanders of the various armed services, wanted to fight the Vietnam War in the

American way. Was North Vietnam the enemy? If so, it must be met head-on. They would start by blockading its coasts and mining the harbor of Haiphong, its best deep-water port. To cut the Ho Chi Minh Trail, they wanted to send ground troops across Laos to the border of Thailand, then build a strong east-west defense line. Such a move should leave the Viet Cong high and dry, unable to replace lost manpower and supplies. Finally, they called for a quick, all-out bombing offensive to stun the enemy and cripple his war effort, if necessary by turning the country into a wilderness. General Curtis E. LeMay, chief of the Strategic Air Command, pulled no punches: "We should bomb them into the Stone Age." No one can say if these plans would have succeeded or not. What is certain is that they were never tried. The President listened to them politely, then turned them down—flat.

LBJ was the only President of the United States to go to war without having any intention of winning. This seems like a harsh thing to say, but it is true, as the President readily admitted. Johnson believed he had important reasons for not seeking a military victory. To begin with, he feared that China would intervene, as it had done in Korea, rather than see a Communist neighbor defeated. If that happened, the Soviets would probably join in, starting World War III. It would certainly be a nuclear war, causing millions of deaths, perhaps even the destruction of the human race. LBJ, therefore, felt that he could not afford to seek a military victory in Vietnam. The President intended to fight a limited war. Victory, for him, did not mean invading the North, crushing its armed forces, and overthrowing its government. The purpose of Rolling Thunder was to eliminate the Viet Cong by persuading Hanoi to end its support. Each bomb that fell was an "exploding telegram," a signal to Hanoi that it must mend its ways. If it did not, the pressure would be gradually increased until it became unbearable. And that point must come soon, for North Vietnam was no match for the world's mightiest nation. The United States had everything—wealth, industry, and modern weapons. North Vietnam had next to nothing. "Veetnam," LBJ noted with contempt, was just a "damn little piss-ant country."[1] An American defeat was unthinkable.

LBJ was wrong. A master politician, his strength was in making deals behind the scenes. In years of political deal-making, he had learned that every man has his price. He could not imagine another leader, albeit a foreigner, turning down his offer. Either he "sweetened" the deal with benefits, or he put on the pressure—hard. In either case, the opponent must yield.

Unfortunately, the President and his civilian advisers misjudged the North Vietnamese. Their error was a blend of arrogance and ignorance. Arrogance made them see Hanoi's leaders in strictly American terms. They imagined that their opposites were "reasonable" men—that is, men like themselves. And that, like themselves, they counted costs in material terms. When so much property worth so much money was destroyed, the North Vietnamese would quit to avoid further loss. Ignorance blinded them to the human factor in warfare. They had no idea of what made the enemy tick. Many North Vietnamese hated communism, but they hated bomb-dropping foreigners more. Though poor, they were not necessarily weak. Their history, their patriotism, their willpower, and their intelligence were sources of strength; indeed, they were weapons. But since these could not be counted and measured, they were ignored by the White House. Thus, failure was built into LBJ's plan from the outset. Hanoi, as we shall see, fought the old American way. It fought to win.

Every aspect of Rolling Thunder was controlled from

89

---

[1] Quoted in Boettcher, *Vietnam: The Valor and the Sorrow*, p. 290.

Washington. LBJ distrusted military men; they were, he felt, too trigger-happy, too willing to take risks. He was cautious. "I won't let those Air Force generals bomb the smallest out-house north of the 17th parallel without checking with me," he asserted.[2] The President would personally direct the air offensive from the comfort of the White House.

LBJ and his advisers met for lunch at the White House every Tuesday afternoon. Secretary of Defense Robert Mc-Namara was a regular guest, as were Secretary of State Dean Rusk, National Security Adviser Walt W. Rostow, and Presidential Assistant McGeorge Bundy. Although they had served in World War II, none had combat experience; generals, who did, were seldom invited. While eating in an elegant dining room hung with paintings of Lord Cornwallis's surrender at Yorktown, they discussed the situation in Southeast Asia. After lunch, they unfolded their maps and selected targets for the following week. Rail lines, bridges, army barracks, oil tanks, factories, and power stations were all prime targets. In addition, they decided on the types and tonnage of bombs to be dropped, the size and flight pattern of bomber formations, and the timing of missions.

Anything that might endanger Russians or Chinese was off-limits to the bombers. LBJ was terrified of harming citizens of the Communist superpowers. Targets within twenty-five miles of the Chinese border were prohibited; this included truck convoys and rail lines carrying war supplies. Planes were forbidden to strike targets within ten miles of Hanoi and Haiphong, whose harbor was jammed with Soviet ships. American commanders were furious when they saw aerial photos of Haiphong: street after street was lined with cannon, tanks, trucks, and ammunition awaiting ship-

---

[2] Quoted in Rowland Evans and Robert Novak, *Lyndon Johnson: The Exercise of Power*, p. 539.

ment to Viet Cong and North Vietnamese Army (NVA) troops. Finally, LBJ forbade attacks on airfields and surface-to-air missile (SAM) sites while under construction, since Soviet advisers worked there. Even when airfields were completed, pilots were prevented from hitting fighters on the ground; they must allow them to take off before opening fire. Only when SAMs began downing American planes were they added to the target lists, but not if their launchers were near dikes.

LBJ was particularly worried about harming North Vietnamese civilians. "If they [airmen] hit people, I'll bust their ass," he growled.[3] Because of him, no attempt was made to destroy the Red River dikes. It was better, apparently, to endanger American pilots than to risk the lives of enemy civilians. To avoid populated areas, he often sent planes on routes that took them closer to antiaircraft batteries. Enemy commanders knew of his concern and made the best of it. Pilot Jack A. Broughton tells of a typical incident in his book, *Thud Ridge*. He was having difficulty hitting a rail yard outside Hanoi because some buildings nearby were a hospital and therefore out of bounds. "If in fact it was a hospital," he remarked, "it must have been a hospital for sick flak [antiaircraft] gunners, because every time we looked at it from a run on the railroad, it was a mass of sputtering, flashing gun barrels."[4]

No wonder airmen resented their Commander-in-Chief. LBJ was sending them into danger, while preventing them from striking key targets or even, at certain times, defending themselves. "We were forced to fight the war with a hand tied behind our back, one eye blinded, and only half a pocket full of ammunition," recalled fighter pilot Mark Berent.[5] This is one of the milder comments. Some of Berent's comrades thought LBJ the best general on Hanoi's side.

91

---

[3] Quoted in Boettcher, *Vietnam: The Valor and the Sorrow*, p. 211.
[4] Jack A. Broughton, *Thud Ridge*, p. 223.
[5] Quoted in Santoli, *To Bear Any Burden*, p. 142.

LBJ's restrictions, however, did not mean that the enemy had an easy time. Far from it. Rolling Thunder was carried out by the mightiest air fleet ever assembled. Part of the fleet was based on carriers stationed in the South China Sea. These vessels were floating airports able to move at a moment's notice. Take, for example, the nuclear-powered U.S.S. *Enterprise,* which carried 5,000 men and could cruise for four years without refueling. If stood on her end, *Enterprise* would be taller than the Empire State Building. She and her sisters carried seventy to a hundred planes: fighters, bombers, tankers, helicopters, and reconnaissance craft. Naval warplanes packed a terrific wallop. The F-4 Phantom was a Navy favorite; used as a bomber, it could deliver 16,000 pounds of bombs; as a fighter, it was armed with Sidewinder or Sparrow air-to-air missiles capable of hitting an enemy eleven miles away.

U.S. Air Force planes were land based, usually in South Vietnam and Thailand. The workhorse was the F-105 Thunderchief, nicknamed "Thud." Armed with six 750-pound bombs and rapid-fire cannon, Thuds flew the largest number of sorties—one mission to and from a target by one plane—against North Vietnam. Thuds were backed by the B-52 Stratofortress, an eight-engined bomber that hauled one hundred and eight 500-pound bombs, as much explosive power as a small atomic missile. Based in Thailand and on the Pacific island of Guam, they flew long-range missions lasting 15½ hours. B-52s seldom ventured north of the DMZ; they were too valuable and LBJ did not want to risk them needlessly.

In order to endure Rolling Thunder, Hanoi had to organize the nation for total war. Everyone and everything had to be directed toward the war effort. The people had to live war, breathe war, make war the center of their daily lives. This was a severe challenge, but the Communists met it with

Operation Rolling Thunder was launched from land and sea. At right, the vast flight deck of a U.S. Navy aircraft carrier on station in the South China Sea. Below, a U.S. Air Force F-100 Supersaber releases a bomb over the jungle.

skill and determination.

Hanoi launched a propaganda campaign like the Viet Cong's, only on a larger scale. "[All] art forms," it ordered, "must be turned into aids in the teaching of hatred toward the American gang. . . . Every poem, every painting and every song . . . must be a bullet shot directly at the enemy."[6] Before long, billions of word-bullets were being fired in North Vietnam. Shop windows displayed books with stirring titles such as *Determined to Defeat the Aggressive U.S. Pirates* and *The Mother Holding the Gun*. Wherever you turned, there were images of LBJ as Uncle Sam, a brute with a hook nose and blood dripping from his teeth. Films like *Resolved to Defeat the Invading American Imperialists* were shown in theaters and schools. Everyone sang the nation's favorite song: "Vietnam, Ho Chi Minh! Vietnam, Ho Chi Minh!" There was no difference between the two, for Uncle Ho and the nation had become one and the same.

Uncle Ho set the example. Dressed in shorts and sandals, he mingled with the people. Wherever he went, he gave the same two-part message. The first part was hopeful: "We shall win!" No doubt about it; if the people stuck together, following the lead of the Communist party, victory was certain. The second part of his message was brutally honest: "Prepare for the worst!" Victory, though certain, would not come cheaply.

There was, however, more to the story. Ho never told the whole truth about the war in the South. Beginning in 1964, regular units of the NVA fought alongside the Viet Cong. Thousands were killed, thousands more wounded. Fearing that the truth would harm civilian morale, and with it the war effort, Ho ordered a news blackout. Families could write to their men, but the letters seldom arrived; soldiers often

---

[6]Jon M. Van Dyke, *North Vietnam's Strategy for Survival*, p. 87.

had no word from home for seven years. If relatives complained, they were accused of "defeatism" and jailed by the secret police.[7]

Unlike the Americans, who reported their losses weekly, the North Vietnamese treated their casualties as state secrets. Families seldom received official notices of the death of loved ones. Those who did were grateful: at least they could properly mourn and then go on with their lives. The majority, not knowing the fate of a husband or son, lived with endless worry. If somehow they learned of a death, they dared not show grief, for anyone who told of soldiers dying got into trouble with the police. To protect themselves and others, they had to hide their pain and go on as if nothing had happened.[8]

Most North Vietnamese never saw a badly wounded soldier. Such men were kept in isolated camps for years before being allowed to rejoin their families. Sometimes this led to tragedy. There was one story everyone knew, that they all believed to be true. It seems that a soldier had been crippled in the South. After a long search, his wife learned his whereabouts and sneaked into the hospital, only to find him without arms or legs. Wild with grief, she ran away screaming and tearing her hair. The soldier, abandoned by the person he loved so much, committed suicide. His wife was sent to prison for killing a soldier. The poor woman had to be "made an example" for the sake of the war effort.[9]

Everyone was supposed to help in the country's defense. Each person, depending upon age and ability, was given a specific task to make him or her feel part of the war effort. In addition to your regular job, you might serve with a fire brigade, join a first-aid team or ambulance unit, repair bomb

---

[7]Chanoff and Doan, *Portrait of the Enemy*, p. 62.
[8]*Ibid*, p. 63.
[9]*Ibid*, pp. 63–64.

damage, or defuse unexploded bombs, work demanding steady nerves and lots of luck. Zealous teenagers formed Youth Shock Brigades to resist invasion attempts. Several brigades were known as "determined to die units," since they had sworn to give their lives as long as they could kill at least one invader.

Women, known as the Long-Haired Army, also played a major role in North Vietnam's war effort. Besides caring for their families and serving in Self-Defense Brigades, they replaced men in the fields and factories, freeing them for military service. They also made up a large part of antiaircraft batteries. But since a pregnant woman was not much use around an antiaircraft gun, birth control became a government priority. Youngsters, in the words of an official statement, had "to think carefully before falling in love, to reflect more deeply before marrying, and to think again and again before having children—for the duration of the war."[10] Accordingly, Hanoi banned marriages for those under twenty. Yet not everyone accepted the ban, and several couples committed suicide rather than be without each other.

To deal with Rolling Thunder, the North Vietnamese tried to limit the damage by showing the bombers fewer targets. This was made easier by the gradualness with which LBJ increased the attacks, giving Ho Chi Minh time to make and carry out his plans. Likely targets were dispersed, scattered over a wide area. Oil, for example, had been stored in large tanks, easily visible from the air. But when the bombs began to fall, it was put into fifty-five-gallon drums that could be stacked along back roads and in bomb craters. The Vietnamese also stored oil drums near dikes, knowing attacks on them had been strictly forbidden.

Key targets were camouflaged. Docks were built to look like parks, with trees and flower beds disguising their true

---

[10]Van Dyke, *North Vietnam's Strategy for Survival*, p. 98.

nature. Motor vehicles were covered with fishnets into which branches, leaves, and even uprooted bushes were inserted. Bombed bridges were replaced by others built underwater. These could be lowered a few inches by day, making them invisible to aircraft; at night they were pulled up for the truck convoys. Tree-lined roads simply vanished; the tops of the trees were bent over until they met, then tied together.

People were protected in similar ways. Millions of city dwellers were evacuated to the country, where the danger was generally less. Those who remained behind were never far from a bomb shelter. North Vietnam built 21 million underground shelters during the time of Rolling Thunder. The idea was to have three shelter spaces for each person: one where you lived, one where you worked, and one along the route you took to work. Some shelters were concrete rooms large enough for a dozen families. The majority, however, were concrete drainpipes with space for one person, or a person holding a small child. These were buried vertically along every street and major road; certain Hanoi streets had a shelter every six feet. When the alarm sounded, you went for the nearest one and pulled the lid, a concrete disc two inches thick, over your head. You were safe from anything but a direct hit.

Entire communities went underground. Vinh Linh, the largest, was a cluster of villages with 70,000 people just north of the DMZ, a heavily bombed area. Thousands of rooms were dug thirty feet beneath the ruined villages and linked by hundreds of miles of tunnels. Markets, warehouses, movie theaters, recreation centers, schools, hospitals, community kitchens, dining halls, and public bathrooms—all were underground, lit by oil lanterns. There was even an underground nursery for infants. During the day, after the all-clear sounded, the babies were lifted to the surface in straw baskets for a

A North Vietnamese airstrip, put out of action during an American air raid in 1965. Note the many overlapping craters, a mark of high-intensity bombing. Most targets weren't so easily spotted, but were camouflaged or protected by bomb shelters. Below, a line of one-person bomb shelters along a street in Hanoi.

few minutes of sunlight. Each family, depending on its size, was assigned a certain number of square feet; the floor was covered with canvas, the ceiling with sheets of nylon, and the walls with old newspapers to give protection from falling dirt. The people tended their crops at night, by moonlight. Those who ventured aboveground in daylight wore large, cone-shaped hats covered with twigs and grass. If a plane appeared, they just sat down and became part of the scenery.

Another form of protection was deadlier. Thanks to its Communist allies, North Vietnam had one of the best air defense systems in the world. Veteran pilots, who had flown in World War II and Korea, said they had never seen anything like it. "Ninety-nine percent of the time as I dropped bombs," an airman recalled, "somebody was shooting at me."[11]

In some areas, every able-bodied person was given a rifle and put on air raid duty. It may seem that a rifle is not much of a weapon against a jet plane. Yet rifles can be quite effective, if there are enough of them. American planes generally flew low to avoid being detected by enemy radar, climbing to bombing altitude only when near their targets. As the planes approached, thousands of civilians stood in trenches and blazed away with rifles, forcing them to go higher. But as they did, they showed themselves to the ground batteries. The Soviets had given North Vietnam 8,000 antiaircraft guns, quick-firing cannon aimed by radar. These guns, pilots agreed, were the worst things in creation. Every time they flew over North Vietnam, said one, they faced "an awesome curtain of exploding steel." Each month antiaircraft gunners fired 25,000 tons of shells at American planes. Most of these shells had arrived through the port of Haiphong.

Not all North Vietnamese weapons were equally danger-

99

---

[11] Quoted in Karnow, *Vietnam: A History*, p. 457.

ous. Their Soviet-built MiG fighters were no match for American planes, which downed them at a rate of two to one. From February 1965 to November 1968, when LBJ canceled Rolling Thunder, Americans destroyed 111 MiGs while losing 55 planes of their own. SAMs, though accurate at close range, could be avoided by suddenly diving toward the ground; the missiles could not turn sharply enough to stay with the planes.

Despite all these efforts, most planes broke through the North Vietnamese defenses. And when they did, people suffered dreadfully. We learn what it was like from a resident of Vinh Quang village, destroyed in July 1967:

> The bombing started at about eight o'clock in the morning and lasted for hours. At the first sound of explosions, we rushed into the tunnels, but not everyone made it. During a pause in the attack, some of us climbed out to see what we could do, and the scene was terrifying. Bodies had been torn to pieces— limbs hanging from trees or scattered around the ground. Then the bombing began again, this time with napalm [jellied gasoline], and the village went up in flames. The napalm hit me, and I must have gone crazy. I felt as if I were burning all over, like charcoal. I lost consciousness. Comrades took me to the hospital, and my wounds didn't begin to heal until six months later. More than two hundred people died in the raid, including my mother, my sister-in-law and three nephews. They were buried alive when their tunnel collapsed.[12]

As we have seen, LBJ wanted to spare civilian lives. Whatever we may think about the war, whether it was right or wrong, he was sincere in this respect. At no time during the Vietnam War were targets selected for any reason other than their military value. Pilots were never ordered to attack ci-

---

[12] *Ibid*, p. 459.

vilians; unlike the Viet Cong actions at Dak Song. Even so, the bombings killed or injured approximately a thousand North Vietnamese each week.

These casualties were unintentional. There is no such thing as a "surgical" air strike, or "pinpoint" bombing, in which only the target is hit. Dropping an iron tube filled with explosives from two miles above the earth is always risky. Any number of things can reduce accuracy. An F-105 pilot in a dogfight with a MiG had to unload his bombs to gain speed and maneuverability; if this happened over a village, it would be flattened. Mechanical "bugs" caused numerous problems. Computer errors in aiming sent bombs off course. Faulty bomb racks caused bombs to be released too soon or too late; at such heights and speeds, a few seconds either way caused bomb "spillage" miles from the target. Tail fins, which keep bombs heading in a straight line, were responsible for more unintended damage. Bombs with bent tail fins often fell outside the target zone, or "box."

Finally, the North Vietnamese brought some of their troubles upon themselves. Storing oil drums and ammunition in or near villages attracted bombers like bees to pollen. So did placing antiaircraft guns in densely populated areas. Jack Broughton's experience with the hospital near Hanoi was not unusual. Antiaircraft batteries were camouflaged as hospitals, complete with red crosses painted on the roofs. Individual guns might also be placed on the roof of any solidly built structures: hospitals, schools, temples, churches. Heavy machine guns poked through the windows of taller buildings. These buildings were legitimate targets. There is no law that says an airman must allow himself to be killed by an enemy who hides behind civilians.

Villagers armed with rifles and machine guns, heroic though they were, invited attack. Dick Rutan, a veteran of 325 missions, described one such incident. During a mission to locate a downed American pilot, he flew close to a North Vietnamese village. Although unhappy about what he had to do, he had no choice:

> The Misty [squadron's] policy was, we never hit a village. . . . I personally only took out one village the whole time I was there. We were doing a rescue, and a .50-caliber [machine] gunner came so close to nailing me I couldn't believe it. The whole town was shooting at us. When the rescue forces came in, I thought that gunner presented a significant danger to them. It was a long, thin village. So we put a smoke rocket at each end of it. We were out of fuel when we did that, and I had some fighters overhead. I said, 'Okay, put all your bombs between the two smokes.' I went out to get more fuel. When we came back, between the two marks there was nothing but dust. Rubble. They totally obliterated the village.[13]

Experiences like Rutan's encouraged some pilots to take matters into their own hands. They became so nervous that they bombed any large building without waiting to be shot at. Sometimes innocent people died as a result; but at other times stored ammunition "cooked off," exploded, for days afterward. A fellow I know, whose job was to report civilian damage, calls these pilots the "mad bombers." There is no way of knowing how many of them there were, or how much damage they did. But they surely existed.

The North Vietnamese even killed their own people during air raids. Russian-built SAMs, unlike American missiles, did not have automatic self-destruct devices. If they missed their mark, they fell back to earth when they ran out of fuel. And since SAMs were often fired near villages, they wiped them out on the return trip. Civilians knew this, but dared not complain. It was a crime to say a village was destroyed

102

---

[13] Quoted in Maurer, *Strange Ground*, pp. 388–389.

by a returning SAM rather than by American bombs.[14]

Rolling Thunder took the lives of about 52,000 civilians out of a population of 18 million. That is a lot of people, but hardly the "aerial holocaust" claimed by Communist propaganda. It is useful to compare the three and a half years of Rolling Thunder with a one-month period during World War II. Allied bombers deliberately targeted German and Japanese cities. Considered necessary for winning the war, these raids involved hundreds of bombers at a time. On February 3, 1945, the American Eighth Air Force hit Berlin, killing 25,000 civilians within a few hours. Ten days later, American and British planes pounded Dresden, killing another 60,000 and injuring 30,000. On March 9, the Americans firebombed the center of Tokyo, leaving 97,000 dead, 125,000 wounded, and 1,200,000 homeless.

Nothing like this happened in North Vietnam. It easily could have, but it did not, thanks to American caution. Indeed, the bombing was not as costly as the enemy expected it to be at the outset. Premier Pham Van Dong later admitted as much, and was proud of it: "Our human losses were not so great as in other wars . . . [considering that] the quantity of bombs and shells used were several times larger than that of World War II. We Vietnamese continued to live, to work and fight."[15]

The premier had reason to be pleased. America had mounted history's largest air offensive against his country. Over 350,000 sorties were flown during Rolling Thunder alone. Throughout the war (1965–1972), 7.8 million tons of bombs fell on all of Indochina—that is, roughly 36 tons per square mile of land. This is four times the tonnage dropped by all the airplanes in World War II. Yet it was for nothing, a complete waste of lives, effort, and money.

[14] Van Dyke, *North Vietnam's Strategy for Survival*, pp. 83–84.
[15] Quoted in Maclear, *The Ten Thousand Day War*, p. 241.

LBJ's exploding telegrams were not read, or were misread, by the North Vietnamese people. Bombing did not break their spirit or turn them against their Communist rulers. In fact, the more bombs that fell, the more angry, the more determined to resist they became. Resistance stirred their pride and sense of history. They, too, became heroes, like their ancestors before them. Besides, theirs was a small agricultural country with few factories, not an industrial giant like Germany or Japan. It needed little to continue the war, and its allies kept the supplies flowing without interruption. The Soviets and China easily made up for bombing losses; indeed, they sent more than was needed. As the war continued, North Vietnam had supplies to spare. Even the bomb craters were turned to good use, as fishponds and storage sites.

Rolling Thunder cost America dearly. In monetary terms, the operation was a disaster. It simply did not pay. Exactly 918 aircraft were lost and 818 airmen killed over the North. Plane losses totaled over $6 billion, not to mention the $500,000 it cost to train each new pilot. Seen another way, it cost $9.60 to do $1 worth of damage! Uncle Sam was simply not getting "the bang for the buck."

There is no way of measuring the damage to American morale. Generals and pilots shared the same feelings of anger and despair. "I can't tell you how I feel," muttered Air Force Chief of Staff General John McConnell. "I'm so sick of it. . . . I have never been so goddamn frustrated by it all. . . . I'm so sick of it."[16]

McConnell's words echoed those of a young lieutenant aboard the carrier U.S.S. *Constellation*. The ship, home for repairs, had just welcomed LBJ aboard for a visit. He was in a nearby cabin, within earshot, when the pilot let go: "We are going through the worst . . . flak in the history of man,

---

[16]Quoted in Boettcher, *Vietnam: The Valor and the Sorrow*, p. 238.

and for what—to knock out some twelve-foot wooden bridge that can be built back in a couple of hours. We can't hit the [Haiphong] docks where they unload the war matériel because we might hit the [Soviet] ships. . . . We've got a great big country with sophisticated equipment, trained pilots, expensive aircraft and it's not worth a damn, it's not worth the loss of planes or the loss of a single pilot—and plenty are being lost, believe me."[17] No one tried to silence him. He was only telling the truth, whether LBJ liked it or not.

It was the same with the Ho Chi Minh Trail, another target of Rolling Thunder. The trail was not a narrow pathway, as its name suggests. It was a network of approximately 12,000 miles of connecting trails, truck roads, bridges, checkpoints, rest camps, supply dumps, fuel depots, repair shops, and barracks. Starting just north of the DMZ, it covered some of the roughest country on earth, winding southward through Laos and Cambodia, with branches extending eastward toward the densely populated areas of South Vietnam: Hue, Da Nang, Pleiku, Saigon, and the Mekong delta.

Using the trail was no Boy Scout hike, but an ordeal to test the strongest person. Before heading south, Viet Cong and NVA soldiers had to build up their strength. Preparing for the journey involved three weeks of grueling physical training. Soldiers went on uphill marches from dawn to dusk. They ran miles wearing backpacks loaded with bricks. They took the training in stride, actually welcomed it, for they were serving their country. Many, according to prisoners of war, did not expect to return alive. Before leaving their villages, funeral services were often held in their honor. They even had a slogan tattooed on their bodies: "Born in the North to die in the South."

105

---

[17] Quoted in Don Oberdorfer, *Tet!*, p. 194.

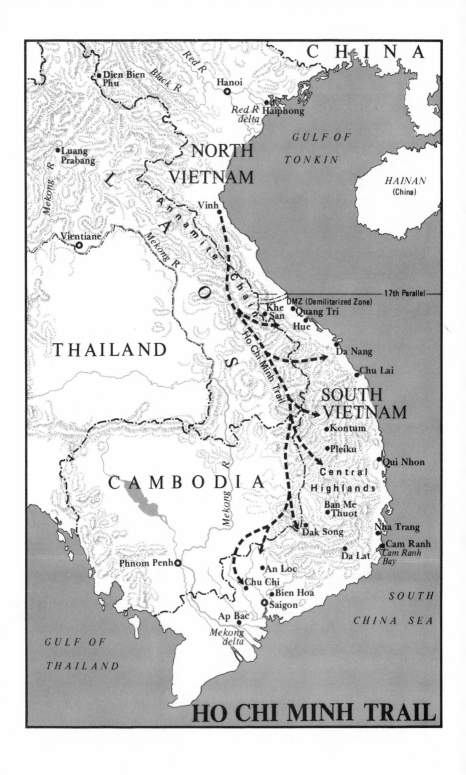

HO CHI MINH TRAIL

On the day of departure, they were brought by truck to a jump-off point near the trail. Each had a weapon and a seventy-five-pound pack filled with clothing, personal items, dried food, and ammunition. If they were NVA soldiers, they exchanged their uniforms for the peasant's black pajamas. They were then made to turn in anything that could link them to North Vietnam or to any other Communist country. "We were invading," explained Colonel Huong Van Ba, "but we did our best to disguise ourselves as native liberators."[18]

In the early 1960s, six months were needed to go from the DMZ to the area around Saigon; a few years later, after many improvements, it took six weeks. Yet no one ever found the going easy. Every foot of the Ho Chi Minh Trail held its own special danger. Soldiers were trampled by stampeding elephants. Tigers stalked their prey; a man would satisfy their hunger as easily as a wild pig. As a rule, though, the smaller creatures were the worst. Poisonous snakes bit scores of men; nearly all survived, thanks to an antidote discovered by NVA doctors. Some places were infested by leeches. They dropped from the bushes and crawled on the ground by the millions. You could not help stepping on them, and their squashed bodies made the ground slippery, causing men to fall. When they did, scores of leeches grabbed hold of any exposed skin and began sucking blood. The best way to remove them was to coax them off with the lit end of a cigarette; pulling them off caused infection. Malaria, a disease carried by mosquitoes, drove people out of their minds with fever, leaving them burned out and wasted. Soldiers, too exhausted to go on, collapsed and died. They were pushed aside and left to the ants.

The Americans tried to close the trail as best they could.

---

[18] Quoted in Chanoff and Doan, *Portrait of the Enemy*, p. 153.

Some of their plans were just idiotic. There was "Lava," the search for a chemical to turn jungle soil into slippery grease. Project Pigeon hoped to tie small bombs onto homing pigeons and send them after NVA trucks. Pigeon was canceled when, during tests, the birds flew into American and enemy vehicles in equal numbers. An army colonel wanted to put man-eating piranha fish into rice paddies. A CIA man favored dropping millions of six-packs of Budweiser beer along the trail. The NVA, he believed, liked this brand, and drinking enough of it would get them drunk enough to come into the open to be shot.

There was nothing silly about Igloo White, an electronic warning system to detect movement along the trail. Igloo White used various gadgets dropped at night from low-flying aircraft. Sensors disguised as tiny trees registered the pressure waves produced by men and machines moving on the ground. Listening devices recorded their sounds. "People sniffers" picked up body heat and odors, especially that of urine, found at all campsites. Information was automatically radioed to planes circling overhead, which sent it to computers at a base in Thailand. The computers noted the sensors' exact location and an officer called in the bombers.

They often hit nothing, since the North Vietnamese learned how to fool Igloo White. Scouts were always on the lookout for sensors. When they found one, they began an elaborate game of hide-and-seek. Tape recordings of crickets were placed near listening devices to cover truck sounds. Or recordings of truck sounds were placed near sensors miles away, causing the Americans to bomb empty jungle. Bags of urine hung along unused sections of trail had the same effect.

The sensors, however, could not always be tricked. Then it was time for "Whispering Death"—the B-52s. These bombers, with their enormous payload, were used regularly against the Ho Chi Minh Trail. Flying in three-plane groups at 30,000 feet, they could not be seen or heard from the ground. The only sign of their presence was the soft whoosh or whisper of bombs moments before impact. But by then it was too late. All hell broke loose as bombs cut a swath a mile long and a quarter mile wide. Flashes of man-made lightning lit the sky. Domes of earth rose into the air, then settled with a gut-wrenching thud. Craters thirty feet across and twenty feet deep opened. Shock waves, visible in aerial photos, snapped trees like matchsticks. Jagged chunks of red-hot steel zinged overhead at bullet speed.

Even the bravest soldiers hugged the ground, feeling helpless and small. Here was fear in its purest form, for nothing you did or did not do made a difference. The bombs had a will of their own. Someone in a "safe" dugout might be ripped apart. A comrade caught standing up might be tossed twenty yards, have every stitch of clothing torn off by the blast, and walk away with nothing worse than a ringing in the ears. Those who lived through a B-52 raid had the experience carved into their memory. "The fear of [B-52] attacks was terrible," said Trinh Duc, a Viet Cong guerrilla. "People pissed and shat in their pants. You would see them come out of their bunkers shaking so badly it looked as if they had gone crazy."[19]

Strange as it may seem, bombs were safer than bugs on the Ho Chi Minh Trail. It is believed that up to 20 percent of those who went south died along the way. Of these, by far the largest number died of disease, mostly malaria, while bombs accounted for only 2 percent of all deaths. And it took an estimated 300 bombs to kill one enemy soldier at a cost of $140,000.

109

It might have been worth the expense, had Rolling Thunder succeeded. But it did not. At no time was the Ho Chi

---

[19] Quoted in Chanoff and Doan, *Portrait of the Enemy,* p. 109.

Minh Trail put out of action. The North Vietnamese made every effort to keep it open. Road repair gangs had 50,000 full-time workers; for big jobs, the NVA could get 150,000 part-timers at a moment's notice. As soon as the bombers left, they swung into action with picks and shovels, clearing the worst damage within hours. NVA troop movements actually increased along with the bombing. American officials estimated that 12,400 troops came down the trail in 1964; by 1967 the figure had risen to 101,263.

Pilots knew they were fighting a losing battle. Dick Rutan spoke from experience when he said: "I never one time saw a road cut or closed. All that was a total waste of effort. Absolute total waste. . . . They were turning jungle into dust. For nothing. . . . It was the most gross waste of bombs I've ever seen in my life."[20]

Rutan was lucky; he came home after his tour of duty. Nearly 700 of his comrades were less fortunate. They were shot down and captured by the enemy. And since Vietnam was America's longest war, their captivity lasted longer than any others'. Their story is an epic of courage, faith, and devotion against fearful odds. It is the story of genuine heroes.

The pilots did not start out as heroes, but were forced to become them just to keep their human dignity. As prisoners of war (POWs), they had certain rights under international law. According to the Geneva Convention of 1949, which Uncle Ho's representatives had signed, they were entitled to humane treatment and decent living conditions. The Communists violated every one of these rules. Downed pilots, they declared, were "Yankee air pirates" without any rights. "You are *not* a prisoner of war," a jailer told Navy Lieutenant Rodney A. Knutson, "you are a war criminal!"[21]

110

---

[20] Quoted in Maurer, *Strange Ground*, p. 387.
[21] Quoted in John G. Hubbell, *P.O.W.: A Definitive History of the American Prisoner-of-War Experience in Vietnam, 1964–1974*, p. 103.

*A captured U.S. pilot being taken
to a Communist press conference in
Hanoi in 1967. Because this photo
was taken by a North Vietnamese
news agency, the prisoner's identity
is not positively known.*

The Bettmon Archives

Captured pilots were kept in North Vietnamese prisons. One, nicknamed Dogpatch, was located in the mountains five miles from the Chinese border. Hanoi and the surrounding area contained ten others, among them the Zoo, Alcatraz, and Skidrow. The largest was Hoa Lo prison in downtown Hanoi. Built by the French, it is surrounded by high walls with jagged pieces of glass, the remnants of old wine bottles, cemented to the top. Americans called it the Hanoi Hilton.

There, as everywhere, living conditions were dreadful. Inmates were locked in dark cells that stank of urine and vomit; cells had no toilets, and wastes were kept in "honey buckets," wooden pails that might be emptied once a week. Hot and humid by day, at night cells swarmed with vermin of every description. Rats, mosquitoes, roaches, and ants made it impossible to get a night's sleep. Food usually consisted of watery pumpkin soup and small loaves of bread crawling with black beetles. Meat might be anything from a scrap of pork fat to the hoof of a cow or a chicken's head floating in grease. One airman recalled having to eat a blackbird, complete with feathers, lying on its back with its feet sticking up. Another was tortured "for insulting the Vietnamese people" after he refused to eat the slops put before him.

The Communists demanded total cooperation. Put plainly, POWs had to betray their country if they hoped to get along in North Vietnam. Military information was a top priority. Airmen were questioned about war plans, weapons, and codes. Interrogators, for example, wanted to know all about people sniffers and similar devices. Equally important, prisoners were to help turn world opinion against the United States. They must confess to "atrocities," denounce America's "unjust war," and condemn the "imperialists" in Washington. And, for good measure, they had to praise their jailers' "humane" treatment.

The vast majority, however, refused. Although held in

enemy jails, POWs were still bound by American law. The Code of Conduct for Members of the United States Armed Forces explained exactly what they could and could not do. There was no way around it for a man of honor. They could give the enemy their name, rank, service number, and date of birth. Nothing else. They must never make statements disloyal to their country. If they did, they were liable to criminal charges upon their return.

The Communists expected obedience and were prepared to do anything to get it. Torture was the accepted method of breaking down resistance. When POWs were questioned after the war, it was estimated that 95 percent of them had been tortured between 1965 and 1969.[22] Things improved in 1969 because of Ho Chi Minh's death that year. Uncle Ho had favored harsh treatment for Uncle Sam's airmen.

Torture was carried out by guards who knew their trade. Since POWs were never told the guards' real names, they gave them nicknames to fit their personalities or appearance. At the Hanoi Hilton, the most hated were Rat, Rabbit, Eel, Cat, Dog, Bug, Greasy, Mickey Mouse, and Dum Dum. Big Ugh was a heavyset brute who grunted as he worked. Fidel—named after Fidel Castro—was a Cuban torture expert on loan to North Vietnam. Pigeye was a sadist, one who enjoyed hurting others. If Pigeye is still alive, there are former POWs who would like to meet him—alone and in an out-of-the-way place.

Before guards resorted to physical torture, they sometimes played mind games with their victims. Instead of causing physical pain, they tried to get their way through fear. To cure Ralph Gaither's stubbornness, a guard put a rifle to his head and pulled the trigger. Click! Nothing happened. The

---

[22]Scott Blakey, *Prisoner of War: The Survival of Commander Richard A. Stratton*, p. 344.

113

gun was empty. Gaither was scared out of his wits, but remained as stubborn as ever.[23] Everett Alvarez, the first pilot to be captured by the Communists, had a cell near a torture chamber for Vietnamese women; the Hanoi Hilton also served as a civil prison. During the night, when the background noise died down, he heard sounds that made his flesh crawl. First came the swish of a whip, then a woman's cries and screams. It went on like that for hours, night after night. The torturer's meaning was clear: the same would happen to him if he did not cooperate. Alvarez refused, and was tortured in turn.[24]

Torture could take many forms. POWs were beaten, deprived of sleep, or made to "hold up the wall" that is, stand for hours with their arms raised, leaning against a wall.

But ropes were the most common form of torture, and the most painful. Hundreds of Americans still bear scars from those ropes. Navy pilot Jeremiah A. Denton, Jr., later a U.S. senator, tells a hair-raising story in his book *When Hell Was in Session*. It is typical of rope-torture victims. When he refused to confess to war crimes, Pigeye dragged him into Room 18, known as the Meathook Room. Denton was forced to sit on the floor while guards tied each arm from the wrist to the shoulder. With every loop, a guard stood on the arm to pull the rope as tight as possible, cutting off blood circulation. The arms were then forced together until the elbows met behind his back and were tied, dislocating the shoulders. Finally, his head was pulled forward until it touched his toes and was tied into place. The feeling was unimaginable. Pain shot through every nerve of his body. They kept it up "until I was unable to control myself. I began crying hysterically, blood and tears mingling and running down my cheeks. I

---

[23] Hubbell, *P.O.W.*, p. 121.
[24] *Ibid.*, p. 68.

feigned unconsciousness several times, but Pigeye was too much of an expert for that. He merely lifted the lids over my eyes and grinned." Denton gave in—for the time being.[25]

POWs resisted as best they could. They resisted in small ways, since it was impossible to beat their jailers by force. Humor was a potent weapon. There are many examples of prisoners raising their morale at the enemy's expense. One of my favorites involves army pilot Dennis Thompson. After being tortured for several days, Thompson agreed to write an article about heroic Vietnamese revolutionaries and read it over the Hanoi Hilton's public address system. But since the guards' English was so poor, he could turn the reading into a farce. "The Vietnamese people," he said firmly, "have proven themselves to be the most revolting people I have ever met in my life. I hope that soon the Vietnamese Communists and all those who have taken care of me and my friends as prisoners will get what they deserve. . . ."[26] The guards were pleased. Thompson's comrades were overjoyed; they put their hands over their mouths to keep from laughing out loud.

Some jokes, however, backfired. Lieutenant Commander Charles Tanner told "Eel" that two fellow officers, Clark Kent and Ben Casey, had been punished for refusing to bomb North Vietnam. Eel, ignorant of American television characters, gave the story to Japanese Communist newsmen, who spread it worldwide. Weeks later, American Communist party officials told the North Vietnamese the truth. They were not amused. Tanner had made them lose face, as they explained in the Meathook Room.[27]

From the beginning, POWs were forbidden to speak to inmates in other cells. Guards constantly patrolled, punishing

115

---

[25]Jeremiah A. Denton, Jr., *When Hell Was in Session*, pp. 86–87.
[26]Quoted in Hubbell, *P.O.W.*, p. 505.
[27]*Ibid.*, pp. 255–256.

those who broke the rule. Some prisoners who shared a cell developed the tap code to send messages over long distances. This code used a twenty-five-letter alphabet in which *C* doubled for itself and *K*. The letters were arranged in a square of five lines with five letters per line.

A B C D E
F G H I J
L M N O P
Q R S T U
V W X Y Z

Messages were sent by tapping on the cell wall or door with bare knuckles or a spoon. To form a letter, you tapped down the left side and then to the right. The word *resist*, for example, would be: .... [four taps, two taps] (*R*); . .....(*E*); ....(*S*); .. ....(*I*); ....(*S*); ....(*T*). Sending and receiving were as easy as talking or listening to another person talk. A man could start a message and it would be passed from wall to wall, cell to cell, within minutes. Jeremiah Denton even invented a voice code in which every grunt, cough, sneeze, and retch indicated a letter's position.

Tap code gave unity, enabling prisoners to help one another and resist their jailers. It helped them feel that, whatever happened, they were not alone. They were people who were cared for and loved. A POW returning from a torture session knew that everyone was pulling for him. As he lay in his cell, the sound of tapping came through the wall: .. ..(*G*); . ..(*B*); ....(*U*). *GBU* meant "God bless you."

Prisoners said that they had never felt closer to God than in their cells. Every Sunday, ". ...(*C*)" would sound from wall to wall. It was the call to church. Everyone would rise, go to the center of his cell, bow his head, and recite the Lord's Prayer. There would be another sound, and everyone faced the east, in the direction of the United States. Then

geration, as airmen knew from experience. Their bases, supposedly under ARVN protection, were open to attack. Not even Da Nang, the largest and most important base, was secure. Hardly a day passed without Viet Cong snipers taking potshots at guards; airmen called it Rocket City, because the enemy constantly fired small rockets over the fence. There was a real danger of South Vietnam's collapsing by the end of 1965.

Determined to prevent this, the President turned his attention to the ground war. Until then few American soldiers had seen combat in Vietnam, and then only as advisers, like my pupil. That changed quickly. Along with more advisers, LBJ sent the first combat units. On March 8, six days after the start of Rolling Thunder, 3,500 Marines landed at Da Nang. Their mission, at least for the time being, was not to fight, but to protect the air base. In April, however, they were allowed to help out if nearby ARVN units got into trouble. In June they received permission to go after the enemy on their own. They were, in fact, to Americanize the war, to take over the bulk of the fighting from the ARVN. President Johnson had decided that only his own "boys" could save South Vietnam.

This was the turning point for America in Vietnam. Once begun, the escalation continued at an ever-quickening pace. The more troops LBJ sent, the more he needed to send to support those already there. Within six weeks, 82,000 troops arrived; by the end of the year, there were 184,300. The numbers rose steadily: 385,300 in 1966; 485,600 in 1967; 536,100 in 1968.

Napoleon used to say that "an army marches on its stomach." It does; and the larger the army, the larger its stomach. Experts in logistics, the science of supplying armies in war, estimated that an American soldier needed eighty pounds of supplies and equipment per day. This in turn meant facilities

---

they put their hands over their hearts and said the Pledge of Allegiance. "We did that every single Sunday we were in North Vietnam," recalled Colonel Jerry Driscol, "whether we were solo, dual, or in one case where I had fifty-five roommates. Every single Sunday."[28]

Several POWs needed all the support they could get. Determined not to be used in any way, they took great risks to defy their captors. For instance, Jeremiah Denton had been tortured into confessing his "war crimes" at a press conference held in April 1966. He stood before an audience of reporters from Communist countries, blinking at floodlights while the cameras rolled. Blinking! That gave him an idea. Feeling that Washington needed to know that POWs were being tortured, he stared into the cameras and began blinking his eyes in a pattern. Slow. Fast. Slow. The reporters thought he had gone crazy, but he was crazy as a fox. Denton's blinks were actually Morse code dots and dashes for T . . . O . . . R . . . T . . . U . . . R . . . E. Again and again he repeated it. TORTURE. TORTURE. TORTURE. Eventually, film clips reached U.S. Naval Intelligence, which deciphered the signals. American officials had suspected that captured airmen were being tortured; now they knew for sure.[29]

Lieutenant Commander Richard Stratton appeared at another press conference. Before he walked on stage, his jailers played a tape recording they had tortured him into making. In it he admitted to murdering civilians and thanked the Vietnamese people for their kind treatment. Stratton's body language, however, told a different story. He came on stage slowly, stiffly, eyes downcast, a blank expression on his face. Suddenly he stopped, held his hands at his sides, and bowed deeply four times. His movements, like those of

---

[28]Quoted in Maurer, *Strange Ground*, p. 412.
[29]Denton, *When Hell Was in Session*, p. 91ff.

a zombie, convinced the audience that he had been mistreated. The same thing had happened in Korea, where American POWs were brainwashed into confessing all sorts of crimes.[30]

Jim Stockdale would not even go on stage. We last met him as the leader of the first wave of bombers over North Vietnam. Shot down in September 1965, he was sent to the Hanoi Hilton and tortured by Pigeye. But he would not give in. Before a press conference, he was handed a razor and ordered to shave. When the guards left his cell for a moment, he slashed the top of his head. Returning, the guards were shocked to find his face and shoulders covered with blood. Angry but determined, they ran for a hat to cover the wounds. That was their second mistake, leaving Stockdale alone once again. Seeing a heavy stool, he began pounding it into his face. His face became puffy, his eyes swollen and bloodshot. They dared not show him to the press in that condition. Nor would they try to do so again.[31]

Although President Johnson knew that prisoners were being tortured, he did not inform the American people. His reason, which veterans still have trouble understanding, was that the publicity would bring further mistreatment by the North Vietnamese. In any case, the POWs were out of the war. There was nothing to do but hold on until it ended and they could go home.

But that day would be a long time in coming.

---

[30]Blakey, *Prisoner at War*, p. 113ff.
[31]Hubbell, *P.O.W*, p. 476.

SEARCH AND DESTROY

It still boils down to suffering, and the thing about Vietnam that still most bothers me is that . . . the human element of what a soldier goes through—and what the Vietnamese went through—is not only neglected: it is almost cast aside as superfluous.

—Sergeant Tim O'Brien

IN THE SPRING OF 1965, A FORMER NINTH-GRADE PUpil of mine, then a Green Beret corporal, came home on leave after a year in the Central Highlands of South Vietnam. We spoke for a while about old times, then I asked how things were going over there. He fumbled for a moment, at a loss for words; he was never handy with words, bless his heart. Finally he thought of Humpty Dumpty, the nursery-rhyme character who fell from a great wall and broke into pieces. Now he had it. South Vietnam was Humpty Dumpty Land, and all Uncle Sam's money and all Uncle Sam's airplanes could not hold it together. His comparison made good sense. For unless Uncle Sam—President Johnson—found a better way, and found it soon, South Vietnam was doomed.

All signs pointed to disaster. ARVN battlefield losses were a battalion (750 men) a week; an additional 5,000 to 7,000 men were deserting each month. The ARVN, an American general noted, controlled "about three or four feet on either side of wherever they were." This was only a slight exag-

to unload, handle, store, transport, and repair whatever arrived from the States. But since few of these facilities existed when the buildup began, military engineers had to start from scratch. Working round the clock, they changed the face of South Vietnam. Eight major airfields, plus ninety smaller landing strips, sprang up within two years. On certain days, each of the larger fields handled more traffic than any airport at home. Seven new deep-water seaports dotted the coast. The largest was Cam Ranh Bay northeast of Saigon, built at a cost of $11 billion. Cam Ranh Bay lay on a beautiful stretch of coast, an ideal vacation spot. When the engineers first arrived, they found just a few shacks atop the sand dunes. When they were done, they left behind a city of barracks, office buildings, docks, airfields, warehouses, oil tanks, pipelines, machine shops, and all-weather roads.

Not only war matériels, but other types of supplies poured into South Vietnam. There were desks, file cabinets, typewriters, and air conditioners for offices. Refrigerated warehouses stored thousands of tons of steak, hamburger, and hot dogs. Forty plants were built to provide ice cream; some forward units even had it delivered by parachute. Especially lucky troops had beer and pizza flown in by helicopter. By the end of 1967, a million tons of supplies were being landed each month, an average of a hundred pounds a day for every American fighting man.

Although the first combat troops were brought by ship, nearly all later arrivals came on planes chartered from commercial airlines. Troops arrived not in complete units, with their buddies, but individually, to be assigned wherever needed. Their first impressions of Vietnam were not good. A strange feeling crept over them as the plane's doors opened and the stewardesses said, "Good-bye, and have a nice war." The stewardesses' smiles seemed forced, as if painted on their faces. Soldiers felt as if they had left Earth and landed on a planet at the far reaches of the galaxy. They were now "in-country," a never-never land called "The Nam"; everything outside of it was "The World."

The first thing you noticed when you left the air-conditioned plane was the heat. Temperatures of over a hundred degrees are normal in The Nam. As you walked down the stairs, sweat seeped from every pore of your body, staining your uniform. The odor was worse, your own and that hanging in the air. "The place smelled like an old urinal. Sweaty, stale and dank. All the nasty smells you can imagine," a soldier wrote.[1] This, too, was normal, for military bases had no plumbing. Each day tons of human waste were collected in barrels, soaked with fuel oil, and set on fire. The stench was stronger or weaker from place to place, depending on the wind; but you never escaped it entirely. Nor could you escape the presence of death. Nearby, you might see work crews unloading aluminum boxes that resembled large tool chests: coffins. New arrivals often saw planes being loaded with the bodies of dead Americans. Such was your welcome in-country.

American soldiers were unprepared for Vietnam. They were young; the average age was nineteen, compared to twenty-six in World War II. Naive and immature, their heads were filled with all sorts of rubbish about the glory of war. They had been raised on World War II movies, particularly those of John Wayne. Although Mr. Wayne had never served in the armed forces, he looked and acted like a hero. In films like *The Sands of Iwo Jima*, he made war an adventure in which the good guys—our guys—were invincible. Americans always won, and did so accompanied by rousing music. Even when they died, death came quickly, neatly, painlessly.

122

---

[1] Quoted in Mark Baker, *Nam: The Vietnam War in the Words of the Men and Women Who Fought There*, p. 48.

You never saw shattered bodies in a John Wayne movie.

Early arrivals felt they were honoring the memory of John F. Kennedy. They were not asking what their country could do for them, but putting their lives on the line for their country. They had a purpose, a cause: to fight communism. Yet they knew so little about either their ally or their enemy; Asian history was not taught in U.S. public schools. More than a few had difficulty finding Vietnam on a map of the world; the first Marines at Da Nang asked the name of the "island" they had just taken. Vietnamese customs seemed odd, to put it mildly. Young soldiers, seeing men holding hands, jumped to conclusions about their sexual preferences. The Vietnamese language sounded like gibberish. Except for a few mispronounced phrases like *didi mow* ("go away"), *dong lai* ("halt"), and *la dai* ("come here"), they had no way to communicate with the people. And much of what they did learn came through painful experience.

Terrorism was often the soldiers' first encounter with the Viet Cong, who were also called VC, Victor Charlie, or simply Charlie. Whatever name they used, the U.S. soldiers came to regard the enemy as a beast in human form. Soldiers' letters and recollections are filled with accounts of terrorism witnessed with their own eyes. The frequency of these accounts, and their similarities, are no accident. They point, instead, to a deliberate policy on the part of the Viet Cong. "Education by terrorism" had been expanded to include all those who were friendly to the Americans.

Soldiers learned that a villager's cooperation or act of kindness could be his death sentence. Entire villages—every man, woman, and child—might be executed if they refused to tell where an American patrol was going. It was the slaughter of children that most shocked the Americans. This was something they had not expected and which infuriated them as little else would.

123

Above, waving Vietnamese children welcome the first U.S. Marines to Da Nang in March 1965. At right, General William C. Westmoreland, commander of American forces in South Vietnam, meets with men of the First Cavalry Division. No amount of training could prepare these troops—on average, the youngest troops in U.S. history ever sent to war—for combat in Vietnam.

Army Lieutenant David Donovan told how it was in his book *Once a Warrior King: Memoirs of an Officer in Vietnam*. The Viet Cong had blown up a school filled with children, and parents brought the survivors to Donovan's first aid team. All were in bad shape, shrieking in pain. "It was a hard thing to deal with," Donovan wrote. "I was psychologically prepared for war as a demonstration of man's inhumanity to man, but I was not prepared for the shock of war as an example of man's inhumanity to children. I felt a deep sense of . . . outrage when I saw myself that our enemy had absolutely no qualms about victimizing innocent children in their campaigns of terror. . . . More than in the exchange of shot and shell . . . more than in the battle line, it was the watching over the agonized death of mutilated children that I met war in all its vile and vulgar glory, and it was there that I grew to truly know my enemy."[2]

Americans, too, became victims of terrorism. No place, it seemed, was safe. Off-duty soldiers could be attacked when they least expected it. Viet Cong agents would pack the hollow tubing of a bicycle with plastic explosive, set a timer, and leave it outside a bar favored by off-duty soldiers. Saigon was notorious for its Honda shooters, youngsters on Honda motor scooters armed with pistols. One would pull up alongside a jeep, shoot the occupant point-blank, and be off in a flash. The wounded might then be murdered in their hospital beds. Viet Cong mortar teams often fired at American hospitals. Not even Cam Ranh Bay was safe; a hundred-man unit once broke into the hospital compound, threw grenades, shot some patients, and made its getaway without losing a single man.

Women could just as easily be terrorists as their victims. A Viet Cong woman might hide a grenade in her blouse or in her baby's diapers. When it was least expected, she would

125

---

[2]David Donovan, *Once a Warrior King: Memoirs of an Officer in Vietnam*, p. 170.

throw the grenade and escape in the confusion that followed. Wherever Americans went, they were approached by women selling Coca-Cola and beer. If the Americans were wise, they passed them by despite their thirst. Drinks became weapons in enemy hands. The Viet Cong liked to put crushed glass in Coke bottles. Doctors had to pump the stomachs of soldiers who bought beer laced with acid. Women who excelled at their work earned the Killer of Americans banner or the title "American-Killer Heroine." The most desirable prize was the Hero American Killer medal, a piece of gold-colored metal with a ribbon of red and yellow silk.

It was not even safe to be near children. The Viet Cong, knowing that Americans liked children, used them in their terror campaign. With training, the children were as effective as any adult. Children of eight or nine would run up and toss a grenade into the back of an army truck. Shoeshine boys might leave their boxes outside a soldier's hangout; the box was a bomb timed to go off moments after the owner set the timer. Even if child terrorists were caught in the act, there was still something to be gained. Truong Mealy, who we met earlier, explained. "American soldiers would have to shoot them. Then the [American people] feel ashamed. And they blame themselves and call their soldiers 'war criminals.'"[3]

Children might actually be turned into living bombs. Toddlers with explosives taped to their bodies were sent into places where soldiers gathered. The children, of course, were not told what would happen, only to go to the nice soldiers. A timer or pressure fuse did the rest. Marine Lieutenant Archie Biggers saw the results at Dong Ha just south of the DMZ: "There was this kid, maybe two or three years old. He hadn't learned to walk too well yet, but he was running

126

---

[3] Quoted in Santoli, *To Bear Any Burden*, p. 62.3

down the street. And a marine walked over to talk to the kid, touched him, and they both blew up. . . . It was a known tactic that they wrapped stuff around kids."[4] Another time, five soldiers died when a child of about five walked into a bar and exploded. Incidents like these made soldiers realize that Vietnam was different. "It was not John Wayne."

President Johnson's goal for the ground war was the same as for Rolling Thunder. Unlike past conflicts, there was no plan for defeating the enemy. American ground forces had no clear-cut mission in Vietnam. There was no target that, once taken or destroyed, would bring victory. LBJ's objective was simply to convince North Vietnam's leaders that they could not win. He would do this not by destroying their war-making ability, an action which he feared might lead to World War III, but by showing that the United States could fight as long as necessary.

General William C. Westmoreland, the American commander in South Vietnam, had to work within the limitations set by his Commander-in-Chief in Washington. Westmoreland—"Westy" to his men—was not allowed to take the war to the enemy. The Ho Chi Minh Trail, not to mention North Vietnam, was out of bounds to his troops. His only choice, therefore, was attrition, the slow grinding down of the enemy until the enemy decided to quit. Each day, Westy was to hunt the VC/NVA, fight them, and kill as many of them as possible. "We'll just go on bleeding them until Hanoi wakes up to the fact that they have bled their country to the point of national disaster for generations," he said.[5] This strategy was called search and destroy—SAD for short.

Although the U.S. strategy included several large opera-

127

---

[4] Quoted in Wallace Terry, *Bloods: An Oral History of the Vietnam War by Black Veterans*, p. 114.
[5] Quoted in Pisor, *The End of the Line*, p. 134.

tions called "sweeps," most of the fighting was done by patrols of 100 or 200 men. SAD involved countless small-unit actions that took place throughout South Vietnam. It was a war without front lines. Groups of soldiers would be brought, or "inserted," into a suspicious area. If, let us say, they found that the Viet Cong held a hilltop, they captured it and withdrew after killing some of the defenders and losing some of their own men. In time, the enemy returned, and the whole thing would have to be repeated. No territory was gained or, indeed, wanted. The hill had no value in itself, but was just a place to hunt the enemy. SAD's only measure of success was the gruesome arithmetic of the body count. Each morning Westy received a report on the previous day's count. If more enemies died than Americans, the operations were a success; if not, a failure. Enemy losses usually outnumbered American by three to one.

It was difficult to take the enemy by surprise. Every operation required detailed planning before it could get under way. Orders had to be issued, troops briefed, supplies gathered, and transportation arranged. From the moment these preparations began, hundreds of people were let in on the "secret." Not that this was done on purpose; far from it. American bases employed Vietnamese civilians to do various jobs; at the Long Binh army post near Saigon, for example, 22,000 workers served 26,000 troops. There were "hooch girls" to clean barracks, make beds, and do laundry. Laborers dug ditches, filled sandbags, and removed garbage. Barbers cut hair. Children polished soldiers' boots, even cleaned their rifles. They overheard the soldiers' conversations, saw the preparations being made. Although the majority were loyal, some were VC/NVA spies. The moment they heard about an operation, they contacted their superiors.

The ARVN was itself riddled with spies. Certain ARVN divisions had dozens of spies among their officers. Several spies, among them Colonel Vo Bac Trinh, held strategic positions. Trinh was a go-between for U.S. and ARVN forces. Whenever Americans planned an operation, Trinh had to inform local ARVN commanders so they would not shoot at their allies. Yet he shared equally with the enemy; indeed, information was often in enemy hands before it reached American units. The colonel returned to Saigon after the war with his true rank—major general in the NVA.

SAD patrols always worked under disadvantages. It was said that the VC/NVA traveled heavy and fought light; that is, they carried a lot while on the move, but fought with only their basic equipment. American soldiers traveled heavy and fought heavy. They called themselves "grunts," because they grunted under the weight of their gear.

The grunt's clothing was heavy, hot, and uncomfortable. He wore boots of leather and nylon, baggy pants with deep pockets, and a long-sleeved shirt. On his head was a steel helmet covered with camouflage cloth. His chest was protected by a flak jacket, an armored vest made of layers of nylon and fiberglass weighing ten pounds.

The grunt was a walking arsenal. Among the weapons carried on patrol were the M60 "light" machine gun, weighing 23 pounds and able to fire 600 bullets a minute, and the M79 grenade launcher, a tiny terror which could fire shotgun shells or hurl grenades 350 yards. Most men carried the M16 rifle; lightweight (8 pounds) and deadly at close range, it had the habit of jamming at the most inconvenient times.

In addition to his weapons, the grunt carried a pack with a coil of rope, collapsible shovel, machete, dry socks, extra underwear, poncho, food, flares, rifle cleaning kit, and personal items. Around his waist he wore a web belt with a long knife, ammunition pouches, first-aid-kit, two water canteens, and hand grenades weighing one pound each. Made with a thin metal skin, these exploded a tightly coiled spring into hundreds of fragments, hence the name "frags" or fragmentation grenades. Last but not least, he had extra belts of machine gun bullets draped across his chest. On average, a grunt carried a hundred pounds of equipment. "[It] really gets heavy. It gets me down," Private Donald Sloat wrote his mother. No lightweight himself, Sloat stood six feet four inches and weighed 215 pounds.[6]

Patrols were brought into a search area by helicopter. The helicopter was the best all-around tool of war in Vietnam. Entire "airmobile" or "air cavalry" divisions, each having 20,000 men, were formed around this homely machine. Helicopters really were the cavalry of the sky. Like the horses of old, they gave mobility, the ability to move swiftly over long distances. But unlike the cavalrymen, airmobile troops could attack from any direction, strike targets in rugged country, and bypass enemy strongpoints. The helicopter flew like a dream, making tight turns, stopping short, hovering, and moving backward and sideways within seconds. More, it could take part in a battle and evacuate the wounded, saving lives that would otherwise have been lost. Large helicopters, called flying cranes, could hoist cannon through the air. "Jolly Green Giants" rescued downed airmen.

No single patrol can show how SAD worked. Given the scattered nature of the fighting, no detailed history of what took place exists. Such an account would be pointless, for one action was much like another—unless you were in the middle of it. So let us put ourselves in the middle of an action somewhere in South Vietnam. Although our patrol never took place exactly as described, it has elements in common with *every* patrol.

On the day of the patrol, grunts lug their packs to the waiting helicopters. Their helmet covers and flak jackets bear

---

[6]Quoted in Stanley W. Beesley, *Vietnam: The Heartland Remembers*, p. 169.

handwritten mottoes: VC GO HOME; TRY YOUR LUCK, CHARLIE; BORN TO KILL; and TIME IS ON MY SIDE. A take-off on the Twenty-third Psalm can be seen on several jackets: "Yea, though I walk through the Valley of the Shadow of Death, I will fear no evil, for I am the meanest son of a gun in the Valley." Mostly this is bravado, an attempt to hide the grunts' fears behind brave words. Other mottoes are not so sure-sounding: JUST YOU AND ME, GOD—RIGHT? and simply, WHY ME?

Whup-whup-whup-whup.

The helicopters' rotors whip the air, tossing up clouds of red dust. Rotors are sharp, and one swipe can chop a man in half; hence the helicopter's nickname, "chopper." These, too, have mottoes painted on their bellies and sides. BE NICE OR I'LL KILL YOU, one warns. Some have war names like WIDOWMAKER, BOUNTY HUNTER, MEAN MACHINE, VIPER, DEATH DEALER, BUSHWHACKER, BRUTAL CANNON, MURDERERS' ROW, and PURPLE PEOPLE EATER.

Grunts run toward the choppers hunched over, holding their helmets to their heads and covering their faces with towels to avoid choking on the dust. They board eight to a machine and sit down four on each side, their legs dangling outside; troop carriers have no doors. Many sit on their helmets, in case a bullet should go through the thin chopper belly as they fly over enemy positions. Although they know that a helmet cannot stop a bullet, they sit on it for the same reason a child clutches a security blanket.

Whupwhupwhupwhupwhupwhup.

The pilot guns the motor. Lift off! The chopper rises straight up, like a high-speed elevator. Reaching cruising altitude, it joins the others and together they move out. The ship rolls and pitches and shakes, for it is light and moving at 120 miles an hour. The sound of the rotors is deafening; exhaust fumes make men cough and bring tears to their eyes.

A UH-1D Iroquois helicopter, top, takes off on a search-and-destroy mission. Above and to right, men on SAD patrols struggle through the rough jungle terrain, fording rivers and crossing fields of sharp-edged elephant grass.

Below, the jungle flashes by in a green blur. And the rushing wind makes everyone wince. Imagine going 60 miles an hour in a car and putting your hand out the window. Now imagine the wind slapping your face at twice that speed. It hurts, and it takes your breath away.

The landing zone (LZ) appears in the distance. As the ships bank for their approach, grunts put their weapons on "rock 'n' roll," full automatic. Plumes of black smoke are rising a thousand feet into the air. Fighters have been raking the LZ with bombs, rockets, and bullets, a precaution against hidden enemy troops. "Please, Lord, let it be cold down there," grunts mutter to themselves. This has nothing to do with the weather; a cold LZ means an unopposed landing.

No such luck today. The LZ is hot. Broiling hot. Suddenly machine guns open up from a tree line. A chopper falters, then goes down, spewing sparks and flame. The tip of its rotor hits the ground, snaps off, and spins across the LZ like a giant sword blade. The rest of the ship explodes, killing everyone aboard.

By now helicopters are arriving one after another. They don't land, but hover inches above the ground while their passengers leave. Hearts pounding, grunts leap out and run for cover. Enemy machine gun bullets stitch the ground, tossing up geysers of dust. Mortar rounds burst, scattering red-hot chunks of iron. "Lying there," a grunt recalled later, "I suddenly wanted to be home in my bed with my parents in the next room."

Just then a piercing whine drowns out the sound of gunfire. An airborne observer, seeing the trouble below, has called in a flock of helicopter gunships. Unlike the troop carriers, gunships are built to fight. There are two models, the UH-1 Huey and the AH-1G Cobra. Each carries machine guns, pods of air-to-ground rockets, and a launcher that shoots grenades with machine-gun speed. Skimming the ground at 200

133

miles an hour, with tiger teeth and cobra fangs painted on their nose turrets, they spray death at anything that stands in their way. Pilots joked that their ships were so powerful that they backed up when all weapons fired at once. Grunts loved them. "I'd marry one of those helicopters if it could scratch my back and cook a respectable meal," Sergeant George Olsen wrote his family.[7]

Daunted by such firepower, the enemy slips into the jungle. They are patient and will deal with the grunts later, on their own terms. Only after they have rehearsed their plan, are sure of its success and the grunts' surprise, will they attack. Until then, the land itself will soften the Americans up for the kill.

Having cleared the LZ, the gunships head home. The grunts are on their own until the end of their patrol, which may last as long as a week. They begin to "hump the boonies," to plod through the back country.

It is a hostile country that begins taking its toll immediately. At first they cross flooded rice paddies through waist-deep mud. Each step becomes a struggle demanding every ounce of energy. Even the strongest men gasp for breath as the straps of their packs dig into their shoulders. The mud sucks at their boots, nearly pulling them off as they lift their feet. "Move your feet, the body will follow," sergeants bawl. Temperatures soar to 115 degrees Fahrenheit in the sun, causing the air to shimmer. Men hunch their shoulders against the heat, but there is nothing to do but go on. The metal parts of their guns become so hot that the grunts have to wrap cloth around them to keep from burning their hands. Everyone has a towel around his neck and uses it often to wipe the sweat from his face.

After several hours of this, they reach the edge of the jungle. The shade from the trees, however, gives no relief. Indeed,

---

[7] Quoted in Bernard Edelman, ed., *Dear America: Letters Home from Vietnam*, pp. 71–72.

the men have stepped into a green hell. The jungle is so thick in places that they have to cut away the brush with a machete every couple of steps. Men trip on roots, fall, and lie panting under their heavy packs; to stand, they grab hold of a tree with both hands while comrades lift their packs. Clearings are filled with saw-toothed elephant grass whose blades are as tall as a man and able to slash open one's face as easily as a razor. Thorns snag men's clothes, and they must tear themselves loose. Every scratch, bathed in salty sweat, stings.

Movement disturbs the wildlife, so that each step is greeted by a chorus of caws, chirps, and chatters. Although there are plenty of snakes and leeches, it is the insects and spiders who rule the jungle. There are half-inch fire ants whose sting feels like an electric needle. There are furry black spiders as large as your thumb and poisonous centipedes too. There are millions upon millions of mosquitoes able to bite through the thickest cotton shirt. There is no avoiding them. The grunts get them in their eyes, noses, and ears, even their mouths when they speak. The creatures seem to thrive on insect repellent.

No air stirs in the jungle, except when it rains. The hot humidity is suffocating, like trying to breathe with a wet towel over your face. During the summer monsoon, rain falls in sheets every day, turning the jungle floor into a quagmire. Decay is everywhere. The ground is spongy with rotting vegetation, which gives off the sour smell of wet garbage. The thick jungle canopy traps moisture, preventing evaporation. As a result, nothing dries completely even in the dry season. Uniforms are always more or less damp. Underpants rot; grunts throw them away rather than have their backsides rubbed raw. Wet feet wrinkle like prunes, blister, and become a mass of painful sores. Personal cleanliness is impossible. Grunts don't shave because the smallest nicks become infected. There is no place to wash. Everyone smells so bad that they can hardly stand themselves.

135

The grunts' canteens are quickly emptied and they must re-fill them from a muddy stream. To purify the water, they add halazone tablets, which give it an iodine taste without hiding its putrid odor. Nevertheless, men develop "Ho Chi Minh's revenge," diarrhea, and are constantly dropping out of line to squat behind a bush. Eating, always a problem in the field, becomes sheer agony. Grunts live on C-rations, or "C-rats," combat rations packed in metal cans. A typical meal consists of "Gainesburgers," ground-beef patties soaked in grease, a few slices of bread, and a small can of fruit in sweet syrup. For variety, there may be ham and lima beans or "weenies and beanies," frankfurters and beans. C-rats are okay for a few days; after that, they are nauseating.

Marine Lieutenant Victor D. Westphall spoke for his comrades in a letter to his brother. Everyone, he said, was miserable and hurt all over. "I know that at one point, my feet about to crack open, my stomach knotted by hunger and diarrhea, my back feeling like a mirror made of nerves shattered in a million pieces by my flak jacket, pack, and extra mortar and machine-gun ammo, my hands a mass of hamburger from thorn cuts, and my face a mass of welts from mosquitoes, I desired greatly to throw down everything . . . and sob."[8]

In the meantime, the enemy is always in their thoughts. They know he is nearby, feel him lurking in the shadows. Yet he does not have to see a grunt to kill him. No, Charlie is a clever fellow who saves his strength. A master of booby traps, he can turn any jungle trail into an avenue of death. Most of his devices have been used in Southeast Asia for centuries. Pungi stakes, though effective, are only part of his arsenal. There is the spike log, a log eight to ten feet long with rusty nails set at all angles. Hidden in the branches of a tree, it swings downward on a vine the moment someone

---

[8] Edelman, *Dear America*, p. 100.

touches a trip wire. The bamboo whip, when triggered, sends a slender bamboo pole tipped with iron spikes whipping into a grunt's face and chest. A man trap is just that: a covered pit with bamboo spears planted at the bottom.

Uncle Sam, however, has given Charlie his best devices free of charge. American ammunition makes wonderful booby traps. The smallest, known as toe-poppers and foot-busters, are captured M60 bullets. A bullet might be set in a bamboo tube and buried with its tip just above ground level; a nail driven through a board acts as a firing pin. The weight of a man stepping on the tip forces the bullet onto the nail, firing it through his foot. Captured grenades are equally effective. Charlie removes the safety pin and slips the grenade into an empty can; a C-ration can does just fine. The can is then tied to a tree or placed underwater in a rice paddy. Touching a trip wire pulls the grenade from the can, which explodes, usually level with a man's crotch or belly. Large mines are made of dud artillery shells and bombs. There is never a shortage of these, since 800 tons of ammunition fail to explode each month. These mines, buried in the ground or hung from trees, can wipe out a line of soldiers. Sergeant Tim O'Brien saw the remains of eight men who detonated such a mine: "Just a mess. It was like a stew, full of meat and flesh and red tissue and white bone."[9]

Booby traps and mines accounted for 11 percent of all American deaths and 17 percent of all American wounds in Vietnam. This is an enormous figure, compared to 3 or 4 percent in World War II and Korea. They also took a lot out of those who were never injured. Seeing a buddy blown apart changed the way a grunt viewed the world. From then on he walked with his eyes glued to the ground, not knowing if he would have a leg after the next step. And not knowing kept him on edge, draining his energies and fighting spirit.

137

---

[9]Quoted in Maclear, *The Ten-Thousand Day War*, p. 160.

Soldiers on patrol had to always be prepared for surprise attack, whether by ambush or booby trap. At right and below, diagrams from a U.S. Army training manual show the workings of the spiked log and the bamboo whip. Bottom, Marines pour rounds into an enemy position.

Figure 4-53. Spike log (mace).

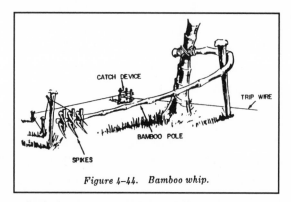

Figure 4-44. Bamboo whip.

Suddenly all hell breaks loose. Ambush! The VC/NVA have been waiting for this time and they strike with everything they've got: rifles, machine guns, and mortar- and rocket-propelled grenades (RPGs). Among the finest infantry in the world, they fight with a fierceness and bravery that takes the breath away. Greenhorns, men under fire for the first time, react with surprise and disbelief. Now they must kill or be killed. Despite their training, killing is not necessarily easy for soldiers. Grunts, particularly those from the South who had been brought up in religious Baptist families, are sometimes unable to pull the trigger. And that split second of hesitation costs some their lives.

Saving lives is "Doc's" job. If grunts adored anyone in the military, it was the combat medic. While the grunts take cover, Doc runs to the wounded, lugging his forty-pound medical kit. He knows he will draw enemy fire, but when he gets hit, he keeps going. Plenty of medics worked till they were blown away. "On two occasions I was treating someone when the Marine next to me, the guy helping me, was hit," said medic David Steinberg. "I figured if I was going to go, it would be while I was doing my job, but I never thought too much, other than doing what I had to do. How do you let down your buddies?"[10]

You *don't* let them down—ever. Not a physician, but a soldier trained in first aid, Doc applies tourniquets to stop bleeding, forces breathing tubes down men's throats, gives mouth-to-mouth resuscitation, and injects morphine to block pain. Morphine is a powerful narcotic made from opium, but even it isn't always effective. Men continue to thrash and scream, unable to escape the pain. Medics in the 101st Airborne Division carried M & M candies for when morphine wasn't enough. They slipped the sweets between a grunt's teeth, saying that they were for the pain and sure

139

---

[10] Quoted in Eric Hammel, *Khe Sanh, Siege in the Clouds: An Oral History*, p. 234.

to work. Occasionally, if a fellow could not be saved, Doc helped him die quietly. This was not considered murder (by the troops), but an act of mercy. Mercy killings occur in all wars, and Vietnam was no exception. Marine medic Jack McCloskey told an interviewer how the wounded begged for death, and how he overdosed at least three men with morphine. Nor was he the only one who did so.[11]

Meanwhile, a radio message is bringing help. Alerted to the ambush, fire-support bases, hilltop artillery positions, lob shells from twenty miles away. Helicopter gunships and fighter-bombers speed to the scene. But more important to the wounded are the Dustoffs. If these medevac helicopters can reach the wounded, their lives will almost certainly be saved. No grunt was ever more than a ten-minute flight from a hospital. The nearest were portable field hospitals built literally on air; that is, their rubberized walls were inflated with compressed air. Air-conditioned, they had everything a modern hospital required: surgeons and nurses, X-ray equipment, preoperative rooms, operating rooms, recovery rooms, pharmacies. Thanks to the Dustoff and the field hospital, the survival rate was higher than in any other war. In Vietnam, 81 percent of seriously wounded Americans were saved, compared to 70 percent in World War II and 74 percent in Korea.

This "mad moment," as the grunts call an ambush, is over in thirty minutes. The enemy breaks contact and slips back into the jungle. Yet the grunts cannot relax. There is plenty to do before nightfall. The weapons of the dead must be collected and the body count reported to headquarters. A final search has to be made for missing Americans. Booby traps make this as dangerous as any battle. Charlie had the habit of booby-trapping American wounded, so that the

140

slightest move blew them and Doc to bits. Sometimes bombs were planted inside dead bodies; if this was suspected, Doc had to feel around inside the wounds with his hands and defuse the bombs before putting the corpse into a body bag. Even a soldier surrending after a battle could be booby-trapped, like the NVA soldier who approached an American unit. He wore a knapsack on his back, had his hands raised, and yelled in English that he wished to surrender. They let him come closer, closer, until he lowered his head and charged. When he reached their position, he set off the bomb hidden in his knapsack. "Man, I wish they were on our side," grunts remarked. "Wow, they *are* hard!"

Night holds its own terrors. Although exhausted, the grunts are too keyed up to rest. On average, combat troops had less than four hours of sleep a night. They might be drifting off when a sound jars them awake. It might be the patter of a rat in the bushes or the slithering of a snake over fallen leaves. Sentries open fire at the slightest noise, waking everyone. They have reason to be jittery, for Charlie is still nearby. He sneaks up in the darkness to taunt the grunts in broken English. "Hey, Marine," he shouts, "tonight you die!" or "You die, you die, Mr. Custer, you die!"

Grunts on patrol saw war in all its ugliness. Modern weapons, products of man's scientific genius, can do things that were unimaginable in the days of swords and muskets. Bullets strike with terrific impact. There are no neat holes, as in war movies. An M60 bullet makes an entry hole the size of a dime and leaves an exit hole as big as a grapefruit. Shrapnel, splinters from grenades and shells, can slice a person to ribbons. Napalm, designed to cover a large area with fire, was particularly nasty. A whitish jelly made of gasoline and other chemicals, it stuck to whatever it touched; trying to wipe it off merely spread the oozing fire. Napalm did not burn flesh, it melted

141

A Medevac helicopter prepares to land in a rice paddy. Below, a wounded soldier is comforted by his friends while awaiting evacuation. A victim of "friendly fire," this man was accidentally struck by grenade fragments from his own forces.

U.S. Army Photo

U.S. Army Photo

it; people's faces actually ran onto their chests, leaving their skulls bare. The United States used 379,369 tons of napalm in Vietnam between 1965 and 1972. It is still legal under international law. All nations that have it have used it in war.

Weapons do not kill only the enemy. Modern war is full of accidents due to "friendly fire," being attacked by your own side. You cannot know when friendly fire will strike, or how, or who. An officer gives the wrong map coordinates, and artillery shells wipe out an eighteen-man platoon. Marine platoons pass nearby in thick jungle, mistake each other for the enemy, and blaze away. Helicopters hit the wrong target. Once, in the A Shau valley, gunships rocketed a colonel's command post, killing two of his men and wounding thirty-five others. Furious, he radioed headquarters, warning that if another chopper appeared, "We're gonna blow his ass out of the sky." That, too, would have been friendly fire. The NVA also made mistakes, like the time a squad destroyed three of its own tanks with rockets.[12]

With the possibility of death everywhere, grunts went in constant fear. At times it was less, at times more, but it never left you entirely. Fear showed itself in different ways. A nineteen-year-old might wake up in the morning to find that his hair had turned white. Men shook, sweated, and drooled uncontrollably. They got "the runs," loose bowels, or were "scared shitless." This is not simply soldiers' slang; men became so frightened that they could not move their bowels for days at a time.

Sooner or later, the strain wore down even the strongest. Men suffered nervous breakdowns, went insane, or committed suicide rather than go on. Sergeant John Houghton told how he felt in a letter to the mother of a dead buddy: "I'm Johnny Boy, and I'm sick both physically and mentally. I smoke too much, am constantly coughing, never eat, always

143

---

[12]Safer, *Flashbacks*, pp. 64–65.

sit around in a daze. All of us are in this general condition. We are all afraid to die. . . . I want to hold my head between my hands and run screaming away from here. I cry too, not much, just when I touch the sore spots. I'm hollow, Mrs. Perko. I'm a shell, and when I'm scared I rattle."[13]

To keep their sanity, grunts had to deal with the emotional experience of death. Men sometimes cried when they first killed. They cried when they saw their buddies die. Tears were contagious, and before you knew it a whole platoon might be weeping. Crying did not show lack of manliness; it was a healthy outlet even for the hardened fighting man. Enemy troops reacted the same way. When NVA soldier Nguyen Ngoc Hung lost his best friend, he said, "I cried. I cried a lot."[14] Unlike the enemy, however, grunts tried to deny death by creating a special language with no word for it. Grunts never died; they were greased, zapped, zonked, wasted, blown away.

Humor, on the other hand, released tension through laughter. Anything could set off hysterical laughter; from a childhood joke to standing among torn bodies and laughing because you were still alive. The wounded laughed so as not to cry. "I'm a commanding general disguised as a private," said a grunt. "I'm here to inspect the hospital facilities, [and] I figured the best way to slip in unnoticed was to blow off my foot."

"If he puts another of these goddamn tubes in my chest," another chimed in, nodding toward a medic, "I'm taking my business elsewhere."

Yet humor could not ease the grunt's worst fear, capture. Airmen were valuable to the enemy on account of their skills; although he treated them harshly, he wanted to keep them alive as bargaining chips in future peace negotiations.

---

[13] Quoted in Edelman, *Dear America*, p. 200.
[14] Quoted in Safer, *Flashbacks*, p. 72.

But ordinary infantrymen had no value at all. Mistreating them was a Communist tradition in Vietnam. Fewer than a third of the French taken in the first Vietnam War were ever heard from again. Most, as far as we can tell, were murdered, starved, or denied medical treatment. Americans, too, were beaten, starved, and humiliated. Words cannot describe the jungle prison camps run by the Viet Cong. Dan Pitzer, for example, was held four years in a forest south of Saigon. He lived in a bamboo cage just large enough to sit up in, and was shown off in villages to prove that Yankees were weaklings.[15]

Pitzer was lucky; he survived. The unlucky ones were skinned alive, sometimes before their friends' very eyes. A patrol led by Arthur E. Woodley, Jr. actually found a victim still alive. His arms and legs were tied to stakes driven into the ground to keep him from moving. He was in dreadful pain, and death was near. He started to cry, begging Woodley to end his agony. Woodley recalls:

> *I put myself in his situation. In his place. . . .*
> *The only thing that I could see that had to be done is that*
>   *the man's sufferin' had to be ended.*
> *I put my M16 next to his head. Next to his temple.*
> *I said, "You sure you want me to do this?"*
> *He said, "Man, kill me. Thank you."*
> *I stopped thinking. I just pulled the trigger. I canceled*
>   *his suffering. . . .*
> *We buried him. We buried him. Very deep.*
> *Then I cried. . . .*
> *I still cry.*
> *I still cry for the white brother that was staked out.*[16]

---

[15] Santoli, *To Bear Any Burden*, p. 92ff.
[16] Quoted in Terry, *Bloods*, p. 240.

•

A village was the SAD patrol's usual destination. Perhaps planes had sighted Viet Cong nearby, or a government worker had disappeared in the area; whatever the reason, the village had to be checked out. Doing so could be as dangerous as any operation in the field. As the grunts approached, they tripped booby traps and mines. A sniper opened fire from a hut; a machine gun cut loose from a rice field. Men died.

The patrol leader had to make a difficult decision. To shoot or not to shoot, that was the question. He knew that Charlie might have turned the village into a combat base complete with trenches, machine gun nests, and escape tunnels. But Charlie could just as easily have only a few snipers posted in the village. The leader could call in air strikes to flatten the place, or hold back for fear of risking innocent lives. If the village was destroyed, he might later find the body of a lone sniper and lots of dead civilians. If, on the other hand, he held back, he might walk into a trap.

The Viet Cong had set things up carefully. Villagers were pawns in their game of guerrilla warfare, to be used, and *used up*, as required. By provoking an attack, they "proved" to the survivors that the Americans were foreign devils. Besides, villagers made fine shields. Main force Viet Cong were taught to take whatever cover was available. According to a captured diary, "We should . . . consider the people as trees to camouflage us."[17] And that is exactly what they did.

In his book *Chickenhawk*, helicopter pilot Robert Mason tells of seeing a group of villagers huddled together. As he passed overhead, a machine gunner opened fire from the center of the crowd. Try as he might, Mason could not frighten away the living screen. They stayed around the gunner and were finally mowed down, apparently because they

146

---

[17] Quoted in Santoli, *To Bear Any Burden*, p. 154.

feared the Viet Cong more than the chopper.[18]

Grunts, however, often entered a village without a fight. But that was no reason to lower your guard. Unless you caught him in action as a Viet Cong, it was impossible to discover a villager's true loyalty. All Vietnamese, as far as the grunt could tell, looked alike, dressed alike, sounded alike. The grunt asked questions, but for every question there were at least two plausible answers. Why are there no young men in this village? Well, they might be ARVN soldiers, or Viet Cong, or with the Viet Cong as forced laborers. That tunnel—is it a family shelter or an enemy escape route? Weapons? Surely finding hidden rifles meant the family was Viet Cong. Not necessarily, since Charlie might have forced them to hold his extra weapons. Women? Children? The elderly? They could smile at you one moment and plant a mine the next. In the end, it all boiled down to the big question: Who is my enemy? There was no way to be certain, unless it was the last thing you ever learned.

Grunts could be sure of just one thing: they had a mysterious enemy who fought by different rules. These nineteen-year-olds saw more horrors in a day than the average person sees in a lifetime. They were exhausted, scared, lonely, homesick, and frustrated. A vicious cycle began in which their frustration turned to anger, and anger to hatred. Hatred is a poison as deadly as any from the chemist's laboratory. It eats away one's humanity, making it impossible to see humanity in others. In short, hatred breeds murder.

There were those who saw the Vietnamese not as people like ourselves, but as subhumans who deserved no pity. In their eyes, Vietnamese were "gooks," "ginks," "dinks," "slopes," and "slants." Helicopter gunships were "gookmobiles" to "de-gook" an area. Jets "ironed" villages flat with bombs; napalm

147

---

[18]Robert Mason, *Chickenhawk*, pp. 184–185.

turned villagers into "crispy critters." Pilots sang sick songs about napalm. Among them was a spoof on "Wake the Town and Tell the People," a 1960s love song:

Strafe the town and kill the people.
Drop napalm on the square.
Get out early every Sunday
And catch them at their morning prayer.

For purposes of the body count, there was the "mere gook" rule, under which any dead Vietnamese, including babies, were considered Viet Cong. Units with the highest scores were rewarded with a few extra days leave.

There were grunts who matched Charlie crime for crime. Vietnam had become for them a war of extermination. Their actions cannot be excused, for they violated both law and morality. Yet they can be understood, insofar as we can understand insanity. For the most part, they came from "average" families and led "normal" lives before entering military service. They might have continued to lead normal lives if they had not gone to Vietnam. What brought the insanity on were the enemy and the conditions under which he made them fight. Personal weakness, the need to follow the crowd, also played a role. When everyone was doing wrong, it was difficult for an individual to stand aside and resist group pressure.

The fact remains that Americans committed war crimes. These were not part of a deliberate strategy ordered by the highest authorities as with the Viet Cong. But they were crimes nonetheless. The thirst for revenge, or "payback," turned entire units into raging mobs. With buddies dying all around them, discipline snapped and they shot whoever crossed their gunsights. Patrol leaders told their men not to take prisoners. Viet Cong were shot after surrendering or tossed from helicopters. Wounded enemies had their throats cut. Enemy dead were mutilated and body parts taken as trophies. Like Stone Age savages, grunts cut off enemy ears, put them on strings, and wore them around their necks until they rotted away. General Westmoreland tried to end the madness. He called it "subhuman" and promised to court-martial anyone caught with human ears. Several soldiers did go to jail, but ear taking was too widespread to be stopped.

The worst atrocity happened at My Lai in central Vietnam, on the coast of the South China Sea. In the weeks leading up to it, C Company of the First Battalion of the Twentieth Infantry had been badly mauled by booby traps and mines. One night, Lieutenant William L. Calley's platoon was kept awake by distant screaming. They thought the Viet Cong were using a public address system to amplify the sound, but they were wrong. In the morning, they found the body of an American who had been skinned alive and bathed in salt water to make him scream at the top of his voice.[19]

C Company was out for blood. Its chance came on March 16, 1968, at My Lai, the base area of the Forty-eighth Viet Cong battalion. There were no young men in the village and no armed Viet Cong, but that made no difference to C Company. Without any provocation, the troops, notably Calley's, massacred between 400 and 500 women, children, and old people. The only American casualty was a fellow who shot himself in the foot.[20]

The My Lai massacre and similar crimes, however, are just one side of the story. Americans in Vietnam showed the full

---

[19]John Sack, *Lieutenant Calley: His Own Story*, p. 126.
[20]After an attempted cover-up, Calley alone was tried for war crimes. Convicted of murder, he received a sentence of life in prison, but was pardoned by President Richard Nixon. Many Americans felt that Calley had done nothing worse than his commanders, or the Commander-in-Chief, when they ordered bombing raids and the use of napalm. Many others felt he should have been put before a firing squad. People still disagree. Today, Calley is the manager of a jewelry store in Georgia.

range of human behavior, and it would be unfair to focus only on atrocities. Thousands of men never saw, heard, or participated in a war crime of any sort. We can find many examples of decency to set against each atrocity. These prove that, on the whole, the American soldier kept his self-respect despite the horrors around him.

Men risked their own lives to protect civilians. Marine Colonel Michael Yunck, for example, refused to call an air strike on a Viet Cong village filled with women and children. As jets circled overhead, Yunck took his helicopter low to pinpoint enemy positions, only to have his leg shot off.[21] There were grunts who sickened at the very idea of harming civilians. One day, Marine Private Reginald Edwards burst into a hut, ready to blast the "enemy." Instead he found "all these women and children huddled together. I was gettin' ready to wipe them off this planet. In this one hut. I tell you, man, my knees got weak. I dropped down, and that's when I cried. First time I cried in the Nam. I realized what I would have done. I almost killed all them people. That was the first time I had actually had the experience of weak knees."[22]

Nor were there only killers at My Lai. There were also heroes, men of strong character and moral courage. When Harry Stanley, a black grunt, refused to shoot children, Calley threatened to arrest him for disobeying an order. Stanley dared him to do just that; he knew the order was illegal and that no one could force an American soldier to commit murder. Calley backed down. Later that morning, helicopter pilot Hugh C. Thompson saw Calley and his men heading for nine people. Thompson landed and told his crew to shoot the Americans if they tried to shoot the Vietnamese.

---

[21] Myra MacPherson, *Long Time Passing: Vietnam and the Haunted Generation*, p. 492.
[22] Quoted in Terry, *Bloods*, pp. 4–5.

Calley, however, had no desire to tangle with armed men. Thompson then radioed for two gunships to fly the people to safety.

For every William Calley, there were scores of men who lived up to their country's traditions of generosity and compassion. The photo collections of the Department of Defense contain hundreds of pictures of nurses, doctors, and combat medics tending to Vietnamese civilians, often on their own time. These photos were not made for propaganda purposes, but as historical records; very few of them have appeared in print. There are also letters in which grunts tell of "adopting" Vietnamese schools and orphanages. Grunts dug into their pockets to buy children clothing and wrote their parents back home to send anything they could spare.

What of the wounded, those crippled by enemy mines and bullets? Lieutenant Lily Adams, an army nurse, saw them at their best. At the hospital at Cu Chi, where she served, grunts lay in beds next to wounded Viet Cong. The VC were so frightened that they hid under the sheets. But she never saw a grunt abuse them in any way. "What I saw was 'Hey, lieutenant, come here quick—the gook over there is in a lot of pain; would you give him a [morphine] shot?' Or 'Here—why don't you give the gook a couple of cigarettes?' I'm talking about guys with no legs asking me to do these things."[23]

SAD patrols dared not venture into certain areas, important as those places were. The Iron Triangle, for example, a triangle-shaped area northwest of Saigon, had been a Communist stronghold since the days of the Viet Minh. Every village was loyal to the enemy. Tunnel systems lay beneath the villages, stretching for miles into the countryside. Unlike the

151

---

[23] Quoted in Kathryn Marshall, *In the Combat Zone: An Oral History of American Women in Vietnam, 1966–1975*, p. 217.

tunnels of North Vietnam, these were strictly military, containing barracks, ammunition dumps, and repair shops. Built one level beneath another, they were so complex that signs had to be posted to help strangers find their way. Attacking these strongholds meant passing through thick jungle—ambush country. The ARVN had given up trying. General Westmoreland vowed to succeed.

Before attacking, it was necessary to defoliate—that is, to strip away the jungle to prevent ambushes. Agent Orange, a herbicide, or plant-killing chemical, was sprayed over the area by planes or helicopters. Within days, the jungle floor was covered with fallen leaves, exposing secret trails and ambush sites. By the end of the war, the U.S. had used 18 million gallons of Agent Orange and other herbicides to defoliate over 5 million acres—about one seventh of South Vietnam's total land mass. Little did the grunts know that Agent Orange was a deadly chemical and would take American lives years after the war ended.

General Westmoreland launched large operations with names such as Starlite, Masher, Silver Bayonet, Piranha, and Dragon Fire. The largest took place in January and February, 1967. The first, Operation Cedar Falls, attacked the Iron Triangle; it was followed by Operation Junction City against a Viet Cong stronghold near the Cambodian border sixty miles from Saigon.

These operations came as no surprise to the enemy. Spies informed him of the targets weeks in advance. Their information was confirmed by the Americans themselves. After being sprayed with Agent Orange, the areas were pounded by artillery and bombers, a sure tip-off. Finally, thousands of troops, led by tanks and armored personnel carriers, came forward. The VC/NVA were not fazed in the least. They just picked up and crossed into Cambodia, leaving sniper units to cover their retreat.

Tracking the enemy. "Tunnel rats,"
such as the man above being lowered
into a tunnel-complex entrance,
searched out individual soldiers.
Defoliation, by herbicide spraying
from the air, napalm drops, and
ground plowing, deprived enemy
troops of cover. At left, a Rome
Plow clears vegetation in the Boi
Loi Woods.

U.S. Army Photo

The Americans arrived to find seemingly abandoned tunnels and villages filled with sullen people. Clearing tunnels was work for the army's "tunnel rats." Small, wiry men able to slip into tight spaces, many tunnel rats were Puerto Rican or Chicano, Mexican Americans. It took a special brand of courage to crawl headfirst down a dark tunnel with only a flashlight and a pistol. There was no telling if Charlie lay in wait at the next hairpin turn. Nor did you know if you would meet the tunnel's "silent sentries." These included bamboo vipers held in place by a piece of string and boxes of scorpions opened by a tripwire. A tunnel rat searched for any documents the enemy left behind and mapped the passageways. When he finished, the tunnels were dynamited. Yet tunnel systems were so complex, and went so deep, that few were destroyed entirely.

Villagers were forcibly removed from their homes. The Americans went about their work step by step, overlooking nothing. It took them only hours to make deserts of places that had been inhabited for centuries. Villages were burned and their ruins blown up; grunts called this "making the rubble bounce." Next, the site was scraped flat by Rome Plows, bulldozers with blades able to uproot the largest trees. Crops were either sprayed with herbicides or burned to keep them out of enemy hands; for he was sure to return when the Americans left. Finally, the villagers were herded together to await the giant Chinook helicopters. Except for some clothes, bedding, and cooking pots, they had become paupers, a blow to their pride. Worse, they had to leave the sacred graves of their ancestors. For some, that was worse than dying. Refusing to leave, they hid beneath the rubble or in undiscovered sections of tunnel. Few survived. In all, 3 million people became refugees.

Refugees were flown to camps located on the outskirts of cities. These shantytowns were worse than anything they had ever seen in the country. The "lucky" ones lived in plywood huts with tin roofs; the less fortunate had homes of cardboard. Boxes that had held refrigerators housed up to ten children; the walls of shacks were made of empty C-ration cartons and read COMBAT MEAL, COMBAT MEAL, COMBAT MEAL from top to bottom. Refugees had no electricity, no running water, no toilets, no hope. They survived by picking through garbage pails or going into the streets. Children formed gangs to steal whatever they could; young women became "bar girls," a polite term for prostitutes. American soldiers bought their favors, and their children, half American, half Vietnamese, may still be seen in the cities. They are the poorest of the poor, outcasts through no fault of their own.

The Saigon government did little to help. Corruption, an old evil, became an epidemic as American aid increased. Everyone who could, reached into Uncle Sam's pockets. An estimated 60 percent of American economic aid was stolen by government officials and ARVN officers. Criminal gangs protected by the police, or policemen themselves, looted American warehouses. Drivers of trucks filled with American goods allowed themselves to be "hijacked" on darkened roads. Anything you wanted—cigarettes, whiskey, television sets, refrigerators, air conditioners, furniture, washing machines, high-tech computers—could be bought on the black market for a fraction of its true value.

If B-52s slowed traffic along the Ho Chi Minh Trail, the enemy could always rely on American supplies. ARVN commanders sold the Viet Cong tens of thousands of American grenades and land mines. Viet Cong agents regularly visited Saigon to buy stolen M16s ($80), M60s ($250), mortars ($400 new, $120 used), and complete combat uniforms ($30). It was also possible to buy stolen tanks and armored personnel carriers.

The Viet Cong always paid in dollars. And the dollars, like

155

the weapons, came from Uncle Sam. To see how, let us take rice as an example. With the fall in rice production due to the war, the United States had to send millions of tons of rice to South Vietnam. Viet Cong agents bribed government officials to divert shiploads of rice to Hong Kong, where other Viet Cong agents sold them for dollars. The dollars were then used to pay more bribes and to buy more American weapons. The Mafia could not have invented a neater racket.

Yet, despite the waste, SAD seemed to be worth the effort. In November 1967, President Johnson asked General Westmoreland to report to the nation on Vietnam. He did so gladly, for wherever he turned, there were signs of progress. Enemy activity had slowed down in most areas. There were fewer raids and less sabotage than in previous years. The body count told its own grim tale. As Vo Nguyen Giap would later admit, 600,000 VC/NVA died between 1965 and 1968. Westy was so sure of victory that he dared Hanoi's leaders to make an all-out attack. "I hope they try something, because we are looking for a fight."

And so were the Viet Cong.

IN THE YEAR OF
THE MONKEY

*All warfare is based on deception. Therefore, when
capable, feign incapacity; when active, inactivity. When
near, make it appear that you are far away; when
far away, that you are near. Offer the enemy
bait to lure him . . . and strike him.*

—*Sun Tzu, 400–320* B.C., The Art of War

AT THE VERY MOMENT GENERAL WESTMORELAND
was giving his challenge, Vo Nguyen Giap was putting the
final touches to a bold plan. A year in the making, it was
the result of lengthy discussions among the Communist leaders. The war was not going as well as they had hoped. True,
their people were determined to go on fighting despite Rolling Thunder. True, the Viet Cong and NVA showed no
signs of wavering. Yet they were dissatisfied; for although
they were not losing the war, neither were they winning it.

South Vietnam was not the obstacle; left to itself, it would
have toppled like a house of cards in a tornado. Everything
ultimately depended on Saigon's ally. American aid, however
misused, was still enough to keep the country going. The
ARVN, inferior as it was, could still count on the grunts to
come to the rescue. American firepower could never be defeated on the battlefield. If the Americans held firm, the war
would drag on indefinitely.

Hanoi decided to force the issue with a massive offensive.

The offensive had several objectives, each one linked to the others. It would bring the war to South Vietnam's cities, which until then had suffered only terrorist actions. Attacks on the cities would shatter people's confidence in Saigon's "puppet" government, destroying its ability to function. ARVN units, taken by surprise, would be overrun, and some would probably turn their guns against the government. Attacks on American installations, especially the U.S. embassy in downtown Saigon, would paralyze the centers of allied power.

Hometown America, however, was the ultimate target. Fighting in the cities would give television cameramen dramatic pictures; would, indeed, bring the war right into American living rooms. Making ordinary people actually feel the war would have all the impact of a battlefield victory. Hanoi's leaders knew that 1968 was a presidential election year. Although elections were a farce in North Vietnam, they recognized the power of voters in a democracy. Their offensive would prove that the war was not about to end, that the VC/NVA were stronger and more stubborn than ever. Discouraged voters, they believed, would rebel. Either they would get rid of President Johnson or force him to beg for peace on Hanoi's terms.

To succeed, the offensive had to take the allies by surprise. This would be difficult, but not impossible. There is a time when Vietnamese take a break from war and politics. Vietnam uses two calendars: the Western calendar, introduced by the French, and the traditional Chinese calendar. The latter follows a twelve-year cycle in which each year is represented by a different animal. The year 1968 was the Year of the Monkey. The New Year holiday, called Tet, begins late in January and lasts a week. Tet is like our New Year's Eve, Christmas, and Thanksgiving rolled into one. It is a time for families to gather and count their blessings. Parents and children burn incense and pray at the ancestors' altar. Everyone goes out in their best clothes, exchanging visits and gifts. Flowers are brought from the countryside to decorate homes, public buildings, even military barracks. For several years, both sides had declared truces during Tet, and 1968 was no exception. While half the ARVN troops prepared to go home on leave for the holiday, Vo Nguyen Giap prepared to strike.

In August 1967, orders began to pour from Giap's headquarters. Planning staffs selected targets and prepared detailed maps. Thousands of tons of Soviet and Chinese weapons went down the Ho Chi Minh Trail on trucks, bicycles, and men's backs. Troops were taken out of action for training and briefings; that is why General Westmoreland thought the war was ending. The Viet Cong—84,000 of them—were to lead the offensive, while the NVA stood by to help as needed. Victory, Uncle Ho promised, was certain. On January 1, 1968, Hanoi Radio broadcast this poem dedicated to the Year of the Monkey.

> *This Spring far outshines the previous Springs,*
> *Of victories throughout the land come happy tidings.*
> *South and North, rushing heroically together, shall*
> *   smite the American invaders!*
> *Go Forward!*
> *Total victory shall be ours.*

Ho's poem was much more than a promise. It was his signal to start the countdown to the Tet Offensive.

So large an operation could not be hidden entirely. Certain information fell into allied hands toward the end of 1967. Electronic sensors detected an unusually heavy flow of traffic along the Ho Chi Minh Trail. South Vietnam's secret police arrested eleven Viet Cong officers in the city of Qui Nhon; in addition to false identity papers, they had tapes with recorded appeals to the people to rebel against the government when the time came. NVA prisoners boasted that all of South Vietnam was about to be "liberated."

These bits of information, plus others, should have been the tip-off. Unfortunately, they were misread by the American high command. Westy knew that something was brewing. What he did not know was when it would start or what its objective would be. Of one thing, however, he was certain: it would not come at Tet, a holiday sacred to all Vietnamese. Nor would the cities be attacked. These were allied strongholds, and attacking them would be suicidal, he insisted. Whenever the blow came, it would fall in the countryside, most likely at a place called Khe Sanh. That conclusion led to the most famous battle of the Vietnam War. Even today, people who may know nothing else about Vietnam know the name of Khe Sanh. The battle began before Tet, continued for weeks after it, and has shaped our ideas about the war ever since.

Khe Sanh is a plateau in the northwestern corner of South Vietnam, fifteen miles below the DMZ and ten miles from the Laotian border. Westy had first visited it upon taking command in 1964. There were still French coffee plantations in the valley below and the remains of a French airfield on the plateau, built during the first Vietnam War. The general immediately saw Khe Sanh's possibilities. It was an ideal jump-off point for raids across the DMZ or for cutting the Ho Chi Minh Trail. Soon after his visit, therefore, Green Berets and local villagers started to repair the airfield and turn the plateau into an outpost. Still, it was nothing special, just one of hundreds of outposts scattered across the countryside.

Khe Sanh became important in the fall of 1967, when American intelligence reports noted an enemy buildup in the area. Huge! Within a few short weeks, two NVA divisions—20,000 men—had been identified, then two others nearby, standing by in reserve. The 304th Division, a leading assault unit at Dien Bien Phu, was part of the strike force. In addition, two artillery regiments had taken positions across the border in "neutral" Laos. Clearly, Giap was about to make his move.

We do not know how Khe Sanh fit into Giap's plans, since he has never fully explained his intentions. But in light of the upcoming Tet Offensive, it was a tempting target for several reasons. Its capture would not only secure the Ho Chi Minh Trail, but allow him to push eastward to the coast, cutting off South Vietnam's two northernmost provinces. Better still, menacing Khe Sanh might draw American forces away from the cities, weakening their defenses at a critical time. Best of all, Khe Sanh had the makings of another Dien Bien Phu. Giap's victory over the French was the high point in his life, and it was natural that he should try to repeat it. If he overran Khe Sanh and captured its defenders, American morale would break, like that of the French before them. Its loss, combined with Tet, would probably cause them to abandon the war. By threatening the base, therefore, Giap was daring Westmoreland to take his bait. He had everything to gain and nothing to lose—nothing, that is, except the lives of his troops. And these meant nothing to him. Years later, he admitted: "Each victory gained in war is worth the cost. Regardless of the cost."[1]

Westy was also thinking of Dien Bien Phu. He had studied the battle and concluded that the French plan was correct, except that they had lacked the means to carry it out. If Giap wanted Khe Sanh so badly, Westy would make him pay for it. He would allow the NVA to mass its troops around the plateau, set up its supply dumps, and get comfortable. Then he would unleash American firepower, turning the place into an open-air slaughterhouse. Each

161

---

[1] Quoted in Safer, *Flashbacks*, p. 15.

commander was spoiling for a fight at Khe Sanh.

The American buildup went into high gear. U.S. Marines and ARVN Rangers, a first-rate outfit, were rushed to Khe Sanh. In all, 6,000 men crowded into an area less than two miles long and a mile wide; another 20,000 to 30,000 troops were held in reserve to the east of Khe Sanh and along the DMZ. Since the road leading to the base was already in enemy hands, giant C-130 Hercules cargo planes were pressed into service. Day after day, round the clock, everything the defenders needed was brought in by air.

Marine Colonel David E. Lownds, the base commander, turned Khe Sanh and five nearby hills into fortresses. His Marines worked hard, often to the sound of music. Many had cassette tape players, and songs by the Beatles, the Temptations, and the Supremes mingled with the noise of picks and shovels; one unit serenaded the unseen NVA with Smokey and the Miracles' "I Love You, Baby." They dug miles of trenches and built hundreds of bunkers, dugouts roofed with wooden beams and layers of sandbags. The entire position was ringed with barbed wire and German tape, twisted coils of wire studded with two-inch razor blades. Buried in front of these were thousands of land mines. Artillery pieces were zeroed in on the approaches. Machine guns were positioned to create interlocking fields of fire; that is, bullets from the guns would crisscross, sweeping an area from every angle.

As the days passed and nothing happened, Marines began to think they were wasting their time. They changed their minds on January 2, the day after Hanoi Radio broadcast Uncle Ho's poem. Early that evening, six men appeared outside the defense lines. They had notebooks and field glasses, and seemed very interested in what was going on. Although wearing Marine uniforms, they failed to give the password when challenged. The guards shot five of them on the spot;

the sixth got away. Sure enough, they were NVA officers; they had been scouting Khe Sanh's defenses in preparation for an assault. From that moment on, the Marines dug faster, and deeper. The enemy was coming!

He arrived at precisely 12:40 A.M. on January 21. He announced himself with a thunderous artillery barrage followed by infantry assaults on the hilltop outposts. Although the attacks were beaten back, a rocket struck Khe Sanh's main ammunition dump. It was the luckiest of lucky shots, and it did more damage than all the others combined. In a blinding flash, 1,500 tons of ammunition blew sky-high. The shock wave flipped helicopters over, swept tents away, and tore steel matting off the runway. Gasoline drums spun through the air, spewing liquid fire. Artillery shells exploded in a chain reaction. One set off a pile of Beehive rounds, each filled with 5,000 steel darts called fléchettes. Lucky to be alive, scores of Marines had fléchettes sticking in their flak jackets and clothing—others had them in their flesh. Unexploded shells rained down, filling trenches completely.

The NVA kept up the pressure in the days that followed. American newsmen, eager to cover something this exciting, pounced on the story. Every night television audiences saw Marines diving for cover, heard the whine of artillery shells, and wondered what they were doing in this godforsaken place. Reporters made the obvious comparison, "Is Khe Sanh to be our Dien Bien Phu?"

President Johnson had the same fear. "I don't want any damn Dinbinfoo," he snapped in his Texas accent.[2] LBJ was tormented by thoughts of the battle. He even ordered the Joint Chiefs of Staff to sign a guarantee—"in blood," as he put it—that the Marines would hold the base. That was a smart move politically. If the base fell, he could blame the

163

---

[2] Quoted in Karnow, *Vietnam: A History*, p. 541.

The siege of Khe Sanh. At right, U.S. Marines rush a wounded comrade to a waiting C-130 transport. The hole in the ramp in the foreground was caused by a North Vietnamese artillery shell. Below, a Marine takes a nap in his bunker. There was little chance for sleep during the almost constant bombardment, and soldiers took it wherever they could find it.

U.S. Air Force Photo

U.S. Marine Corps Photo

military for deceiving him. If it held, he could take the credit at election time.

Khe Sanh, however, was no Dien Bien Phu. It was never—*never*—in danger of falling. There were vital differences between the two bases. Except for being outnumbered, every advantage lay with the Americans. Dien Bien Phu had been encircled from the high ground, Khe Sanh *was* the high ground. At Dien Bien Phu, the French air force had been too small for its mission. At Khe Sanh, the U.S. Air Force ruled the sky.

Airpower was Westy's Sunday punch. The Khe Sanh battlefield covered roughly ten square miles. This area was strewn with people sniffers and sensors able to hear a footstep or locate a warm truck engine beneath the jungle canopy. Specialized planes orbited overhead to monitor the sensors, snap photographs, and intercept enemy radio messages. All information was relayed to the control center of Operation Niagara in Saigon. Niagara, Westy's air defense plan, was to be carried out by 2,000 attack planes, 3,000 helicopters, and a fleet of B-52s. Their mission was simple: deluge the enemy with high explosives and napalm. The result was the most concentrated use of air power in the history of warfare.

American air power devoured the enemy. Anyone caught outside the defense perimeter could trigger his own personal air strike. No enemy soldier was too unimportant to be attacked. One morning, Corporal Walt Whitesides, an air force ground spotter, saw an NVA soldier digging a foxhole. A radio signal brought *two* jet fighters. "The poor guy," said Whitesides, "evidently wasn't too well set in because he immediately set to with his entrenching tool to deepen his hole. The two jets swooped in and he quickened his digging. On the second pass, one of the jets dropped two 250-pound bombs almost on top of him. I could see the guy rise with the bomb cloud. We gave the pilots 'One confirmed,' and the grunts around us cheered."[3]

The B-52s came in relays. Three planes dropped their payloads every ninety minutes, for a daily average of 5,000 bombs. Remember, this is 1,250 tons of explosives each day, concentrated in a small area. The bombing was so intense that airmen likened the area around Khe Sanh to the surface of the moon. It was impossible to walk a straight line for more than a few feet without falling into a bomb crater.

Marines welcomed the B-52s, affectionately known as BUFFs—Big Ugly Fellows. Crews were so good at their job that they could place a string of bombs within four hundred yards of the base. That is about as close as you can get without dropping them in the defenders' laps. "One hiccup," an airman observed, "and we would have decimated the base." This was no exaggeration.

Watching a B-52 strike was an awesome experience. One afternoon, Marines were told to get down in their trenches; the BUFFs were about to hit a nearby ridge. "It was still overcast at the appointed time," a lieutenant recalled, "and we all looked up at the sky. Nothing. Three or four minutes later, we heard this eerie sound—a *bubba-bubba-bubba* sound, like when you put a balloon on your bicycle wheel so the spokes hit it. Suddenly the whole ridgeline exploded from one end to the other. . . . It was a sight to behold, a mountain blowing up in front of us."[4]

Despite the bombings, the NVA would not back down. Its soldiers fought as bravely as their fathers at Dien Bien Phu. Marines, who know about courage, were astonished, particularly by the antics of Luke the Gook. His real name, of course, remains unknown, but his nickname was given in respect for a man who became a legend among Khe Sanh vet-

---

[3] Quoted in Hammel, *Khe Sanh, Siege in the Clouds*, p. 229.
[4] *Ibid*, pp. 157–158.

erans. Luke had lugged his machine gun to a shell hole within range of the airstrip. Every time a plane landed or took off, he let go a stream of bullets. Marine snipers, who saw his face clearly through their rifle scopes, could not pick him off; he knew just when to duck. Mortar shells raked his hole, gunships rocketed it, but he had a charmed life. Once an F-4 Phantom went for him with its machine guns, bombs, and rockets. He shot it down. Finally, jets swooped in with napalm. A wave of fire rolled over his hole for ten minutes, blackening the earth around it in a wide circle. And when the fire burned out—up popped Luke the Gook with his machine gun. The Marines cheered. "We gave Luke a standing ovation and never bothered him again," a veteran recalled.[5]

Luke's comrades could not close the airstrip, as they had done at Dien Bien Phu. They destroyed only four cargo planes during the entire battle, but the wreckage was cleared, making way for others to land. Helicopters worked their usual wonders, as when they delivered six field guns to replace those blown up by the enemy only hours before. Super Gaggles, cargo carriers escorted by gunships, swooped in like flocks of wild, death-dealing birds. Additional supplies came by parachute each day. There was even room for "goodies" to raise men's morale. Mail from home was a joy. Occasionally gallon tubs of ice cream plummeted from the sky and broke open in the mud. The Marines weren't fussy; they scooped it with their bare hands, lapping it up, mud and all. Uncle Sam, however, could be a pain in the neck, as when he sent W-2 income tax forms to the embattled leathernecks.

Life at Khe Sanh was as nasty as any SAD patrol. In his book *Dispatches*, a Vietnam War classic, Michael Herr describes its sights and smells. "Everything I see is blown through with smoke, everything is on fire everywhere . . .

167

---

[5] *Ibid*, p. 264.

every image, every sound comes back out of smoke and the smell of things burning. Some of it, like smoke from an exploding round in the air, breaks cleanly and has a comfortable distance. Some of it pours out of large tubs of shit being burned off with diesel fuel, and it hangs, hangs, taking you full in the throat even though you are used to it. Right there on the strip a fuel ship has been hit, and no one who has heard that can kill the shakes for an hour."[6]

The dark, dank bunkers stank of mildew and unwashed bodies. At night they swarmed with rats as large as American house cats. Scurrying and tumbling over each other, they ran over the faces of sleeping Marines, or burrowed into their packs and pockets for food. More than one fellow was bitten in the face. Yet, when the shock passed, there were those who managed to smile. A rat bite was a first-class ticket out of Khe Sanh, since victims had to be evacuated for anti-rabies treatment. This involves twenty painful injections in the stomach; but it was better than catching a bullet in the same place. Some men, unable to endure the strain of battle, daubed their toes with peanut butter to get a "safe" rat bite. Desperate men shot themselves in the foot, or held up an arm to attract a sniper's bullet.

Nevertheless, the Marines held on until Giap decided to withdraw. On April 7, U.S. ground troops reopened the road and linked up with Khe Sanh's defenders.[7] The Marines had lost 205 men during the battle. Although Giap has never revealed his losses, it is believed that between 10,000 and 15,000 NVA were killed. Now, if victory is measured in terms of holding ground and slaughtering the enemy at better than seventy to one, then the Americans won at Khe

---

[6]Michael Herr, *Dispatches*, pp. 108–109.
[7]Khe Sanh was abandoned on June 17. It had served its purpose, the American high command said, and was no longer worth keeping. Many Marines were resentful, feeling that they had suffered and sacrificed for nothing.

Sanh. But, as Giap says, numbers do not tell the whole story. He has a point; for while American attention was focused on Khe Sanh, Tet exploded across South Vietnam.

In the days before zero hour, thousands of Viet Cong guerrillas entered the cities and towns without being challenged. Since many people normally travel before Tet and a truce was in effect, the police simply waved them through the checkpoints. They came disguised as peasants bringing produce to market, as ARVN troops returning home on leave, as tourists, and as Buddhist monks. Four thousand Viet Cong simply walked or rode Hondas down the main streets of Saigon. Once inside, they rented hotel rooms or made their way to "safe houses," the homes of Viet Cong agents and sympathizers. Their weapons arrived separately, hidden in the false bottoms of trucks and vegetable carts. To make sure they worked, guerrillas test-fired them during fireworks displays.

The Tet Offensive began in the early hours of Wednesday, January 31, 1968. Moving with split-second timing, the Viet Cong struck South Vietnam's five largest cities, thirty-six out of forty-four provincial capitals, sixty-four district capitals, and scores of smaller towns. Every major airfield was mortared by Viet Cong commandos. One of General Westmoreland's aides, tracing the attacks on a map at headquarters, likened them to a pinball machine lighting up. But if the allies were surprised, so too were the Viet Cong. The people of the cities did not join them; they just stood aside and let the warriors slug it out among themselves. Allied troops rallied and counterattacked in force. In most places the Viet Cong were defeated within the first hours or days of the offensive.

169

Serious fighting took place in Saigon. It began when nineteen Viet Cong blew a hole in the wall of the U.S. Embassy compound in the center of the city. As the symbol of American power, the embassy's capture would show the world that the United States was a "paper tiger" and could not win the war. At the same time, other Viet Cong units assaulted Westy's headquarters and those of South Vietnam's navy, artillery, and armored forces. There was even an effort to free Viet Cong held in Saigon's central prison. All these attacks were crushed by noon of the first day. The men at the embassy died on the lawn without setting foot in the buildings.

The battle of Saigon, however, continued for another week. The Viet Cong, realizing that head-on assaults were useless, formed pockets of resistance in various parts of the city. Groups of fighters took refuge in crowded neighborhoods, using the residents as shields. They did not expect the Americans to unleash their firepower in the very heart of the capital. They were wrong.

General Westmoreland was determined to root out the Viet Cong at all costs. Day after day, gunships hovered over the rooftops, spraying bullets and rockets into the houses below. Tanks rumbled through the streets, firing their cannon point-blank at enemy strongholds. Entire streets went up in flames, and civilians died alongside their Viet Cong captors.

American gunfire, however, was not the only cause of civilian deaths. Wherever the Viet Cong took control, they let loose a reign of terror. "Tyrants and bloodsuckers"—that is, anyone who served the government—were marked for death. Soldiers home on leave, policemen, and office workers were either shot in cold blood or after a mock trial. To show their power, the Viet Cong forced residents into the streets to watch "people's courts" pass death sentences.

One Viet Cong learned that justice can be a double-edged sword. The man, dressed in a checkered shirt and black shorts, had been captured by South Vietnamese troops. After beating him up, they tied his hands behind his back and dragged him before General Nguyen Ngoc Loan, chief of the National Police. Loan, a sour-faced man with a quick temper, was in a foul mood. Without saying a word, he raised his pistol, put it to the man's head, and fired. Eddie Adams of the Associated Press happened to have come by moments before. The instant Loan pulled the trigger, Adams snapped the shutter of his camera. The result was one of the most dramatic pictures of the Vietnam War. The photo, at right, appeared on television and in newspapers across the world, winning numerous prizes for photojournalism.

Opponents of the war made the most of Adams's picture. It showed, they said indignantly, that the United States had no business in South Vietnam. Here, an unarmed man was shot in cold blood without even the pretense of a trial; it was plain murder, and the American people were paying the murderer's salary. The truth, however, is not that simple. Adams later discovered that the victim was a Viet Cong lieutenant. But not your ordinary run-of-the-mill lieutenant. He had personally killed a police major—General Loan's best friend—and stabbed the man's wife and six children to death. "I'm not saying that what [Loan] did was right or wrong," says Adams. "But I ask, if you were the general, and they killed your people and their children, how do you know what you would have done?"[8] There is no easy answer to Adams's question.

Meanwhile, a ferocious battle had broken out in Hue. Vietnam's ancient capital was a beautiful city of neat houses bordering wide, tree-lined avenues. Known throughout Asia as a center of learning, it had a university, founded by the French, and the famous Quoc Hoc High School whose graduates included Ho Chi Minh, Vo Nguyen Giap, and Ngo Dinh Diem. At the heart of the city loomed the Citadel, a fortress of stone towers and brick walls twenty feet thick,

171

[8] Quoted in Santoli, *To Bear Any Burden*, p. 184.

The Battle of Saigon. Above, Eddie
Adam's Pulitzer Prize–winning picture of the execution of a Viet Cong
officer. Right, a member of the Thirty-
eighth Ranger Battalion fires into a
Viet Cong position in Cholon, the
Chinese section near Saigon. Though
the Viet Cong attack was halted in a
week, these and other images of chaos
in the capital city convinced the American public that Vietnam was a losing
cause.

surrounded by moats filled with water diverted from the Perfume River. Strong as it was, by the twentieth century the
Citadel had become less a fortress than a museum. The Imperial Palace, which lies within its walls, was filled with art
treasures and precious books dating back a thousand years.
Scholars, not soldiers, lived in its outlying buildings, amid
peace and quiet.

That quiet was shattered on January 31. Just as their comrades were invading the U.S. Embassy compound in Saigon,
Viet Cong and NVA troops burst into Hue. Meeting little
resistance, they overran nearly the whole city, including the
Citadel. Within hours, they had dug in for the battle that
was sure to come. Little did they know that it would last
twenty-five days.

U.S. Marines and ARVN units were ordered to retake the
city without delay. Unfortunately, these orders were easier
to give than to obey. The first allied troops to arrive met a
storm of bullets, mortar shells, and rockets. They took cover,
but could do little without heavy weapons. At the beginning,
American planes and artillery were kept out of action for fear
of damaging historic buildings. But when it became clear
that the enemy was dug in deeply, Saigon gave the go-ahead
to blast them out by any means. Hue would be destroyed in
order to "save" it from Communist rule.

Fighter planes swooped in low with rockets and napalm.
U.S. Navy ships stood offshore, lobbing thousand-pound
shells at enemy positions. Tanks and cannon blazed away at
close range. But in the end, as always, the grunts had to finish
the job. They fought room by room, house by house, street
by street. The "front" could be anything from a narrow hall-
way in a burning building, to a winding alley choked with
rubble, to a sewer beneath the streets. Fog and drizzle combined with smoke to blanket Hue in a grayish haze. It was
slow going, a grunt noted, with every inch of ground costing

a drop of blood. Enemy fire was so intense that the Dustoffs could not land. Hundreds of wounded had to be taken out on top of tanks or on the backs of their comrades. One Marine officer learned how much his men loved him when he was wounded; with bullets cracking all around, they lay on top of him, shielding him with their own bodies. Those who had not been physically wounded showed the strain by bursting into tears or having nervous breakdowns.

Two Marines had an experience they would tell their grandchildren about. They had started down an alley, crouching to avoid snipers, when one of them suddenly looked up. There, standing before him, were two North Vietnamese soldiers. They, too, must have been worried about snipers, for they hadn't noticed the Americans. All four men froze, unable to believe their eyes. To open fire at such close range would have killed everyone. So they did the wise thing: they turned tail and ran in opposite directions.[9]

The enemy were finally cornered in the Citadel. According to World War II veterans, the fighting there was heavier than anything they had been through in Europe. Finally, on the morning of February 25, after a ten-day siege, ARVN Rangers took the last enemy position. Yet there were no VC/NVA to be seen except for the dead and a handful of prisoners; the others had escaped during the night. Myron Harrington, a Marine company commander, described those last days:

> As a marine, I had to admire the courage and discipline of the North Vietnamese and Viet Cong, but no more than I did my own men. We were both in a face-to-face, eyeball-to-eyeball confrontation. . . . After a while, survival was the name of the game as you sat there in the semi-darkness, with the firing going on constantly, like at a rifle range. And the horrible

---

[9]Keith William Nolan, *The Battle for Hue*, p. 107.

smell. You tasted it as you ate your rations, as if you were eating death. It permeated your clothes, which you couldn't wash because water was very scarce. You couldn't bathe or shave either. My strategy was to keep as many of my marines alive as possible, and yet accomplish our mission. You went through the full range of emotions, seeing your buddies being hit, but you couldn't feel sorry for them because you had others to think about. It was dreary, and still we weren't depressed. We were doing our job—successfully.[10]

The same could not be said of the ARVN. Grunts admired certain outfits, like those at the Citadel. They were hard men; several had SAT CONG—KILL COMMUNISTS—tattooed over their hearts. They wore the tattoo knowing full well that, if captured, the enemy would carve it out before shooting them. Yet, on the whole, the ARVN fought as poorly as ever. Uncle Sam could give them weapons and training, but not the will to win.

Grunts knew that ARVN units avoided battle, and despised them for it. At Hue, ARVN soldiers, including full colonels, took off their uniforms and fled to refugee camps on the city's outskirts. For three weeks they hid behind the Americans, taking no part in the fighting whatsoever. But stealing from their countrymen was another matter; that they did with enthusiasm. "The ARVN," a Marine sergeant grumbled, "were an unruly lot and they made sure to stay far to the rear of the advancing Marines. . . . We'd see them after a pitched battle, driving up in trucks to loot the buildings we had just captured. There was a lot of bitching among the Marines about this and I think if the ARVN ever enjoyed any fighting reputation with the Marines, they lost it in Hue."[11]

Shortly after retaking the Citadel, Marines found the re-

---

[10] Quoted in Karnow, *Vietnam: A History*, p. 533.
[11] Quoted in Nolan, *The Battle for Hue*, p. 86.

mains of several civilians buried in a shallow ditch. That was not unusual; many civilians had died during the battle and had been hastily buried to avoid disease. These bodies, however, had one thing in common: a bullet in the back of the head. They had been murdered. In the months that followed, mass graves were uncovered in and around Hue. Only then did the full extent of the tragedy become clear.

The VC/NVA had planned every part of the Hue operation carefully. Before the attack, agents had prepared lists of "cruel tyrants and reactionary elements." Exactly what this meant became clear in the first days of February. After taking the city, Viet Cong officers with bullhorns ordered government workers, police, and those known to be sympathetic toward America to report for "reeducation." Anyone who tried to hide would be found and shot, they threatened. At the same time, special squads combed each neighborhood. Each had a clipboard with names, addresses, and identity card photos of thousands of individuals. Among them were teachers, writers, political activists, religious leaders—anyone who might speak out against Communist rule.

What followed was the worst atrocity of the Vietnam War. Defenseless civilians were tied and taken in batches to be shot, stabbed, burned, or buried alive. Hundreds of Roman Catholics, including priests, were dragged from Phu Cam Cathedral and killed. Whole family units were exterminated. In one well known case, a community leader was shot, together with his wife, son, daughter, and a man and woman servant and their baby. But this did not satisfy the Viet Cong; every living being in the house had to die. The family cat was strangled and the dog clubbed. The goldfish were scooped out of their bowl and thrown on the floor. Then the killers left, having avenged themselves for whatever offense the man had committed.[12]

176

---

[12] Pike, *The Viet Cong Strategy of Terror,* p. 57.

Although 2,800 bodies were eventually recovered, hundreds of other people vanished from Hue and have never been accounted for.

During the battle for Hue, 147 Marines were killed and 857 seriously wounded. ARVN casualties numbered 384 dead and 1,800 wounded, largely in retaking the Citadel. The VC/NVA lost 5,113 men in Hue, plus 89 captured; we have no information about the number of wounded or those who died of their injuries. An estimated 80 percent of Hue's buildings lay in ruins, leaving 116,000 homeless out of a population of 140,000. For Hue, as for all of Vietnam, 1968 was the worst Year of the Monkey on record.

Although the siege of Khe Sanh dragged on, the recapture of Hue ended the Tet Offensive. In terms of its military aims, Tet was a colossal disaster. Not only had Giap's forces failed from the outset, they lost an estimated 50,000 men. Nowhere did the people welcome them or turn against the Saigon government.

Tet shattered the Viet Cong. The results of eight years of steady growth were tossed away in a month. Viet Cong leaders admitted to losing half their forces, including large numbers of experienced officers. In many areas which it had terrorized for years, the Viet Cong simply vanished. Gone was the myth of a southern rebellion. By crippling the Viet Cong, Tet proved that the National Liberation Front was just that—a mask for a North Vietnamese invasion. From then on, the NVA would have to do most of the fighting.

Nevertheless, Hanoi's loss was not Washington's gain. American forces had indeed won a smashing victory. But wars are more than battles lost and won. They are also political struggles, struggles for people's hearts and minds. By winning Tet, American leaders lost something far more precious than a city or a combat base thousands of miles from

The end of Tet. Top, women in white mourning clothes weep over the coffins of their loved ones, some of the hundreds of civilians slain by Communist murder squads in Hue. Bottom, U.S. Marines move cautiously through the rubble of Hue.

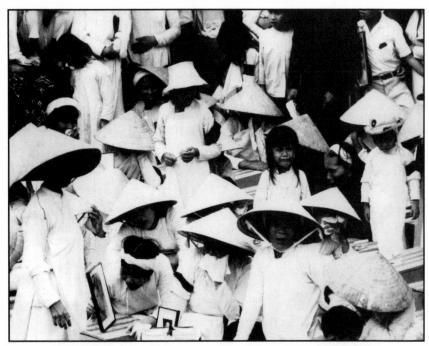

home. They lost the trust and respect of their own people. This is the ultimate tragedy of Tet: a battlefield victory for the United States became a still greater political triumph for the enemy. Hanoi had brought the war home to America.

BRINGING THE
WAR HOME

We have met the enemy, and they are us.

—Pogo

WAR PROTESTS ARE AS AMERICAN AS APPLE PIE.
Americans have never gone to war gladly or, once involved,
been unanimous in their approval. Long before there was a
United States of America, there were Americans who rejected all forms of violence for religious reasons. These people, known as pacifists, believed that God's word was the
highest law. And since the Almighty commanded "Thou
shalt not kill," fighting was sinful under any and all circum-
stances. Nonpacifists, however, also held strong beliefs about
war. Although they felt that war is right under certain conditions, they might oppose a particular war as unjust, unwise,
or unnecessary.

Protesters' methods differed as widely as their beliefs.
Quakers, for example, refused to fight even if attacked. But
that did not prevent them from defending themselves peacefully. In the days of piracy, Quaker merchants "armed" their
ships with wooden cannon to scare away sea rovers. In 1846,

Henry David Thoreau, a famous writer, opposed the Mexican War by refusing to pay his taxes, a tradition that continues to this day. During the two world wars, conscientious objectors chose jail rather than violate their ideals by fighting; others became medical workers, risking their lives to save the wounded.

Although opposition to the Vietnam War resembled that of past wars, it differed in several important ways. Never before had so many Americans denounced the actions of their government. Never before had so many Americans expressed such hostility—indeed, hatred—toward their own country. Never before had so many Americans seen the enemy's cause as just and hoped for his victory. How this came about is a complicated matter that still stirs angry debate. We cannot join the debate here. All we can do is present the basic facts and allow readers to judge for themselves.

The debate began with the Gulf of Tonkin Resolution. Senators Ernest Gruening of Alaska and Wayne Morse of Oregon were the only members of Congress to vote against the resolution. Senator Gruening saw it as the start of a long, senseless war against people who were no threat to American interests. "All Vietnam," he said, "is not worth the life of a single American boy." Senator Morse went further, insisting that the resolution robbed Congress of its war-making power and gave it to the President. If Congress felt so strongly about North Vietnamese aggression, then it ought to act, he said. But let it act in the American way, by declaring war. To do otherwise, would allow Lyndon Johnson to wage "a Presidential war" over which we, the people, would have no control.

181

Senator Morse had a strong argument. According to the U.S. Constitution, only Congress may take the nation into war. The Founding Fathers believed in government by the people. And since it was the people who fought wars, only they could agree to them through their representatives in Congress. A declaration of war is no legal formality. It tells the world that the American people have decided to fight and that the armed forces have their support. That support allows the government to do certain necessary things. Taxes are raised to pay for the war. The reserves are mobilized in case more fighting men are needed. Laws against treason, defined as giving aid and comfort to the enemy, automatically go into effect. News reports are censored to prevent information leaks and keep up morale on the home front.

President Johnson, however, dreaded a declaration of war. LBJ, we recall, hoped to do two things: save South Vietnam from communism and complete his Great Society reforms. Asking Congress for a declaration of war would be the same as asking Americans to choose between guns or butter. They would pay for the war or reform, but not both. The Gulf of Tonkin Resolution, therefore, enabled him to go ahead with both at once. It made the war "legal," except that its legality smelled like a politician's clever trick. Thus Vietnam became "Lyndon's war," but not the American people's war. They would go along with it for a while, but he had to win quickly or risk losing everything.

Doubts about the war grew as the casualties increased. By 1966, Senators Gruening and Morse were joined by prominent members of Congress. J. William Fulbright of Arkansas, Chairman of the Senate Foreign Relations Committee, held hearings on all aspects of the U.S. role in Vietnam. Fulbright, a chief backer of the Gulf of Tonkin Resolution, now demanded that LBJ deescalate without further delay. Congressman Thomas P. "Tip" O'Neill of Boston spoke for the "doves," as the war's opponents were called; its supporters were known as "hawks." The war, said O'Neill, was a costly blunder that must not be allowed to continue.

Meanwhile, Vietnam had become an issue outside the halls

182

of Congress. This was partly due to television, the chief source of news for the majority of Americans. Unfortunately, commercial television is not very helpful in forming intelligent opinions. It is basically entertainment aimed at holding viewer interest while advertisers push their products. To do this, its pictures must first catch the viewer's attention. Yet a picture is not worth a thousand words. Words allow you to understand an event in terms of what came before and after, and how these relate to one another. Pictures are merely thin slices of time. They record the high points of an event, which film editors then compress into two-minute stories containing the most exciting moments. In this way television makes the unusual, dramatic, and violent seem like the normal. What is seen on the screen becomes, in effect, reality to the viewer. This was recognized by Walter Cronkite, one of television's leading reporters, who said: "We are charged with a responsibility which, in all honesty, we cannot discharge. We do such a slick job that we have deluded the public into thinking that they get all they need to know from us."[1]

Vietnam was our first television war. Americans were bombarded with images of exploding shells, splashing napalm, chattering machine guns, wounded grunts, piles of enemy dead, burning villages, and weeping women and children. Seven hundred reporters covered the war for television and the newspapers. Yet their reporting was one-sided, and with good reason. Neither the Viet Cong nor the NVA believed in freedom of the press. They did not invite cameramen to film the maiming of schoolchildren or the skinning of captured grunts. Allied actions, however, were freely reported, for this was an undeclared war and newsmen could do much as they pleased. Most actions were ordered for

183

---

[1]Quoted in Timothy S. Lowry, *And Brave Men, Too,* pp. 43–44.

sound military reasons. But since television demands the dramatic, the reasons for them were seldom explained or were explained inadequately. As a result, viewers got the impression that allied forces were largely to blame for the war's horrors.

Those pictures made a deep impression upon young America. Unlike their parents, who had struggled through World War II, the generation that came of age in the 1960s grew up at a time of amazing prosperity. As the first generation to be raised on television, they learned to be consumers from childhood. Television taught them that whatever they "needed," from Hula Hoops to breakfast cereals and stylish clothes, could be theirs for the asking, if their parents were willing to pay. Middle-class young people took economic security for granted, along with a college education followed by a good job and happiness ever after.

Having grown up in a land of plenty, they never knew the anxiety of being without work, or how it felt to go hungry every day of your life. Freed from want, they began to think that perhaps there was more to life than clothes, cars, houses—possessions. And the more they thought, the more disillusioned they became, for their country was far from perfect. American society seemed artificial, materialistic, greedy, and crude. The richest country on earth still had millions of poor people. Those who were poor *and* black carried a double burden, due to racial bigotry.

College students showed their concern by taking part in the civil rights movement. During the early 1960s, hundreds of them spent their vacations in the South, working in voter registration drives and demonstrating against racial injustice. One organization, the Students for a Democratic Society (SDS), hoped to change America in ways favorable to the less privileged—poor people, blacks, Hispanics, and factory workers. Vietnam, however, would change everything.

184

Once the United States became involved, SDS turned toward revolution as the only way to bring social justice.

By 1965, Vietnam overshadowed any other cause. For countless young people, the war symbolized all that was wrong with their country. Television, which had shaped their outlook since childhood, brought the war into their living rooms every evening. It was not a pretty picture. Rich America, with its high-tech weapons, was killing poor people on the other side of the globe. The President, who they had been taught to respect, had lied. Despite promises not to send American boys to fight in Asia, LBJ was waging an undeclared war. The time for lies had passed. Ending the war became a moral crusade.

On March 24, 1965, three weeks after the start of Rolling Thunder, the first teach-in took place at the University of Michigan at Ann Arbor. Students and faculty gathered for an all-night session of speeches, debates, and lectures on U.S. policy in Vietnam. That policy, they agreed, had led to an illegal war fought by immoral means—bombing, napalm, body counts. In the weeks that followed, teach-ins were held at colleges and universities across the country. Students stated their case peacefully, logically, as civilized people should. But there were limits to their patience, and there was no telling what might happen if the President refused to listen.

Black people were particularly disturbed by Vietnam. From the very beginning, they were more likely to oppose the war than whites. Having welcomed the Great Society, they feared—rightly—that the war would take funds away from social programs that served their needs. Besides, the very nature of the war effort was unfair to blacks. Blacks made up 13 percent of the forces in Vietnam, about the same as their population at home. Yet Defense Department figures showed that 28 percent of blacks had combat assignments; between 1965 and 1967, blacks accounted for 23 percent of American

185

combat deaths. Thus blacks were fighting and dying at twice the rate of whites. Talk about racial discrimination!

Dr. Martin Luther King, Jr., America's foremost civil rights leader, lent his name to the antiwar movement. King saw a connection between racial injustice at home and the war in Vietnam. On April 4, 1967, he gave a fiery speech at New York's Riverside Church. "A time comes when silence is betrayal," he said, his voice rising with emotion. "That time has come for us in relation to Vietnam." He told of his hopes for the Great Society and how, at long last, the nation had begun to deal with its social problems. "Then came the buildup in Vietnam and I watched the program broken . . . as if it were some idle political plaything in a society gone mad with war . . . and I knew that I could never again raise my voice against the violence of the oppressed in the ghettos without having first spoken clearly to the greatest purveyor of violence in the world today—my own government." He went on to describe America's sins against the Vietnamese people. "We have destroyed their land and their crops. . . . We have corrupted their women and children and killed their men. . . . Somehow this madness must cease. We must stop now."

King's speech was immediately criticized, by both the civil rights movement and White House officials, who described King as either a fool or a Communist. Surely, they said, there were greater purveyors of violence than the U.S., such as the rulers of the Soviet Union and China, dictators who had butchered millions of innocent people. Yet nothing could prevent King from protesting the war. To him, it was a sin, and being silent in the face of sin was an evil in itself.

Antiwar protests took different forms. Most dramatic were the deaths of those who turned their hatred of the war against their own bodies. It began with Norman R. Morrison, a Quaker who committed Buddhist-style suicide. On

November 2, 1965, he took his fifteen-month-old daughter, Emily, to the Pentagon, the headquarters of the Defense Department outside Washington. Placing her on the ground, he stepped away, poured gasoline over himself, and struck a match. Pentagon workers managed to drag the child to safety, but could not save her father. The nation was horrified. People questioned the sanity of one who, to protest killing, killed himself in front of his own child; friends saw him as a martyr who gave his life to show solidarity with the innocents in Vietnam.

Morrison's suicide inspired others to follow his example. Within three weeks, Alice Herz, an 82-year-old Quaker, and Roger Allen LaPorte, a Roman Catholic, burned themselves to death. Joan Fox and Craig Badiali, recent high school graduates, later took their lives with auto exhaust fumes. Craig left a note explaining his reasons: "If I sound strange, it's because I am insane with sorrow and distress. Please make them see! Love and peace, Craig."[2] Between 1965 and 1969, eighteen Americans committed suicide to protest the Vietnam War, eight of them by fire.

Meanwhile, the largest antiwar movement in American history was taking shape. Its members were drawn from all walks of life, representing a cross section of the nation. Ordinary citizens were joined by college professors, lawyers, businessmen, and scientists. Baby expert Dr. Benjamin Spock delivered antiwar speeches, entertainers Pete Seeger and Joan Baez sang antiwar songs. Religious leaders marched with Dr. King at the head of antiwar demonstrations. Quakers, showing concern for their fellow men, donated medicines to North Vietnam, some of which later turned up in Viet Cong tunnel hospitals. Student groups collected blood for the Viet Cong to show that not all Americans supported "Johnson's war."

187

[2] Quoted in Eliot Asinof, *Craig and Joan: Two Lives for Peace*, p. 123.

Demonstrators appeared in front of the White House, Congress, and the Pentagon. Women wheeling baby carriages picketed the Dow Chemical Company, chief manufacturer of napalm, and Honeywell, Inc., a producer of fragmentation bombs, calling them "merchants of death." Citizens marched in the hundreds, and the hundreds of thousands, in towns and cities across the land. They carried signs demanding a halt to the killing. STOP THE BOMBING, NO MORE NAPALM, STOP THE WAR IN VIETNAM, BRING THE TROOPS HOME, CHILDREN ARE NOT BORN TO BURN. They displayed posters with slogans like WAR IS NOT HEALTHY FOR CHILDREN AND OTHER LIVING THINGS, VIETNAM FOR THE VIETNAMESE, and SHAME ON AMERICA. They chanted easily remembered questions and answers:

> *What do we want?*
> *Peace!*
> *When do we want it?*
> *NOW!*

A phase from a song by The Beatles resounded wherever demonstrators appeared.

> *All we are saying is,*
> *Give peace a chance.*

Younger marchers scribbled a motto on their jackets: MAKE LOVE NOT WAR.

Demonstrators portrayed the horrors of war in startling images. In New York City, there were "die-ins" where people sprawled in the gutter like dead villagers after an air strike. Groups in skeleton costumes carried musical instruments and played "The Marine Hymn." Marchers carried enlarged photos of a Vietnamese mother and her wounded child into St. Patrick's Cathedral to remind worshipers of the Sixth Commandment. The Bread and Puppet Theater, a troupe of street performers, appeared as oversized dummies of ghosts carrying maimed children and as Uncle Sam drenched with blood. Not everyone, of course, appreciated their artistry. Onlookers might denounce the demonstrators' loudness and "bad taste," but the protesters had a ready reply: people were dying in Vietnam, which was in even worse taste. Besides, if you could not express yourself in America, where on earth could you? Protest is a form of free speech, protected by the Constitution. It is an American's birthright.

The Selective Service System, or draft, was deeply resented by people in the antiwar movement. It was, they claimed, a type of slavery in which young men were "robotized," trained to be "mindless killing machines." Upon reaching the age of eighteen, every American male had to register with his local draft board. Once a month each draft board received its quota from Selective Service System headquarters in Washington. The board, whose members were private citizens volunteering their time, then ordered a certain number of men to take a medical examination. Those who failed were classified 4−F, ineligible for military service. Those who passed went into the army; the navy, Marines, and air force usually had enough volunteers.

Draft resistance took different forms. An estimated 170,000 men proved their religious opposition to war and were excused as conscientious objectors. Others, equally sincere, openly defied the law. Barry Bondus of Big Lake, Minnesota, broke into the local draft board and poured two buckets of human feces over its records; he, his eleven brothers, and their father had worked overtime filling the buckets. Elsewhere, a group of devout Catholics burned the records of the Catonsville, Maryland, draft board. Among the group's leaders were the Berrigan brothers, Philip and Daniel, priests admired for their work among the poor.

Hundreds of thousands refused to register for the draft or,

189

having done so, publicly burned their draft cards. No antiwar demonstration was complete without young men shouting, "Hell no, we won't go!" An estimated 150,000 did not go; they fled the country. Canada received the largest number, about 80,000; most of the others went to Sweden and Mexico. Not all of these, however, opposed the war. There were cowards among them, a fact some admitted after the war. Nevertheless, 3,250 young men did go to jail for draft-related offenses.

Millions of others quietly played it safe. Draft dodging was easy, if you had the money and know-how. This made the system unfair, in that it allowed the well-to-do to escape while poor people, minorities, and the uneducated bore the brunt of the war.

College students were automatically classified 2-S—that is, deferred (temporarily excused) from military service. Upon graduation, they were called for a medical examination. At that point they might turn to draft counselors, regular visitors at college campuses. Draft counselors knew everything about winning a 4-F classification. They could, for example, suggest a doctor skilled at finding "illnesses" you never knew you had. But even if you were drafted, you stood little chance of seeing combat. Army records show that men with college degrees had a 42 percent chance of going to Vietnam, high school graduates a 64 percent chance, and high school dropouts a 70 percent chance. If they did go to Vietnam, most college graduates fought from behind office desks.

It is interesting to compare this with the enemy experience. Although draft evasion was never a serious problem in North Vietnam, not everyone was eager to go south. As draft calls increased, people realized that casualties were also increasing. Hundreds of families tried to keep their sons out of the army. Communist officials, among them the mayor of Hanoi, helped their sons avoid the draft, usually by sending them to study abroad. Ordinary folks hid their sons when the draft notice arrived, or bribed doctors to disqualify them from service. To fail the physical, draftees chewed raw tobacco leaves to raise their blood pressure, rubbed iodine into their eyes, or "accidentally" broke their trigger fingers.[3]

President Johnson's failure to end the war deepened the frustration and sense of moral outrage among his antiwar opponents. As always when people feel strongly about something, there were those who got carried away by their emotions. They became extremists, radicals who saw America as the center of evil in the world. Although a tiny minority in the antiwar movement, they had an influence far beyond their numbers. That influence further disunited the country, aided the enemy, and may have prolonged the war.

Certain Americans saw their country as a menace to the human race. Tom Hayden, a founder of SDS, thought it rotten to the core. "The truth is," he said, "that we live under a system which requires violence because it is based on the exploitation of man by man. . . . Nobody in the world is safe from the 'ugly Americans' who come to take their land, their resources, and their cultural identities." Thus, to him, the Vietnam War was no error, but the logical outcome of a wicked system's "drive for world domination."[4]

Hayden was the soul of moderation compared to fellow SDS members. They used the German "Amerika" to spell their country's name because they *knew*, beyond any question or doubt, that America was as guilty of genocide as Hitler's Germany. As for genocide, the murder of millions of innocent people, the numbers speak for themselves. The com-

191

[3] Chanoff and Doan, *Portrait of the Enemy*, pp. 44, 64–65, 124.
[4] Quoted in Nancy Zaroulis and Gerald Sullivan, *Who Spoke Up? American Protest Against the War in Vietnam, 1963–1975*, p. 90.

bined populations of the two Vietnams actually grew from 34.8 million in 1965 to 42.6 million in 1973.

If America was evil, it followed that its enemy must be good. North Vietnam was idolized by radicals as the land of the free and the home of the brave. It was, indeed, their version of America in 1776. The American Revolution had fought the greatest power on earth with a ragged army and a yearning to be free. North Vietnam stood for that ideal in the modern world, they insisted. Its struggle, according to *The Vietnam Songbook*, a collection of antiwar songs, "embodies the hopes of all humanity." People who had never lived under a dictatorship sang the praises of Uncle Ho, the latter-day George Washington:

> *No More Johnson,*
> *No More Johnson,*
> *No More Johnson, over me.*
> *And before I'll be fenced in,*
> *I will fight for Ho Chi Minh*
> *And go home to the North and be free.*[5]

Vietnam came to torment Lyndon Johnson. Antiwar activists made him the most vilified president in American history. LBJ, they said, was not merely wrong, or even stupid, but wicked and devilish. He was spared no insult, charged with every crime imaginable. Speakers branded him a tool of the weapons manufacturers, for whose benefit he was supposed to have started the war. He had, according to some, assassinated John Kennedy to gain the presidency. People who might have hesitated to predict tomorrow's weather were absolutely sure that he was planning to escalate the Vietnam War into World War III, beginning with an atomic attack on China.

192

---

[5] Quoted in Barbara Dane, ed., *The Vietnam Songbook*, p. 129.

Antiwar activists promised never to allow the President a moment's peace. And they were true to their word. College students burned him in effigy during campus rallies. Cartoonists depicted him as a gross, crude bully with a ten-gallon hat. He became the subject of songs—funny songs, ugly songs, obscene songs. Song writers portrayed him as America's Hitler, the Beast of the White House. For instance, in Bill Frederick's "Hitler Ain't Dead," we learn:

> *Hitler ain't dead,*
> *Hitler ain't dead,*
> *Hitler ain't dead,*
> *He just talks with a drawl.*[6]

Wherever the President went, demonstrators followed with signs reading IMPEACH LBJ, JOHNSON WAR CRIMINAL, and JOHNSON MURDERER. Whenever he spoke in public, he drew catcalls, curses, and chants. The chant "Hey, hey, LBJ, how many kids did you kill today?" made him shudder. It was as if he had struck down every innocent victim with his own hand. In protesters' eyes, freedom of speech was a sacred right of all Americans—except the highest elected official in the land. Since they did not like what he had to say, they tried to prevent everyone from hearing him.

The man who enjoyed "pressing the flesh," going out among the people, became a prisoner in the White House. LBJ had to be careful, for each day's mail brought its share of death threats. "I feel like a hitchhiker caught in a hailstorm on a Texas highway," he told Bill Moyers, an aide. "I can't run. I can't hide. And I can't make it stop."

193

While the President watched the Great Society turn against him, radicals championed the Viet Cong as defenders of human rights. "Now we are all Viet Cong," Tom Hayden

---

[6] *Ibid.*, p. 103.

was reported as saying during a visit to Communist Czecho-slovakia.[7] Did he mean that we are all terrorists? Certainly not. Although quick to condemn allied atrocities, antiwar activists hardly noticed those of the Viet Cong. One would have to search for a long time to find a reference to them in their articles and speeches. Onlookers at protest rallies frequently noted the absence of pictures of Viet Cong terror victims or demands that *they* stop the slaughter *now*.

Radicals preferred to ignore Viet Cong terrorism, or to explain it away. The massacre at Hue, said photographer Philip Jones-Griffith, never happened; it was propaganda invented by America to blame the enemy for civilian deaths caused by its own forces.[8] How he could have known this, let alone proven it, remains a mystery. Indeed, America was even held responsible for Viet Cong actions. By making it impossible for the Viet Cong to fight effectively, the argument goes, American firepower *forced* them to use terrorism.

The tone of antiwar protests began to change as the war went on. Radicals, skilled at playing to the television cameras, became noisier and more provocative. Marijuana was smoked openly at demonstrations, Viet Cong flags were displayed, and the American flag was burned.

The first major outburst took place on October 21, 1967. One hundred thousand people had gathered at the Lincoln Memorial in Washington. The vast majority, young and old alike, had come to protest the war peacefully. After the rally, 30,000 marched on the Pentagon, their goal, according to a student leader, to "storm the nerve center of American militarism." Suddenly, a large crowd broke from the main body, scaled a low fence, and charged the sprawling building. Turned away by lines of troops, they sat down in the plaza

194

---

[7]Quoted in Charles DeBenedetti, *An American Ordeal: The Antiwar Movement of the Vietnam Era*, p. 193.
[8]See Nolan, *The Battle for Hue*, p. 184.

The antiwar movement takes to the streets. Top, protestors gather around the Pentagon in 1967. Scores were arrested when they tried to break into the building. Bottom, a young man burns his induction notice while his father looks on during an anti-draft rally.

facing the troops. "Ho! Ho! Ho Chi Minh! NLF is gonna win!" they chanted as SDS members hoisted the Viet Cong flag on the Pentagon flagpole. Demonstrators, knowing the troops had orders not to strike back, cursed them, kicked them, and spat in their faces. Finally, the troops were sent to clear the area, which they did with clubs and rifle butts.

Protests by ordinary citizens, let alone radicals, affected American forces in South Vietnam. Although no official survey has been done, letters and interviews show much anger on the part of fighting men. Grunts called demonstrators "peaceniks," "Vietniks," "freaks," and other names we cannot repeat. Students were especially resented. Grunts could not understand those "spoiled brats" who threw temper tantrums over things they did not understand. "I'm fighting for those candy-asses because I don't have an old man to support me," exclaimed one soldier.[9]

Grunts felt that the antiwar movement insulted the dead by degrading the cause they served. A typical reaction came from Marine Corporal Kevin Macaulay. "Dear Mom and Dad," he wrote from Khe Sanh. "My morale is not the best because my best buddy was killed the day before yesterday. . . . He caught a piece of shrapnel in the head. I carried him over to the aid station where he died. I cried my eyes out. . . . It bothers me to think of these so-called Americans who shirk their responsibility to their country. If I even get close to a peace picket he will see part of the Vietnam War in my eyes."[10]

The enemy, however, had only nice things to say about protesters. Hanoi encouraged the antiwar movement, and drew encouragement from it in return. Uncle Ho and Premier Pham Van Dong often sent greetings and thanks to their

---

[9] Quoted in Edelman, *Dear America*, pp. 80–81.
[10] Quoted in William H. Chale, *The Unfinished Journey: America since World War II*, p. 338.

"dear American friends" for "giving us support." Protesters were hailed as "our heroic comrades-in-arms." Norman Morrison, for example, was well known among the VC/NVA, his picture posted in the windows of trucks on the Ho Chi Minh Trail to inspire drivers to bring more weapons to their forces. Newsreels of demonstrators carrying Viet Cong flags were shown throughout North Vietnam and in jungle camps in the South. Statements by antiwar leaders were read over Radio Hanoi. Each picture, each statement, became a pep pill, energizing the North Vietnamese and Viet Cong. Since so many Americans opposed the war, it was only reasonable to assume that the nation had no stomach for fighting. Victory, therefore, was only a matter of time. All they had to do was keep fighting—and killing Americans.

Vietnamese Communists saw the antiwar movement as a handy weapon to use against the United States. This does not mean that they controlled its leaders or lured them into betraying their country. Investigations by U.S. government agencies failed to uncover any illegal activities. There is no evidence that any group, even the most radical, took money from Hanoi or followed its orders. Yet the fact remains that Hanoi did try to influence them in hopes of turning the American people against the war.

One method was to have North Vietnamese officials meet antiwar leaders in Cuba, Czechoslovakia, and France. During these meetings, they gave them advice and discussed the issues they should push when they returned home. The French Sûreté observed their meetings in Paris, noting who attended and what was discussed. Its findings were quietly passed on to American diplomats.

Another way of influence was through American newsmen. Although the details of this effort remain secret, we do have some fascinating clues. Truong Nhu Tang, NLF minister of justice, spent much of his time on propaganda.

Truong knew his enemy well. "[The] American media," he says, "is easily open to suggestion and false information given by Communist agents. The society is completely hypnotized by the media."[11] His agents fed stories to several well known reporters in Saigon, who took them at face value. The stories, critical of American actions, were then sent home to fuel antiwar sentiment. Truong, however, was only one of many specialists working on the media. Pham Xuan An, for ten years a star reporter for *Time* magazine in Saigon, was also a Viet Cong colonel.

Perhaps the best means of spreading propaganda was to invite foreigners to North Vietnam. American visitors were generally opponents of the war. All those who made the trip, radicals, clergymen, lawyers, writers, journalists, and entertainers, were manipulated in one way or another by the enemy. Their hosts gave them the full treatment. Communist officials spoke of their "sincere wishes" for a just and lasting peace. Briefing officers dished out the latest information on American "atrocities." Guides took them on tours of villages destroyed by American "air pirates."

The villages were real, but there was no way of knowing why they had been bombed. Communists claimed it was part of the U.S. "genocide plot." They did not say whether a SAM missile had fallen into the village, or if it had contained antiaircraft guns, or had been a storage site for ammunition. With the military target destroyed, there was nothing left but the ruins, and bricks cannot speak for themselves. Visitors, however, seldom asked probing questions. The majority came with their minds already made up, wanting to believe the worst about Rolling Thunder. The North Vietnamese gladly filled them in on the "facts."

Certain visitors found North Vietnam the total opposite

---

[11] Quoted in Santoli, *To Bear Any Burden*, p. 156ff.

of their own country. North Vietnam seemed, to them, a paradise inhabited by loving, gentle, courageous people. Susan Sontag, a well-known arts critic, could not contain her joy at visiting this marvelous land. She found the Communist nation an "ethical society" whose government "loves the people." The only problem was that they "aren't good enough haters." America, by contrast, was founded on genocide and the cruelest system of slavery in modern times. Sontag, who is white, saw America as the land of white devils. And, said she, "the white race *is* the cancer of human history."[12] Her view of North Vietnam is nonsense. Her view of America and white people is racist nonsense—nonsense on stilts. Yet she was not alone in her views.

American POWs became pawns in a vicious game played by their captors. As we have seen, Hanoi regarded them as assets in its propaganda effort. Its aim was to break the prisoners' spirit, indoctrinate them with antiwar ideas, and then use them to further the antiwar effort in the United States.

Jailers treated the activities of the antiwar movement as major events. Articles about them from the *New York Times,* the *Washington Post,* and *Time* and *Newsweek* magazines were constantly read over prison radios. Photos of protesters carrying Viet Cong flags decorated prison hallways. Prisoners were required to read pamphlets and speeches by antiwar leaders. Jeremiah Denton learned their contents the hard way. He had been tortured by Mickey Mouse, one of the "gentle" North Vietnamese guards. Before ending the session, Mickey made him promise to copy passages from an antiwar book by Dr. Spock. He obeyed, since the baby doctor's words hurt less than the guard's fists.[13] Denton's comrade, Navy Lieutenant Everett Alvarez, had to read similar books. In addi-

199

---

12 Susan Sontag, *Trip to Hanoi,* pp. 26–76; *Partisan Review,* Winter, 1967, pp. 51–58.
13 Denton, *When Hell Was in Session,* p. 182.

tion, he was forced to denounce the war in letters to Senator Fulbright and student activists.

Letter writing was important to the North Vietnamese. They would force a POW to give the names and addresses of his family members. The information was then passed to contacts in the West, who tried to get them to make antiwar statements in return for promises of good treatment for their loved ones. One of these contacts was Cora Weiss, a wealthy New Yorker chosen by Hanoi as a go-between with prisoners and their families. "She was absolutely horrible," recalls Janis Dodge, a POW's wife. "She told me—and many other wives and mothers—that if I wanted to correspond with my husband I would have to go through her. And she wanted the families to make antiwar statements. I told her that I didn't want to talk with her."[14]

Gullible visitors accepted North Vietnamese claims about good treatment for POWs. Upon returning to America, they repeated the claims to congressional committees, newspaper readers, and television audiences. POWs, they claimed, lived in clean, roomy quarters, had proper medical attention, and ate well; Susan Sontag believed an NVA officer who said POWs received larger rations than Vietnamese, "because they are bigger than we are." Naturally, visitors were not allowed into the cell blocks, much less the Meathook Room in the Hanoi Hilton; nor were representatives of the International Red Cross. The closest they came to POWs were staged interviews with men who had been forced to meet them, and then tortured if they did not give a good performance.

200

The most disliked visitor among POWs was actress Jane Fonda, who toured North Vietnam in July 1972. During that time she left no doubt that she admired the Communists and hoped for their victory. Smiling broadly and clapping her

---

[14]Quoted in Santoli, *To Bear Any Burden*, p. 243.

hands for joy, she approached an antiaircraft gun used to shoot down American planes. Then she put on a North Vietnamese combat helmet and posed for photographs looking through the gunsight. As if that wasn't enough, she made ten broadcasts over Radio Hanoi aimed at demoralizing American fighting men. Accusing the United States of crimes against humanity, she warned pilots, men "paid to commit murder," that they had better think twice before carrying out orders; obedience made one "a war criminal," like the Germans who had served Adolf Hitler. In effect, she urged them to disobey lawful commands in the face of the enemy. Her broadcasts were beamed to the inmates of the Hanoi Hilton day and night, until the men felt they were going out of their minds. "It was hard to keep going," says Captain Eugene "Red" McDaniel. "I felt betrayed and hurt . . . I don't think the right to dissent extends to the capital city of the enemy in time of war."[15]

Fonda's broadcasts won her the nickname "Hanoi Jane." Men who served their country honorably have never forgiven her for the pain she caused them. True, she had not committed treason; for if there is no declared war, there can be no treason. Nevertheless, they blame her for the deaths of countless Americans by raising North Vietnamese morale and keeping them in the fight. Her actions still anger Senator John McCain of Arizona. McCain was a POW in 1972, when the North Vietnamese ordered him to have his picture taken with her and make antiwar statements. When he refused, guards broke both his arms and locked him in a three-by-six-foot box for five months.[16] A fellow POW, Lieutenant Commander David Hoffman, did meet her at a news conference. At first he refused, but his captors were very persuasive. They broke his arm, then attached

201

---

[15] Quoted in Christopher Andersen, *Citizen Jane: The Turbulent Life of Jane Fonda*, p. 10.
[16] *Ibid.*, p. 10.

it to a rope and hung him from it until he agreed to the meeting.[17]

Despite President Johnson's growing unpopularity, a majority of Americans still supported the war. Americans like a winner and, by late 1967, the allies appeared to be just that. Then came the Year of the Monkey.

The Tet Offensive took America by surprise. It needn't have, for the President had been briefed by General Westmoreland weeks earlier. He knew something big was on the way, but did nothing to prepare the nation, an awful blunder. As a result, people were shocked at learning how easily the "defeated" enemy could strike South Vietnam's "secure" cities and military bases. Overnight the nation lost confidence in LBJ's leadership. He seemed confused, frightened, unwilling to go for the knockout blow. A total of 222,351 Americans had been killed or wounded during the Johnson years, 1964 through 1968. Enough was enough. If, after so much bloodshed, he could not say when the war would end, it was time to get out.

The sense of shock was magnified by the news media. Historians believe that the media, particularly television, did a poor job of covering Tet. Part of the reason was that newsmen, too, were taken by surprise. In the hubbub and confusion, they failed to get their facts right. Early reports of the fight at the U.S. Embassy, for example, told how the Viet Cong occupied five floors of the building and described guards battling them "through the carpeted offices." In fact, as we have seen, the invaders were shot dead on the front lawn. Worse, television did what it does best: simplify. There was plenty of fighting, and bodies, and ruins, and tears during Tet. Reporting them is the journalist's duty. But by focusing

---

[17] *Ibid.*, p. 256.

BRINGING THE WAR HOME

on, say, a burning street in Saigon, they gave the impression that the whole city—no, the whole country—was ablaze. This was simply untrue.

In going after the "big story," there were those who tried to make news rather than report it. Dick Burnham, an American official, recalls a television reporter asking about the "horrendous" disaster of Tet. When Burnham explained that things were going quite well, the reporter cut him off, saying he didn't want to hear such lies. So the reporter questioned several other officials until he got the answers he wanted to hear, which were broadcast to the American people a few days later.[18] Others may actually have damaged soldiers' morale with their questions. At Hue, a reporter asked a paratrooper: "How do you feel fighting over here knowing that everybody back in the States is against the war?" "Lost any friends?" another asked a Marine. "How do you feel about it?"

The media became the voice of gloom and doom. Tet was presented to the American people as an enemy, not an allied, victory. There were no ifs, ands, or buts about it. "The Tet Offensive had been a tremendous Communist victory," declared the *New York Times* of March 10, 1968. Reporters for NBC and CBS, the leading television networks, agreed. Indeed, they said the Communists would surely overrun Khe Sanh. CBS correspondent Murray Fromson reported from the scene: "Here the North Vietnamese decide who lives and who dies . . . which planes land and which ones don't and sooner or later they *will* make the move that *will* seal the fate of Khe Sanh."[19] This sounded dramatic, but there was not a word of truth in it.

203

The enemy found all of this very interesting. Hanoi, knowing a good thing, deliberately sent American news re-

---

[18] Maurer, *Strange Ground*, p. 308.
[19] Quoted in William M. Hammond, *Public Affairs: The Military and the Media, 1962–1968*, p. 364. Italics added.

ports into South Vietnam. Viet Cong units, reeling in defeat, were told they had actually crushed the enemy. In the Mekong delta, villagers had the bad news before American servicemen stationed nearby. And since it came from the American press, they asked, "Why would the Americans say they lost if they had won?"[20]

The strain of governing a nation and fighting a war left its mark on President Johnson. He had pounding headaches, slept poorly, and had nightmares. Suddenly, in the midst of a conversation, he would lash out at his critics. The Communists, he'd say, were out to get him. They controlled the television networks, poisoning people's minds against him. His critics were not loyal citizens with sincere doubts about his policies. Oh, no; they were "traitors," "simpletons," "nervous Nellies," "cut and run" cowards with "no guts." LBJ called Senator Fulbright, once a dear friend, "Senator Halfbright."

Tet was the last straw.

The storm broke just as the nation was gearing up for the 1968 presidential campaign. Until then, Johnson felt confident of reelection. Suddenly, everything went topsy-turvy. By the end of the first week of Tet, he faced a battle within his own Democratic party. Like the public at large, many Democratic congressmen and senators had lost confidence in him. On March 12, Senator Eugene McCarthy of Minnesota challenged him in the New Hampshire primary. McCarthy, an outspoken dove, lost by a slim margin. LBJ was stunned, but there was more to come.

New York Senator Robert Kennedy announced his candidacy four days later. Once a firm supporter of his brother's Vietnam policy, he had believed that America must try to

204

save an ally from communism. But as the war escalated, and hopes of success faded, he became convinced that the whole effort was wrong. LBJ despised "Bobby" as a traitor and feared him as a political rival. Of all his opponents, Kennedy was the most dangerous. A tough political fighter, he might well take the nomination, humiliating Johnson as no one had ever done before.

On March 31, the President faced the television cameras. He looked tired and upset, but he spoke with dignity. He spoke not about war, but about peace in Vietnam. Although the enemy's Tet Offensive was a failure, he admitted that the war was far from over. For the sake of peace, therefore, he announced a freeze on the number of American troops in Vietnam, a cutback on the bombing of North Vietnam (it was halted completely a few months later), and his plan to start peace talks as quickly as possible. Then came the shocker: he would not seek his party's nomination for another term as president. Vietnam had destroyed his presidency.

If LBJ expected things to calm down after his announcement, he was sadly mistaken. The next five months were a time when the nation seemed to be coming apart. On April 4, Dr. Martin Luther King, Jr., was felled by an assassin's bullet in Memphis, Tennessee. For the next week, the black ghettos exploded in anger and grief. Cries of "Burn, baby, burn!" echoed in cities across the land. Black mobs took to the streets in over a hundred cities, breaking windows, looting stores, and setting fires. In Chicago, twenty blocks of the downtown business district went up in flames. Riots in Washington made it necessary to mass troops on the White House grounds.

A wave of student strikes followed the ghetto riots. During the last week in April, over a million college and high school students walked out of class to protest the war. Although the protests were orderly, one got out of hand. On April 23, the

The year of the Tet Offensive, 1968, was also a year of violence at home. Top, a free-for-all breaks out on the Columbia University campus during the student occupation. Bottom, an antiwar demonstrator, blood streaming from his head, confronts a Chicago policeman. Almost one hundred were injured and two hundred arrested during the demonstration, one of many during the Democratic National Convention.

Columbia University chapter of SDS led a takeover of several campus buildings. The issues, according to its leader, Mark Rudd, were racial injustice and the university's role in military research. When the students refused to leave the buildings, police cleared them by force.

Columbia was a milestone for the antiwar movement. "We manufactured the issues," Rudd later admitted. Radicals deliberately provoked police violence, hoping to spark student uprisings throughout the country. The word *uprising* is no exaggeration; for they had crossed the line between peaceful protest and violent revolution. Their aim was to end the war by overthrowing the American system of government and replacing it by a "people's democracy"—that is, a dictatorship ruled by themselves.

Meanwhile, Robert Kennedy went from one primary victory to another. He seemed a shoe-in at the Democratic nominating convention to be held in Chicago in August. But on June 6, he was shot by Sirhan Sirhan, a young Palestinian angered by Kennedy's support of Israel. Kennedy's death opened the way for Vice President Hubert Humphrey, a supporter of Johnson's Vietnam policy. Humphrey entered the race and, thanks to his influence with party leaders, soon became the Democratic favorite. His strongest opposition came, naturally, from the antiwar movement. The entire movement, from religious pacifists to the American Communist party, planned to go to Chicago to protest the war and campaign for Eugene McCarthy.

They were to be joined by a new group, the Youth International Party—Yippies for short. The Yippies were the brainchild of Jerry Rubin, a college dropout who claimed to have taken his ideas from the Lone Ranger! Rubin had strong likes and dislikes. His book *Do It!* was dedicated to the things he liked: "Dope, Color TV, and Violent Revolution." America, which he scorned, needed a revolution.

207

He did not disguise his aim. "Our tactic is to send niggers and longhair scum into white middle-class homes . . . breaking the furniture and smashing Sunday school napalm-blood Amerika forever. . . . *When in doubt, burn.* Fire is the revolutionary's god. . . . Burn the flag. Burn churches. Burn, burn, burn."[21] Rubin also had a warm spot in his heart for killers. Robert Kennedy's assassin was all right in his book; "Sirhan Sirhan is a Yippie," he said. Likewise for Charles Manson, leader of a gang that murdered actress Sharon Tate and three of her friends. After visiting Manson in jail, Rubin claimed "his words and courage inspire us."[22] The Viet Cong were fine fellows, too, patriots who fought for high ideals. In quieter times, most people would have ignored Jerry and his Yippies as doped-up lunatics. But the Year of the Monkey was anything but quiet—or sane.

Radicals had no intention of behaving peacefully in Chicago. SDS leaders called for a "little Tet Offensive" to bring the city to its knees and disrupt the Democratic convention. Rubin's Yippies had more ambitious plans. Yippie headquarters in New York vowed to put LSD, a dangerous drug, into Chicago's water supply. Yippies would stage mass "nude-ins" at Lake Michigan and flood sewers with gasoline from service stations to burn the city to the ground. Convention delegates and their wives would be kidnapped.

Mayor Richard Daley took the Yippies at their word. Part of his city had already been burned in April, and he was not going to allow them to finish the job. Chicago's twelve-thousand-man police force, supported by 11,000 army and national guard troops, was put on alert. Daley's show of force had the desired effect. Fearing violence, hundreds of thousands of ordinary people, the backbone of the antiwar movement,

---

[21] Jerry Rubin, *Do It!*, pp. 111, 127.
[22] Quoted in David Caute, *The Year of the Barricades: A Journey Through 1968*, p. 446.

stayed home. In the end, only five thousand demonstrators came to the Windy City during the last week of August.

That week saw an American tragedy acted out before the television cameras. Radicals had come for a showdown, and that is what they got. Policemen were taunted by long-haired, foul-mouthed, marijuana-smoking young people. "Pig! Pig! Pig! Pig!" they chanted, shaking their fists in the air. "Kill the pigs!" "Nazi Pigs!" "Oink, oink, oink, oink!" Policemen were spat upon and sprayed with paint. They were pelted with stones, bottles, burning rags, and balloons filled with urine. Protesters tried to haul down the Stars and Stripes and replace it with their Viet Cong flags. Finally, on August 28, police discipline snapped. What followed, in the words of an official report, was a "police riot." Swarms of policemen attacked the protesters with clubs. Not only did they beat them, they beat anyone they could reach: innocent passers-by, newsmen, convention delegates.

Jerry Rubin was delighted. "We wanted exactly what happened," he said. "We wanted . . . to create a situation in which . . . the United States would self-destruct. . . . The message of the week was of an America ruled by force. That was a big victory."[23]

The United States, however, was stronger, and angrier, than Rubin imagined. Television audiences had watched the doings in Chicago with disgust: disgust at America-haters and at the Democrats, who seemed unable to manage their own party, let alone a nation at war. Although Hubert Humphrey was nominated and fought a hard campaign, Richard Nixon, the Republican candidate, defeated him by a narrow margin.

History is full of fascinating "ifs." One of these concerns Sirhan Sirhan. If his bullet had missed Robert Kennedy,

---

[23] Quoted in Milton Viorst, *Fire in the Streets: America in the 1960s*, p. 456ff.

things would have been different for America. Bobby was the strongest of all the Democratic candidates. Had he lived, he would probably have beaten Nixon, as his brother had done eight years before. Had he become president, it is likely that he would have brought the war to a speedy end, perhaps on terms favorable to the enemy. But this was not to be.

When Richard Nixon was inaugurated in January 1969, the United States had been fighting in Vietnam for the three years and nine months. Nixon would need four more years to reach a settlement. During that time, another 122,708 Americans would be killed or wounded.

America's Vietnam War still had a long way to go.

MR. NIXON'S
WAR FOR PEACE

*That guy, Nixon; he's okay. He brought my
kid back from Vietnam.*

—A soldier's father

T HE INAUGURATION OF RICHARD M. NIXON SIGNALED
the end of an era. A shrewd politician with a keen interest
in foreign affairs, Nixon was a staunch anti-Communist. Fifteen years earlier, as vice president under Eisenhower, he
had urged the use of American forces at Dien Bien Phu. As
President, his aim was still to halt the spread of communism,
which he saw as pure evil, the work of the devil. Yet Nixon
was also a realist who recognized the power of the Soviet
Union and China. Both countries, he believed, threatened
world peace. Vietnam was a side issue, albeit a troublesome
one for the United States. But as long as the war there continued, it kept him from dealing effectively with the Communist giants.

That conclusion led Nixon to rethink the Vietnam War.
Three Presidents had committed America to the defense of
South Vietnam. It was a sincere effort, but one that had
failed. Given the realities on the battlefield and at home,
Nixon decided that he could not allow the war to drag on

year after year. "I'm not going to end up like LBJ, holed up in the White House afraid to show his face in the street," he told an aide soon after taking office. "I'm going to stop that war. Fast."[1]

Stopping a war, however, can be harder than starting one. If Nixon hoped to succeed, he had to solve two problems. First, the war must end in such a way that the world would not see it as an American defeat. Antiwar people demanded an immediate end regardless of what happened to South Vietnam. But Nixon dared not "cut and run," as he put it. There had to be "peace with honor." Abandoning an ally was both dishonorable and an admission of weakness that would bring further Communist aggression. Second, he must persuade Hanoi to make peace, or at least to leave South Vietnam alone—exactly what LBJ had failed to do.

"Vietnamization" was Nixon's solution to the first problem. The opposite of escalation, its aim was to give the war back to the South Vietnamese. In May 1969, after the 101st Airborne Division had 476 men killed and wounded at a place called Hamburger Hill, he halted large-scale SAD operations. The following month, he announced the withdrawal of American troops from Vietnam. Withdrawal would be gradual, beginning with 25,000 men, but would continue until none remained. To fill the gap, South Vietnam would receive massive aid, enabling it to defend itself, perhaps even to win, on its own. If, after a certain time, the country fell to the Communists, it would be seen not as an American defeat, but as a South Vietnamese failure. Thus, Nixon would not be the first American President to lose a war.

The plan worried South Vietnamese and Americans alike. President Nguyen Van Thieu doubted his country's ability

212

to stand on its own. American officers agreed, calling the plan a formula for disaster. The ARVN, they noted, was as inept and corrupt as ever; indeed, things would get worse as the Americans left. Vietnamization was a cruel hoax, merely a polite term for "changing the color of the bodies." Nixon replied that the South Vietnamese had to fight their own battles, but they could count on his full support. He would not let them down; they had his word as President of the United States.

Vietnamization was well under way by late 1969. Generous amounts of American money enabled the ARVN to expand to 1.1 million men. ARVN firepower grew as a million brand-new M16 rifles were sent and withdrawing Americans left their weapons behind. Within a year, the ARVN had plenty of small arms, tanks, patrol boats, artillery, helicopters, air transports, and jet fighters; in time it would have 2,000 planes, making it the fourth largest air force in the world. Fully equipped army camps, airfields, and docks were also turned over to the South Vietnamese.

Weapons, however, were only part of Vietnamization. Behind the scenes, the Central Intelligence Agency (CIA) launched the Phoenix Program, a plan to annihilate the Viet Cong at the village level. Working with the South Vietnamese secret services, CIA agents pooled all their information about Viet Cong activities. Lists were made of Viet Cong organizers, village leaders, terrorists, propagandists, and tax collectors. These were given to American, or American–South Vietnamese strike teams. The American teams consisted largely of Army Green Berets or Navy SEALs, an elite commando unit; SEAL stands for sea, air, and land.

William Colby, head of the Phoenix Program, claimed its purpose was not to kill Viet Cong, but to arrest them and hold them for questioning. If they were killed, he claimed, it was during shoot-outs while resisting arrest. He may be-

213

lieve that, but Americans who took part in actual missions tell a different story. Phoenix, they say, was an assassination program.

Unlike SAD patrols, which arrived in daylight and searched villages in the hope of finding Viet Cong, the men of Phoenix fought terror with terror. Theirs was a barbaric war with no mercy given or expected. Operating in fourteen-man teams, they wore black peasant pajamas and worked at night. They might slip into a village, find their man, and "terminate with extreme prejudice"—that is, slit his throat while he slept. They would then place a calling card in his mouth: the ace of spades. Other Viet Cong were kidnapped and taken for questioning. If possible, they were brought back to base; if not, questioning took place in the jungle, by torture. But not all of their victims were Viet Cong. Corrupt South Vietnamese officials often placed their rivals' names on the hit lists.

A Green Beret named Yoshia Chee went on several Phoenix operations. Years later he gave a chilling account of his work.

We'd try to get all the information we could—supply dumps, meeting points, dates, times, hospitals, more collaborators' names. . . . It's pretty unpleasant to talk about this, but there were some ways of torturing people without really getting into the Dark Ages. You've got to always have shock on your side. One of the favorite things was popping one of their eyeballs out with a spoon. It won't kill the guy. The eye can be fixed. But it's awfully painful and shocking. Just imagine having one of your eyeballs hanging out. I would talk—if I had one of my eyeballs hanging out, I'd say I killed Kennedy. I'd agree to do anything in the whole world. . . . Another thing we did was look for Viet Cong hospitals. We'd get word that a hospital was operating in an area, and we'd try to find it. We got a couple. Our duty was to wipe out the whole hospital. . . . The

214

thing was to go in there and get the doctors. Get the nurses. Get the patients, too. . . . Of course, our hospitals got hit, too. But we weren't supposed to be doing that. . . . We were high most of the time . . . on Methedrine. They gave it to us for endurance. . . . So most of the time we were stoned. We had to be stoned. I can't see anybody in their right mind doing the stuff I did.[2]

The Phoenix Program, brutal as it was, hurt the Viet Cong badly. By mid-1971, the toll was 28,978 Viet Cong officials captured and 20,587 killed. Communist leaders admitted after the war that Phoenix weakened their hold on the countryside, forcing thousands of Viet Cong and NVA troops to retreat to bases in Cambodia. Unfortunately for Cambodia, President Nixon had plans for those bases. Big plans.

Nixon's strategy in Cambodia was tied to his second objective, persuading Hanoi to leave South Vietnam alone. Early in 1969, he told an aide about his "madman theory." Everyone knew of his hatred for communism, he said. He now wanted the North Vietnamese to think that he was losing his mind and might do anything to stop the war. If they did not make peace soon—well, he had his finger on the nuclear button. One press of that button and Hanoi would cease to exist. He, Richard Nixon, would not be trifled with by a gang of aging revolutionaries. No wonder political rivals called him Tricky Dick.

Had Nixon been serious about using nuclear weapons, he would, indeed, have been crazy. But he was only playing on the enemy's fears. To make his "insanity" believable, he decided to bomb VC/NVA bases in Cambodia. It would be a direct signal to the enemy that if they were unreasonable, he would bomb them as they had never been bombed before.

215

When he got through, Hanoi would look back on Rolling Thunder as the good old days.

Cambodia was an appropriate target. Not only did the Ho Chi Minh Trail pass through eastern Cambodia, but for ten years the Communists had controlled large areas, or "sanctuaries," along the border with South Vietnam. These sanctuaries contained supply dumps, fuel depots, training centers, hospitals, truck parks, repair shops—everything an army needed. It was also believed that the Central Office for South Vietnam (COSVN), the Communists' main headquarters, was located in Cambodia.

Grunts knew all about Cambodia. They would watch from their hilltop outposts as enemy troops trained a few miles away, within easy artillery range. But mostly the enemy's artillery fired: shells and rockets constantly came from across the border. In broad daylight, the grunts saw battered VC/NVA units slip into "neutral" Cambodia to be carried to rest camps by fleets of waiting trucks. The enemy, in turn, marveled at American stupidity. Nguyen Thong Lai, leader of a Viet Cong unit, said that fighting the Americans was easy because of the restrictions they placed on themselves. "We knew that the American commanders had strict orders . . . to respect the Cambodian border. Whenever we were chased by the enemy, we knew we could retreat across the frontier . . . into the safe zone and get some rest. We were protected by international law. Also, we knew there was a large antiwar movement in America who would not allow the American army to cross over the border."[3] That was true in the days of LBJ. But Tricky Dick was different.

In March 1969, Nixon launched Operation Menu, his air offensive against Communist sanctuaries in Cambodia. For the next fourteen months, B-52s flew 3,630 sorties and

216

---

[3] Quoted in Santoli, *To Bear Any Burden*, p. 146.

dropped 110,000 tons of bombs. To avoid embarrassing all parties, the bombing was kept secret. Cambodian ruler Prince Norodom Sihanouk had known about the sanctuaries from the beginning. Cambodians have hated the land-hungry Vietnamese for centuries, and Sihanouk was no exception. But since his country was weak, he kept quiet, hoping it would be left alone as a neutral country; indeed, he allowed the Communists to send shiploads of weapons through the port of Sihanoukville. Protesting the bombing would tell the world that he had permitted his territory to be used for war against a neighbor. The North Vietnamese said nothing, because they had always lied about their presence in Cambodia. Nixon kept the bombing secret to avoid an outcry from Congress, which feared a further escalation.

Operation Menu, however, turned out to be a disappointment. It was an updated version of Rolling Thunder and therefore doomed to failure. Early in 1970, General Creighton Abrams, Westmoreland's replacement, sent an urgent message to the White House. Unless the Cambodian bases were cleaned out, he warned, further troop withdrawals would endanger the forces remaining in South Vietnam. To avoid this, on April 30, 1970, Nixon sent allied forces into Cambodia. The action, he said in a televised speech, was not an invasion but an "incursion"—that is, the troops would remain in the border areas and pull out within sixty days. Their aim was to keep the enemy off balance, which they did by destroying thousands of tons of supplies.

Although a military success, the incursion was a disaster in every other respect. It was a disaster for Cambodia, which was already in deep trouble. Prince Sihanouk had been overthrown soon after the start of Operation Menu. The new ruler, General Lon Nol, immediately asked for U.S. aid to fight Cambodia's own Communists, known as the Khmer Rouge (Red Cambodians). Nixon's incursion further com-

217

plicated matters. Striking the VC/NVA base areas did not drive them from Cambodia; it forced them westward, *deeper* into the country. There they linked up with the Khmer Rouge, supplying them with all the weapons they needed. Until then, the Khmer Rouge had numbered less than 3,000 poorly armed guerrillas. Thanks to the incursion, it grew by leaps and bounds, plunging Cambodia into civil war.

Nixon's announcement also sent shockwaves across the United States. An angry Congress repealed the Gulf of Tonkin Resolution and barred future action in Cambodia. (When the ARVN invaded Laos in 1971, it went alone and took an awful beating.) Student strikes shut down more than 400 colleges, forcing several to cancel classes for the rest of the semester.

The worst incident occurred at Kent State University in Ohio on May 4. After radical students burned down one of the buildings, the governor sent National Guard troops to restore order. Rioting followed, in which students threw stones at guardsmen, hit them with clubs, cursed them, and shouted, "Pigs off campus!" A number of guardsmen, believing they heard a shot, opened fire, killing four students and wounding nine others. In fact, no one had shot at them; all the dead students were hundreds of feet from the troops, unable even to reach them with stones. The guardsmen had panicked, with tragic results.

Millions of Americans had no regrets about Kent State; some actually welcomed it. For five years they had watched student protests, seen students carrying Viet Cong flags, heard students insulting the nation. Those privileged youngsters were attacking their most cherished values: steady work, security, patriotism, the flag. A *Newsweek* poll showed that a majority supported Nixon on Cambodia and that six out of seven blamed the students rather than the National Guard for the killings at Kent State.

The secret bombing of Cambodia, ordered by President Richard Nixon, left, brought antiwar protest to a new level. Below, a young woman cries in horror by one of the four students killed at Kent State University during a demonstration against the bombings. This widely published photo became a symbol of student rebellion and an incitement to further demonstrations.

This was underlined by events in New York, where the city hall flag had been lowered to half-mast in memory of the slain students. Angry "hard hats," construction workers, marched on city hall, beating antiwar protesters and forcing the mayor's office to raise the flag to full staff. Their message was blunt: students, like everyone else, are accountable for their actions. If they provoke violence, they must pay the price. The public had not only lost patience with the war, but with those who protested against it. Too many people had come to agree with Governor Ronald Reagan of California. Asked about student radicals, Reagan said, "If it takes a bloodbath, let's get it over with."[4]

The American fighting man was losing patience as well. Morale had been high in the 1960s, when soldiers believed in their cause and their ability to get the job done. Vietnamization, however, was an admission that the war could not be won. Whatever sense of accomplishment they might have had in the early years vanished once the pullout began. By the end of 1971, there were 156,800 troops remaining in Vietnam, and the number continued to fall steadily. Those who remained behind knew they were just holding on while the ARVN learned to stand on its own feet—if that was possible. Yet they were still fighting, still dying, still being crippled. At the same time, they felt the folks back home did not appreciate their efforts. "The whole thing stinks," as one grunt put it none too delicately.

Returning veterans were haunted by the horror of Vietnam, by the horror of what they had seen and done there. An organization, Vietnam Veterans Against the War, was formed to demand an immediate end to the war. Antiwar protesters were one thing, antiwar veterans were something

220

4Quoted in Zaroulis and Sullivan, *Who Spoke Up?*, p. 308.

else. These men had earned the right to speak, and speak they did.

On April 23, 1971, two thousand Vietnam Veterans Against the War marched on Washington. They dressed not in civilian clothes, but in the remnants of combat-worn uniforms. At the head of the column were amputees and grunts in wheelchairs like Ron Kovic, author of *Born on the Fourth of July*, a moving account of one man's ordeal. Policemen, no admirers of protesters, watched silently, some with tears in their eyes. Arriving at the Capitol, the marchers paused. Then, as a father wearing his dead son's army jacket blew taps, they threw their Purple Hearts, Bronze Stars, and Silver Stars onto the steps. Said one veteran, explaining his action: "I just want to ask for the war to end, please."

Draftees wanted the same thing. Unlike their older brothers, their heads were not filled with romantic rubbish about war. Ever since junior high school, television had burned its images of Vietnam into their minds. Speeches about "duty," "honor," and the "Communist menace" no longer rang true. They had no desire to go to Vietnam, or to return from it in an aluminum box. Music, in many ways *the* language of the Vietnam generation, expressed their deepest concerns. These were captured in a song by Phil Ochs that swept the country in the late 1960s:

> It's always the old who lead us to war,
> It's always the young who fall. . . .
> Call it "peace" or call it "treason,"
> Call it "love" or call it "reason."
> But I ain't marchin' anymore.

221

Draftees were targeted by antiwar activists. In the early 1970s, the activists set out to cripple the war effort by weakening the discipline and loyalty of America's armed forces. Groups of antiwar lawyers and clergymen promised to help draftees who refused to serve in Vietnam. Show business groups gave antiwar performances outside military bases. Using songs, jokes, and skits, they described the military as a mindless meat grinder that was consuming the young. A song by the rock group Country Joe and the Fish sent the message with the force of an artillery shell. Its title is "I-Feel-Like-I'm-Fixin'-to-Die-Rag":

And it's 1, 2, 3, what are we fighting for?
Don't ask me I don't give a damn
Next stop is Vietnam
And it's 5, 6, 7, open up the Pearly Gates
Well there ain't no time to wonder why
Whoopee we're all gonna die.

Well come on mothers throughout the land
Pack your boys off to Vietnam
Come on fathers don't hesitate
Send him out before it's too late
Be the first on your block
To have your boy come home in a box.

Draftees brought antiwar attitudes to Vietnam or developed them after a short time in-country. The result was a crisis unlike any in American history. Marine Colonel Robert D. Heinl, Jr., an expert on military affairs, described it in a 1971 report entitled "The Collapse of the Armed Forces." Heinl's emphasis was on the word *collapse*. Step by step, he showed how the war in Vietnam was tearing the armed forces to pieces. This had nothing to do with defeats in battle, but the feeling that the war was no longer worth fighting. "By every conceivable indicator," he wrote, "our army that now remains in Vietnam is in a state approaching collapse. . . . [D]istrusted, disliked, and often reviled by the public, the uniformed services today are places of agony for the loyal, silent professionals who doggedly hang on and try to keep the ship afloat."[5]

Signs of collapse were everywhere. Anyone with eyes to see and ears to hear knew that army morale had reached rock bottom. Grunts simply did-not want to fight anymore. They painted peace symbols on their flak jackets and helmet covers. They pinned badges to their shirts with slogans like GIVE PEACE A CHANCE! and PEACE NOW! There were antiwar fasts, as in Pleiku, where a medical unit refused Thanksgiving turkey as an antiwar protest. But, as always, music went to the heart of the matter. Soldier songs took on quality of sadness and disillusion. You heard it in the pounding rock 'n' roll beat of "We Gotta Get Out of This Place," for a while the troops' unofficial theme song. Old tunes were changed to suit new ways of thinking. One version of "Detroit City," a sentimental country and western ballad, expressed the grunts' fondest wish:

I wanna go home, I wanna go home,
O I wanna go home.

This did not mean that grunts cowered in their foxholes, shivering at the slightest sign of trouble. Far from it. They were as brave as ever—when they had to be. But with the American role ending, they saw no reason to risk their lives. No one, the saying went, wanted to be the last grunt to die in The Nam.

Soldiers did everything they could to avoid combat. Some deserted—that is, ran away from their units for at least one month. Before 1968, the number of deserters had been lower than in World War II and the Korean War. By 1971, however, desertions rose to 74 per thousand troops. Another 177

223

---

[5]Robert D. Heinl, Jr., "The Collapse of the Armed Forces," *Armed Forces Journal*, June 7, 1971, p. 30.

per thousand were absent without leave (AWOL), gone for less than thirty days. Combining the numbers gives 251 per thousand. In other words, one quarter of the troops ran away for some period of time while on active duty. The Marines went still further; they had the highest desertion rate in their history. Runaways hid with their Vietnamese girlfriends or in seedy hotels until found by the military police. Deserters received a dishonorable discharge after serving time in prison. Those who had gone AWOL were fined, reduced in rank, and returned to their units. No deserter, as far as we know, joined the enemy.

Those who stayed with their units had ingenious ways of avoiding combat. A popular method was "working it out," by which men refused an order, forcing their commander to bargain with them to decide exactly what they were willing to do. Another method was "search-and-avoid," setting out on patrol while keeping out of harm's way. A squad might leave camp and settle down for the night a hundred yards from the forward outposts. In the morning, it returned to camp and reported "no contact."

If these methods failed, there was always mutiny, open re-volt. Entire units refused to obey their commanders' orders. On August 26, 1969, for example, a company of the 196th Infantry refused to attack a North Vietnamese position. Later that year, members of the First Air Cavalry Division, a top-notch outfit, refused to advance along a dangerous trail. Mu-tiny is a serious offense under military law, carrying the death penalty or life in prison at hard labor. George Washington ordered mutineers to be shot by firing squad. In Vietnam, however, officers generally looked the other way. No one was executed and few went to prison for mutiny.

Pity the officer who pushed his men too far. Unpopular officers might be chewed out, cursed, spat on, even threat-ened in public. Only a fool ignored a threat. The killing of officers by their own men is as old as warfare itself. In the United States, the first known incident happened on the night of January 1, 1781, when soldiers of the Continental Army killed a captain. But most such murders took place during battle, when they could be blamed on the enemy. After all, one bullet hole looks pretty much like another.

Murder was a real possibility in Vietnam. Incidents of "fragging"—killing officers with fragmentation grenades—increased sharply after 1969. An unpopular officer might receive a warning, such as a smoke grenade rolled under his cot. If he did not mend his ways, he might find that he had a price on his head. Grunts would pool their money and offer rewards of $50 to $1,000 for his murder. The largest reward, $10,000, was for Major General Melvin Zais, who had ordered the assault on Hamburger Hill. Luckily for Zais, he left Vietnam before anyone could collect. Unlucky officers were fragged as they slept; one got it while in a shower reserved for officers. Between 1969 and 1971, there were 520 officers attacked and 85 killed. These were the reported cases; scholars believe that nine out of ten attacks went unreported. It is impossible to tell how many were fragged or shot in the back during battle. Word of an officer's death brought cheers in the camps of certain outfits.

Increased drug use was another sign of trouble. Drugs were nothing new in Vietnam. The French, we recall, had done a booming trade in opium, importing tons of it each year from the Golden Triangle. French soldiers became addicted as easily as the Vietnamese, whom they robbed for money to buy opium from their own government. During the first Vietnam War, the Deuxieme Bureau, France's version of the CIA, was a major player in the Laos drug trade, using the profits to finance its operations. Before going into battle, the Viet Minh, Viet Cong, and North Vietnamese drugged their troops to stiffen their courage. At Khe Sanh,

225

Marines found drugs on the bodies of NVA soldiers. During the fight for Hue, some walked like zombies into American machine gun fire. When Marines searched their gear, they found packets of heroin, syringes, matches, and bent spoons— just like the "fixings" of junkies back home. Enemy troops used so much marijuana that you smelled it on their clothes during close-in fighting.

Drugs were readily available to American troops, thanks to their allies. South Vietnamese air force planes, gifts from Uncle Sam, landed regularly at secret airstrips in the Golden Triangle, usually in Laos. On the return flight, they dropped their cargoes by parachute or brought them in through Tan Son Nhut, Saigon's airport. Delivery was no problem, since corrupt officials were involved at every level of the drug racket. Corruption reached into the Customs Service, the National Police, the ARVN high command, even into the presidential palace. The chief advisers of President Nguyen Van Thieu and Vice President Nguyen Cao Ky ran the largest drug operations; drug money helped both men further their political careers and stay in power.[6] Americans, too, became involved in this filthy trade. In 1970, an air force major assigned to the U.S. Embassy was arrested at Tan Son Nhut with $8 million worth of heroin aboard his plane.

Drugs were sold openly in the streets and around American bases by local women and children. Marijuana was a "bargain" at ten cents a joint. Heroin cost $2 a capsule, compared to $50 in the States, and was ten times more pure. Early in the war, soldiers were careful about when and where they used drugs. They might use them while off duty, but rarely in the field, where everyone had to be alert. Grunts had rules about drugs, and God help anyone who disobeyed. There were no second chances. More than one fellow fell

226

[6]Alfred W. McCoy, *The Politics of Heroin in Southeast Asia*, pp. 149–223.

with a "sniper's" bullet in his back. At Khe Sanh, a private ignored warnings about smoking marijuana on duty. His platoon mates broke both of his arms. Rough justice, surely, but it saved lives.

Vietnamization changed everything. As the pullout went forward, drug use became a cancer eating away at the American forces. Unlike the enemy, who took drugs to stiffen his courage, the grunt used them to escape the war. By using drugs, you could "desert" without ever leaving camp. Yoshia Chee had a lot to run away from: "What I decided to do was completely obliterate my brain the best way I knew how, which was opium. When I wanted to put away the war, opium was the best thing in the world."[7] Having put away the war, he later found that it was even harder to get rid of his opium habit. Drug use was a no-win situation all the way.

In 1971, a Defense Department study found that 50.9 percent of the troops stationed in Vietnam had used marijuana, 28.5 percent had taken heroin or opium, and 30.8 percent had experimented with LSD. During that same year fewer than 5,000 American soldiers were treated in hospitals for combat wounds; four times that number, 20,529, had to be hospitalized for drug abuse. Worse, drugs caused needless deaths. Army records tell of tipsy guards opening fire and killing fellow Americans. The rule about drug use in the field was also being ignored, with awful results. An infantry company once stopped for a pot party, got high, and was promptly zapped by the Viet Cong.

Racism—white and black—was an equally serious problem. There were actually two Vietnam Wars: in the combat zones and in the rear areas. Blacks and whites got along best when facing a common danger. Newsman Wallace Terry

227

---

[7] Quoted in Maurer, *Strange Ground*, p. 361.

deals with this subject from the viewpoint of the black soldier in his book *Bloods: An Oral History of the Vietnam War by Black Veterans*. The men he interviewed told how the Viet Cong tried to persuade them to turn their weapons on their white comrades. Through radio broadcasts, posters, and pamphlets Viet Cong propaganda told them that whites were their true enemy.

These tactics failed because blacks and whites needed each other for survival. As the saying went, "Same mud, same blood." There was no time to notice the color of a man's skin when you had all you could do just to stay alive. In fact, danger often brought the races closer together than they had ever been at home. Arthur E. Woodley, Jr., a black paratrooper, became friends with a member of the Ku Klux Klan, and ended up saving the Klan member's life. Another black, a combat engineer, rescued a Klan member who had been pinned down by Viet Cong fire. The Klansman later said that incident changed the way he thought about black people. He could never hate them again.[8]

Racism, however, reared its head in the base camps. Black rage, which had exploded after the assassination of Dr. Martin Luther King, Jr., continued to smolder in the military. Black soldiers, feeling like second-class citizens, often kept to themselves. They tried to live in all-black barracks, speaking in "mothertongue," black slang. Blacks went in for Afro haircuts, wore bracelets woven from the bootlaces of dead comrades, greeted each other with special handshakes, and listened to soul music. Racial insults flew thick and fast. Whites, some of them, displayed Confederate flags and called blacks "nigger," "coon," "spade," and "spook." Blacks, some of them, used terms like "whitey," "ofay," "redneck," "honkey," and "the man."

228

---

[8] Terry, *Bloods*, pp. 25, 246.

The year 1971 saw an all-time low
in combat soldiers' morale as racial
tension and drug use increased. Top,
in the midst of an army drug crackdown, two GI's exchange vials of
heroin in the barracks. Bottom, black
soldiers, gathered for the birthday of
the slain civil rights leader Martin
Luther King, Jr., raise their fists in
the Black Power salute.

By 1971, the Americans were fighting among themselves. "Everybody seemed to be at everybody else's throat," recalled helicopter pilot Fred Hickey. "You had to speak softly, mind your own business, sleep with a weapon at all times, and only trust your closest buddies, nobody else."[9] Race riots broke out in several army camps. Soldiers fragged soldiers because they happened to be the "wrong" color. Men on leave ambushed one another in back alleys with guns and knives. In the navy, race riots erupted on the aircraft carriers U.S.S. *Constellation* and *Kitty Hawk*.

Time was running out for America in Vietnam. The nation had known many disasters in its history. Now, for the first time, an entire army was crumbling from within. President Nixon knew it. The Joint Chiefs of Staff knew it. To save the army, it had to be withdrawn from Vietnam without delay. And that meant going to the peace table.

In May 1968, after LBJ's withdrawal from the elections, peace talks began in Paris between Saigon and the NLF. The talks went nowhere. Since Hanoi controlled the NLF, the Saigon representatives would speak to no one but the North Vietnamese. The North Vietnamese, calling the Saigon government Washington's "puppet," would speak only to the Americans. For over a year, both sides did little more than make propaganda speeches and argue over the shape of the table.

President Nixon decided that no real bargaining could take place in public. In August 1969, he wrote Ho Chi Minh to ask for secret talks without either Saigon or the NLF. Uncle Ho agreed a few days before his death on September 3, at the age of seventy-nine. On February 20, 1970, Nixon's national security adviser, Dr. Henry Kissinger, began talks in

230

---

[9]Quoted in Karnow, *Vietnam: A History*, p. 632.

Paris with Hanoi's representative, Le Duc Tho. A smiling, soft-spoken man with white hair, Tho was one of the five top leaders of North Vietnam. As a devoted Communist, he had spent many years in French jails, which only made him more determined to drive out the foreigners. Kissinger would find him a sly, stubborn negotiator, like Kissinger himself.

Both sides jockeyed for position during the negotiations. The United States, said Kissinger, simply wanted a cease-fire followed by the withdrawal of foreign (American and North Vietnamese) troops. Kissinger, who had been briefed on the madman theory, presented himself as a peace-loving man serving a lunatic, President Nixon. If Hanoi was not "sensible," he noted grimly, Nixon might really go off the deep end; the bombing of Cambodia was just an example of how violent he could be. It was a fine performance, but Tho stood firm. He knew that removing northern forces would enable the ARVN to crush the Viet Cong, already weakened by Tet and the Phoenix Program. The only foreigners in Vietnam, he said, smiling, were the Americans. Let them leave and allow the Vietnamese to work things out for themselves. And the best way to do that was by a coalition government in which the NLF shared in ruling South Vietnam. In other words, allow the Viet Cong, backed by the NVA, to take over without firing a shot. Neither Nixon nor Kissinger would buy *that*.

Meanwhile, Vo Nguyen Giap was planning another offensive for 1972. Although it was to be in South Vietnam, its target, as with Tet, was the United States. Once again the nation was in a presidential election year. With only 24,200 American troops remaining, the offensive would force Nixon to choose between two evils. If he reescalated, sent more men to aid the ARVN, he would surely lose the election; the American people were fed up with Vietnam and would not tolerate such an action. But if he did nothing, Vietnamization would be proven a failure. Nixon's only hope would then be to withdraw the remaining troops quickly and beg Hanoi for peace terms.

On March 30, 1972, 120,000 North Vietnamese troops and thousands of Viet Cong swung into action. What became known as the Easter Offensive began with an assault straight across the Demilitarized Zone. NVA troops, freshly equipped with Soviet artillery, rockets, and tanks, took Quang Tri city and sped toward Hue. Elsewhere, they attacked Kontum and Pleiku in the Central Highlands and An Loc, only sixty miles north of Saigon. The South Vietnamese, taken by surprise as usual, fell back in disorder, abandoning a billion dollars worth of equipment.

Hanoi might have overrun the entire country had it not been for Richard Nixon. This man was as unlike LBJ as day is from night. What LBJ considered reckless, Nixon thought courageous. "We have the power to destroy [the enemy's] war-making capacity," he wrote Kissinger soon after the Easter Offensive began. "The only question is whether we have the *will* to use that power. What distinguishes me from Johnson is that I have the *will* in spades."[10]

Nixon meant what he said. Rather than send more troops, he launched Operation Linebacker. Once again American planes appeared in the skies of North Vietnam. Ignoring the danger to Soviet ships, Nixon ordered the mining of Haiphong harbor. Thousands of tons of bombs struck transportation and storage facilities. Among those bombs were the new "smart bombs," electronic marvels guided by laser beams. In the South, hundreds of B-52s and fighter-bombers blunted the enemy advance, allowing the ARVN to rally. The drive on Hue was halted and lost ground was recovered.

232

[10]Richard Nixon, *RN: The Memoirs of Richard Nixon*, p. 607.

By mid-June, the Easter Offensive came to a halt. Never-theless, Hanoi had made its point: Vietnamization was a fail-ure. But Nixon had also made a point: he was willing to renew the air war in a terrifying fashion. Enemy soldiers hated him so much that they named their dogs "Nic-son."

Both sides returned to the peace table. This time they were willing to make concessions. The U.S. dropped its de-mand for the removal of NVA troops, while the North Vietnamese gave up their scheme for a coalition govern-ment. On October 18, 1972, agreement was reached on a four-point settlement. The first point called for a cease-fire in place—that is, fighting would stop and each side would keep the land it occupied when the cease-fire went into ef-fect. Points two and three provided for a U.S. withdrawal within sixty days, followed by the return of American pris-oners held by Hanoi. Finally, a "National Council of Rec-onciliation" would deal with the political settlement at a future date.

President Thieu was stunned by the agreement. It was a betrayal, he snapped, a dirty deal made behind his back and without regard for the South Vietnamese people. The cease-fire in place meant that NVA troops—*invaders*—could stay in their positions. That was insane. The United States had originally gone to war to save his country from the Viet Cong; now it was going to leave the Viet Cong's master in control of the territory it had conquered. Worse, with the Americans gone at last, South Vietnam would be doomed. He, Thieu, would be doomed. Kissinger would have to do better, he insisted.

233

Negotiations resumed after the November election, in which Nixon trounced the Democratic candidate, Senator George McGovern of South Dakota. Yet distrust on both sides made progress impossible. Kissinger explained Thieu's objections, only to have Le Duc Tho brush them aside. Tho countered with his own demands, saying that the original deal was no longer good enough. Talks finally broke down on December 13. The next day, Nixon sent an ultimatum to Hanoi. His message was sharp—no, brutal. Hanoi must return to the table within seventy-two hours—or else. There would be no second warning. When it refused, Nixon ordered Operation Linebacker II to begin.

On the morning of December 18, 1972, the crews of B-52 bombers assembled in their briefing rooms on the island of Guam. Before them on a stage were target maps hidden behind curtains. After a few brief remarks, an officer opened the curtains, revealing the routes to and from the targets. There was a gasp as crewmen realized what their destination would be. Suddenly they began to cheer and whistle. "We're going downtown," they cried, slapping each other on the back. Unlike Rolling Thunder, which had spared Hanoi and Haiphong, Linebacker II would be a maximum effort against the enemy's two largest cities.

Nixon was not as reckless as might be imagined. His orders were to hit only targets of military importance. The rules against harming civilians were far stricter than during Rolling Thunder. Once they began a bomb run, pilots were not to dodge antiaircraft fire even if it was coming at them; anyone who did risked court-martial. They were to go straight in, allowing the bombardier to make sure he was aiming at the right target. If he was unsure of the target, the plane was to turn away and drop its payload into the ocean. In view of what was said later, it is important to remember that civilians were never targets of Linebacker II. Americans actually died in order to avoid unnecessary loss of innocent lives.

B-52 raids began on December 18 and lasted for eleven days, with a day off for Christmas. It was not a merry Christmas. These who had cheered on Guam changed their tune over North Vietnam. Enemy defenses had been strengthened since Rolling Thunder, a fact airmen learned to their regret.

It was hell over Hanoi. During the first week, the B-52s flew into a storm of fire and steel. "If you could take the largest Fourth of July fireworks display and multiply it one million times, you would have an idea of the scene as we approached the final portion of our bomb run," recalled Major Billy Lyons.[11] As they neared their targets, streaks of white light rose into the night sky at three times the speed of sound. SAMs! Exploding antiaircraft shells opened into huge fiery "roses." Planes disintegrated, splashing their fuel in long flaming streaks across the sky.

It did not take the bomber crews long to figure out what was wrong. Linebacker II's planners were sending them on the same approach route each night. The enemy, noticing this, set up his weapons along the route, turning it into a corridor of death. The crews' morale sagged. Back at Guam, "you could smell the fear," an officer noted grimly. Airmen booed their commanders during briefing sessions. Entire crews reported sick, the airman's version of mutiny.

The air force chiefs got the message. From then on they sent planes in from different directions, confusing the enemy defenses. Better still, they ordered attacks on SAM storage sites, destroying approximately 1,300 missiles within a few days. Another 1,100 SAMs were fired at American planes, but nearly all went astray; they were not very accurate and could be thrown off course by the bombers' electronic jamming gear. By Day seven, Hanoi had run out of SAMs. It was wide open. Now you could smell fear in the city below. It was a sweet smell to inmates of the Hanoi Hilton.

235

POWs knew something was up when the air raid sirens

---

[11] Quoted in Karl J. Eschmann, *Linebacker: The Untold Story of the Raids over North Vietnam*, p. 96.

sounded and the first bombs landed. As they listened, they heard not single bombs, but long strings of explosions. And since only one plane carried such payloads, they realized that the war had entered a new stage. Nixon was taking off the gloves and using the Big Ugly Fellows!

Men ran to their cell windows to wave and shout encouragement up at the sky. "I jumped around and yelled with delight," said Captain Frank D. Lewis. "I remember that I cried with pleasure. I didn't feel alone anymore. . . . I prayed for the men, the crews, and the aircraft they flew. To me they had become the hand of God that had reached out to bring me an inner peace and strength with which I could endure this cruel land." A comrade, Colonel John P. Flynn, simply turned to his cellmates and said, "Pack your bags—I don't know when we're going home, but we're going home."[12]

The guards were no longer their usual, bullying selves. Bullies are cowards, and these ran true to form. As the ground shook, some became frozen in fear, weeping uncontrollably. Others headed for the shelters—individual manholes—and pulled the cement lids over their heads; shelters were for guards, not prisoners, a violation of international law. One POW saw a guard, "trembling like a leaf, drop his rifle, and wet his pants."

Antiaircraft crews, however, stuck to their guns. Colonel Bill Conlee, who was there, claims they used the POWs as a shield. Believing that the Americans would not harm the prisoners, they fired their weapons from the roof of the Hanoi Hilton and from the streets just outside its walls.[13] That was a smart move, for B-52 crews knew the prison's location and tried to keep their bombs at a safe distance.

---

[12] Eschmann, *Linebacker*, p. 178, 237.
[13] *Ibid*, p. 178.

Hundreds of NVA truck drivers, trusting the U.S. crews' aim, parked their vehicles on the prison grounds each night.

Nevertheless, the "Christmas bombing" brought cries of outrage from all over the world. A West German newspaper called it "a crime against humanity"; "Genocide," said a newspaper in Buenos Aires, Argentina. Anti-American demonstrations rocked London and Paris. But the harshest criticism came from within the United States itself. Newspapers used terms like "Holocaust," "another Hiroshima," and "carpet bombing" to describe the attacks. *New York Times* columnist Anthony Lewis denounced those who ordered the bombing as "men without humanity"; they were guilty of "mass murder" and "a crime against humanity," he said. Senator George McGovern termed the raids "the most murderous aerial bombardment in the history of the world" and "a policy of mass-murder that's being carried out in the name of the American people." President Nixon, critics agreed, had taken LJB's place as the American Hitler.[14] Dr. Kissinger became "Dr. Killinger."

These charges were exaggerations. They were due in part to Communist propaganda, which showed lurid pictures of bomb damage and dead civilians. But more importantly, Hanoi's claims were accepted over the word of the U.S. government. This was not simply a case of anti-Americanism. The government's lies were coming home to roost. LBJ had lied about not intending to fight in Vietnam and the Tonkin Gulf incident. Nixon had kept the Cambodian bombings secret; when the truth finally came out, people felt violated by their own leaders. The *New York Times* had recently printed the Pentagon Papers, a collection of documents stolen by Dr. Daniel Ellsberg, a former Defense Department employee. These documents exposed the government's errors, lies, half-

237

---

[14] Martin F. Herz, *The Prestige Press and the Christmas Bombing, 1972*, pp. 42–47.

truths, and deceptions on Vietnam going back to the Eisenhower years. Thus, by late 1972, it was easy to disbelieve any claim from the White House.

Yet criticism of the Christmas bombing bore little relation to the truth. Civilians had indeed been killed, but not deliberately. The crowded Kham Thien district of Hanoi was struck when a string of bombs meant for the nearby rail yards went astray. An entire street, the Rue Thu Kien, was flattened when a burning B-52 released its bombs over the city. Bach Mai Hospital, located about a thousand yards from a military airfield, was hit by bombs that fell short, killing eighteen. In addition, there is a good chance that others died when SAMs fell back into the very cities they were supposed to protect.

Hanoi officially gave its losses at 1,318 dead and 1,261 wounded during the whole of Linebacker II; Haiphong reported 305 dead. This is hardly the "mass murder" critics claimed. Actually, the Hanoi-Haiphong death toll was smaller than the number of civilians killed by the North Vietnamese bombardment of An Loc, or the refugees ambushed as they fled Quang Tri city during the Easter Offensive.

Hanoi Mayor Tran Duy Hung tells his own story about the bombings. A group of American antiwar activists happened to be in town during the whole period. When they urged him to claim 10,000 dead, he refused; he could not say such a thing, he explained, because his government's credibility was involved. If the United States later killed so many people, "nobody would believe us."[15] Foreign reporters noted that Hanoi and Haiphong were almost completely undamaged.

The Christmas bombing cost the United States thirty planes, including fifteen B-52s downed by SAMs. Five B-52

---

[15] Karnow, *Vietnam: A History*, p. 653; Herz, *The Prestige Press and the Christmas Bombing*, p. 55.

crewmen were killed in action or died of their wounds; thirty-three became prisoners of war. But they succeeded where Rolling Thunder had failed. In less than two weeks, Hanoi's importation of war supplies dropped by 85 percent. The men of Linebacker II had done their duty. They had struck the enemy's war-making ability while sparing as many civilians as possible. Airmen still wonder whether such an all-out effort could have won the war at the outset, as the generals had suggested to LBJ. No one will ever know the answer.

What we do know is that Linebacker II forced Hanoi back to the peace table. At the same time, it allowed Nixon to bear down on Thieu—hard. Nixon gave him an offer he dared not refuse. America was leaving the war; that was a certainty. If Thieu accepted the cease-fire terms, Nixon promised his full support in the event Hanoi broke its promises. But if Thieu refused, Nixon promised an immediate cutoff of American military and economic aid. Thieu gave in.

On January 23, 1973, Kissinger and Le Duc Tho reached agreement in Paris. Except for minor changes in wording, it was the same one Thieu had rejected in October.

So ended the longest war in American history. The Vietnam War had been a disaster in every way. The Americans lost 45,941 in battle, 10,298 died of accidents and disease, and 300,635 were wounded between January 1961 and January 1973. Except for World War II, Vietnam was America's costliest war—$140 billion—enough to pay for a hundred Great Society programs. Yet these sacrifices paled before those of the Vietnamese. During those same years, 220,357 ARVN were killed in action and 499,026 wounded; the VC/NLF lost 666,000 soldiers. God alone knows how many civilians died as a result of the war; the best estimate is a million North and South.

North Vietnam welcomed the agreement as a triumph equal to that of Dien Bien Phu. The moment it was signed,

239

Radio Hanoi broadcast the full text. For forty-eight hours, it was read and reread, reaching every corner of the land. It was, announcers said, a victory for the Vietnamese people. More, it would enable North Vietnam and the Viet Cong to go on to the final victory.

The agreement did nothing for the Saigon government. With the Americans leaving, and the VC/NVA holding large areas of the countryside, its days were numbered. Of that Henry Kissinger was certain. On January 24, a day after the breakthrough in Paris, he had a conversation with John Ehrlichman, one of the President's top aides. Ehrlichman asked how long South Vietnam could survive under the agreement. "I think that if they're lucky they can hold out for a year and a half," Kissinger admitted.[16] He was off by nine months; Saigon fell in April 1975.

Mr. Nixon's war for peace had brought peace to his own country. We may question whether it was the "peace with honor" he intended. But for the two Vietnams, the Paris agreement was the peace that never was.

---

[16]John Ehrlichman, *Witness to Power: The Nixon Years*, p. 316.

THE PEACE THAT
NEVER WAS

Who among us was not touched,
or even wounded, in some way by the Vietnam War?

—*Jack Wheeler, Veterans Day prayer, 1983*

GIA LAM AIRPORT, HANOI, FEBRUARY 12, 1973. THREE C-141 Starlifter transports stood on the tarmac outside the main terminal, each with a large red cross and the Stars and Stripes painted on its tail. They had come for the first batch of POWs to be released under the cease-fire agreement with North Vietnam.

Moments after the planes arrived, six buses filled with Americans drove up to the boarding area. The passengers wore drab civilian clothes, which their captors had given them during their last night at the Hanoi Hilton. Arranging themselves in columns of two, they listened as a prison official called out names and service numbers. As his name was called, a man would step forward and walk toward an air force colonel waiting to greet him. Among the first to be called was Rodney Knutson, a prisoner for over seven years and the first to be tortured by the Communists. Knutson halted in front of the colonel, snapped a salute, and said: "Sir,

Knutson, Rodney Allen; lieutenant junior grade, United States Navy. Reporting my honorable return as a prisoner of war to the United States."

One by one the men were taken aboard the gleaming airplanes and shown to their seats. When the airplanes were full, the pilots taxied to the starting line. Then they gunned their engines and the planes shot forward. Faster and faster they went, until they left the ground with a thunderous roar. Being airborne was like being reborn. Instantly, the men sprang from their seats. Weeping and laughing, whooping and hollering, they shook hands, slapped each other on the back, and kissed the air force nurses who'd been sent to care for the sick. They were going home.

During the following weeks, 651 POWs returned from Hanoi. It was a strange homecoming, marked by joy and anger. The nation, delighted to have them back, welcomed them with open arms, as heroes. Now, for the first time, it heard from their own lips about the tortures they had endured. These were not pleasant stories, but some of the POWs harshest words were aimed not at their torturers, but at the American antiwar movement. Rodney Knutson and Richard Stratton held press conferences to denounce the antiwar movement for having "aided and abetted the enemy." POWs singled out Jane Fonda for special criticism, because of her broadcasts over Radio Hanoi. She gave no excuses, in response, but continued to attack the POWs, now calling them "hypocrites and liars" for daring to claim that they had been tortured.

242

The grunts who returned, either during the war or after the cease-fire, had a different experience than the POWs. It had been an American custom to welcome troops home in special ways. Towns would declare a holiday, close schools, and have the local drum and bugle corps lead them down Main Street. Cities held colorful parades with millions of

Going home. Top, American POWs cheer as their plane takes off from Gia Lam Airport, Hanoi, in February 1973. It would be almost ten years before their sacrifices would be recognized with the dedication of the Vietnam Memorial in Washington, D.C. (bottom).

cheering, flag-waving civilians lining the route. These homecomings were more than big parties at public expense. They were the nation's way of honoring its fighting men. The United States had sent them to do a job in its name, and for that reason they deserved its respect and gratitude. The job done, the country received them back, as a family receives a loved one after a long, perilous journey.

The Vietnam veteran was unlike any in American history. There were no welcoming ceremonies for him, no parades, or banners, or flowery speeches. He returned as he had gone, not as part of a unit with other hometown boys, but as an individual. Thanks to the jet airplane, he usually came straight from the battlefield, without having time to calm down or reflect on what he had been through. His most vivid memories were still of death and dying; often he left camp aboard a helicopter loaded with the bodies of comrades. Within forty-eight hours, he was in the States, Vietnam's dirt still under his fingernails.

His welcome was individual as well. Families and friends showed their affection, each in their own way. Strangers were also kind—occasionally. He might find, when paying for a meal in a restaurant, that the cashier refused to take his money. A passerby might tap him on the shoulder just to say, "Glad you made it, son." Some native American tribes, true to their warrior traditions, were especially thoughtful. In Oklahoma, tribes honored their veterans at powwows, sang sacred songs, and did the ancient dances for braves returning from the warpath.

244

Others—a great many others—had a sadder homecoming. Vietnam was the first war America had ever lost. It was unpleasant to think about, and people preferred to erase the memory of it from their minds. To mention Vietnam in polite company was considered bad manners. If a veteran forgot himself, people looked away in embarrassment or politely changed the subject. John Kerry, later elected to the U.S. Senate from Massachusetts, was bitter at his reception. "The country didn't give a shit about the guys coming back, or what they'd gone through," he recalled. "The feeling toward them was, 'Stay away—don't contaminate us with whatever you've brought back from Vietnam.' "[1] Such attitudes forced veterans to keep painful memories bottled up inside, where they hurt all the more.

Veterans might also meet open hostility. In one study, a third of the veterans interviewed said they were insulted upon their return.[2] The most moving account is a collection of veterans' letters edited by Bob Greene, a syndicated columnist for the *Chicago Tribune*. Greene had heard all kinds of stories about mistreatment. They were so outlandish, so un-American, that he decided to find the truth for himself. In his column he asked veterans to write him about their homecoming experiences. Greene was amazed at the flood of letters that came from every part of the country. Several hundred of these were printed in a 1989 book, *Homecoming: When the Soldiers Returned from Vietnam*. It is a sad book to read.

Never have American fighting men been so poorly treated by their own people. The reason lies in the remark a woman made to a soldier just off the plane from Vietnam. She walked up to him, gave him a hug and a flower, and "told me it wasn't me, but the government." That woman deserves our admiration for her good sense and decency. She understood that no person should be punished for the sins of another. If we are guilty, it is because we, personally, have done wrong. Unfortunately, there were those who could not separate the war from the warrior. They saw no difference between a "bad" government policy, the Vietnam War, and

245

---

[1] Quoted in Karnow, *Vietnam: A History*, p. 27.
[2] McPherson, *Long Time Passing*, p. 37.

those called upon to carry it out. If the war was bad, then, they reasoned, the warriors must be either fools or criminals—probably both. It is the other side of the argument that all antiwar people were traitors because they denounced the war. Both arguments, of course, are false.

Extremists formed vigilante squads to punish returning veterans. Groups of protesters roamed airports, where they were sure to find men to torment. "Were you part of those who burned, raped, and pillaged for our government?" they might ask. At least there was a way out with that question: a veteran could say no and keep walking, fast. But few got off so easily. Veterans might be met by youngsters waving Viet Cong flags and chanting, "How many babies did you kill today?" The most common insults were "hired killer," "murderer," "baby killer," "baby burner," "rapist," "soldier pig," "war monger," and "mercenary." One soldier was told by an elderly woman, old enough to be his grandmother, that he was an "army asshole." Needless to say, these people knew nothing about the men they insulted, who they were, or what they had done in Vietnam. They only knew that the men were soldiers, and that was crime enough in their eyes.[3]

A few overstepped all bounds of decency. Bob Greene's book contains scores of incidents in which veterans, including army chaplains in uniform, were spat upon. At Chicago's O'Hare Airport, a soldier in a wheelchair was covered with spittle; another, on crutches, was knocked down and jeered by protesters. In San Francisco, wounded men on stretchers were pelted with garbage and soiled diapers while being loaded into ambulances. "Where did you lose your arm? Vietnam?" a college boy challenged an amputee.

246

"Yes," the soldier replied.

---

[3]Bob Greene, *Homecoming: When the Soldiers Returned from Vietnam*, pp. 21, 24, 25, 30, 38, 42, 51, 248.

"Good. Serves you right," was the boy's reply.

The abuse became so vicious that soldiers were advised to change into civilian clothes as soon as they landed from Vietnam. It was dangerous, and humiliating, to be seen in an American uniform in an American airport.[4]

Even the dead were abused. On several occasions, protesters spat and threw mud on coffins draped with the Stars and Stripes.[5] In Williamsburg, Virginia, students demonstrated outside the home of a widow who had lost her only son in Vietnam; they burned the flag and called him a baby killer.[6] I remember a similar incident from my junior high school teaching days. One of my pupils burst into tears during home room. It seems that the day after her brother's funeral, her mother received a telephone call. "Serves him right. Peace now!" the caller said, and hung up. The caller did not give his name. Such people never do.

Veterans found their way back into civilian life as best they could. The vast majority went on to lead satisfying, productive lives. Nevertheless, the road back could be very bumpy. War is not television; you cannot escape it by switching channels. Soldiers carried the battlefield with them, in memory and spirit, long after the guns fell silent. Nightmares jolted them awake, sweating, shaking, sobbing, screaming. Ordinary things triggered flashbacks, buried memories too painful to recall. A schoolteacher, for example, once passed the students' locker room, with its odors of sweat and dirty socks. Instantly he was back in Vietnam, nauseous at the stench of bloody bandages. Walking as quickly as he could, he went to his office, shut the door, and cried for thirty minutes. Unexpected noises—auto backfires, sirens, thunder—sent veterans diving for cover. These reac-

247

---

[4] *Ibid*, pp. 76, 181, 195, 196.
[5] *Ibid,* p. 30; Willenson, *The Bad War*, p. 264.
[6] Greene, *Homecoming*, p. 30.

tions are not unique to Vietnam veterans. In earlier wars, they were known as "shell shock" and "battle fatigue." During the 1960s, a new term was used to describe them: PTSD, post-traumatic stress disorder.

Enemy troops were no different. Those who have interviewed former Viet Cong and North Vietnamese soldiers report the same reactions as Americans. They have nightmares, cry for no apparent reason, and are extremely nervous. Some committed suicide. Bui Tin, a retired NVA colonel and veteran of Dien Bien Phu, has never gotten over the B-52s. "I still have the B-52 problem; I sometimes panic when I hear a loud noise," he said in 1989.[7] Many comrades share his feelings.

The U.S. government could have done more to help veterans. To its eternal shame, these men ranked low on its priority lists. In *Born on the Fourth of July*, Ron Kovic, paralyzed by a bullet wound, describes veterans' hospitals as hellholes of filth, neglect, and despair. America, politicians boasted, was the richest nation on earth. But although they always found money for weapons, there was never enough for veterans' needs. A week before his reelection in 1972, President Nixon vetoed the Veterans Medical Care Expansion Act, calling it too expensive. Keep in mind that each B-52 cost $7,946,780, and that fifteen were lost during Linebacker II, plus the billion dollars worth of equipment abandoned by the ARVN during the Easter Offensive. "Why couldn't a tiny fraction of that money have been spent on us?" veterans asked. Why indeed!

248

Veterans continue to pay the price for the Vietnam War. The herbicide Agent Orange contains dioxin, a chemical known to cause cancer and birth defects in the children of those who have been exposed to it. Cancer rates are higher

---

[7] Quoted in Safer, *Flashbacks,* p. 25.

among those who sprayed the herbicide or took part in SAD operations where it was used. The U.S. government has never admitted that Agent Orange caused their illnesses. In May 1984, a suit brought by 20,000 Vietnam veterans against the herbicide's manufacturers was settled for $180 million without going to trial. This is a step forward, but there is still a long way to go. There is no telling how many South Vietnamese suffer the effects of Agent Orange poisoning. Visitors to the affected areas report unusually large numbers of birth defects in children and farm animals. They are part of the ongoing cost of the Vietnam War.

More than 2,500 American servicemen are listed as missing in action (MIA) in Southeast Asia. In war, it is impossible to account for every MIA. Men are disintegrated in explosions, burned to ashes, drowned and their bodies never recovered. But in Vietnam, 166 MIAs are known to have been captured alive. Their fate is unknown—at least in the United States. Their families are resentful, blaming Washington for not pressing Hanoi for a full explanation. Perhaps they will learn the truth someday. Meanwhile, their agony continues.

Many veterans still feel used, abused, and betrayed. They blame the government for tricking them into fighting a war they were not allowed to win. "Yes, I'm bitter, and probably always will be," says Scott Brooks-Miller of Spokane, Washington. "We were not politicians—most of us couldn't even vote. We simply did what we were asked to do, just as our fathers and grandfathers and all the generations preceding did. But because it was an unpopular war, we took the brunt of the anger of the American people. I was spit on. . . . As far as I'm concerned, let the politicians fight the next war. They aren't getting my sons."[8]

249

---

[8] Quoted in Greene, *Homecoming*, p. 18.

American veterans are not alone, however. Vietnamese from all walks of life feel cheated by those they trusted.

The Communists never intended to live up to the Paris agreement. They had not fought for thirty years to be content with a divided country. The ink had scarcely dried on the paper when Hanoi began to break its promises. General Van Tien Dung, Giap's right-hand man, was ordered to plan the final campaign. Under cover of the cease-fire, Dung paved large sections of the Ho Chi Minh Trail, turning them into all-weather roads for trucks, tanks, and mobile artillery. To keep vehicles rolling at top speed, a fuel pipeline was laid alongside the trail and giant storage tanks were buried at key points along the way. NVA troops poured down the trail day and night; 45,000 came in 1973 alone. The ruins of Khe Sanh were occupied, its airstrip was rebuilt, and SAM missiles were installed.

President Nixon protested these violations but was powerless to stop them. In the spring of 1973, a war-weary Congress banned further combat operations in, over, and off the shores of Indochina. In addition, it made drastic cuts in U.S. aid to South Vietnam. Aid fell from $7 billion in 1972 to $2.3 billion in 1973 and $1 billion in 1974.

President Thieu saw these cuts as a death sentence passed by an unfaithful ally. So did General Dung, who said they forced Thieu to fight "a poor man's war." This was true in part. The ARVN had been trained to fight an American-style war, which meant using massive firepower. Now ammunition had to be rationed to eighty-five bullets per man per month and four shells per cannon per day. Spare parts became scarce, making it necessary to take parts from working equipment. Hundreds of tanks and trucks were scrapped for lack of parts at the very time North Vietnam was receiving increased aid from China and the Soviet Union. Even so,

South Vietnam did not collapse for lack of weapons. It had in reserve enough weapons for several months of heavy fighting. No battle was ever lost for want of ammunition. Its real problems were the old ones of corruption, inefficiency, and low morale.

The Communists were further encouraged by Richard Nixon's fall from power. In the recent election campaign, seven men were arrested during a break-in at Democratic party headquarters in the Watergate Towers in Washington. The burglars, it turned out, were working for the President's reelection committee. Although Nixon had not ordered the break-in, he tried to cover up the involvement of close aides. That is obstruction of justice, a serious crime under American law. People were outraged; for if the president broke the law, then lied about it, there was no one you could trust. Rather than risk an impeachment trial, Nixon resigned the presidency in August 1974. Vice President Gerald Ford immediately took over the highest office in the land.

Hanoi decided that victory lay within its grasp. Its strategy was a two-year program of escalating attacks in 1975, followed by the knockout blow in 1976. This would not be another Tet, a guerrilla action supported by North Vietnamese regulars. Known as the Ho Chi Minh Campaign, it would be a full-scale invasion spearheaded by columns of tanks backed by heavy artillery. The Communist leaders knew they were taking a risk by openly violating the Paris agreement. When pushed to the wall, the Americans might send the B-52s in a final act of desperation. This time, however, North Vietnam had more and better SAMs. American combat troops? They would surely tip the balance in favor of Saigon. But there was no chance of their return. "They won't come back even if we offered them candy," joked Premier Pham Van Dong.[9]

251

---

[9] Quoted in Karnow, *Vietnam: A History*, p. 664.

On January 1, 1975, the NVA broke out of its Cambodian sanctuaries. In less than a week, it overran the border province of Phuoc Long fifty miles north of Saigon. For the first time the NVA took, and held, a South Vietnamese province. Phuoc Long, however, was not the main effort. It was a test to see what President Ford would do. By doing nothing, Ford in effect signaled Hanoi that it could go all the way. It did.

The big blow fell during the second week of March. It landed at Ban Me Thuot, a city in the Central Highlands. Hundreds of NVA tanks literally crushed the defenders, spreading panic in all directions. The panic set off shock waves that reached all the way to President Thieu's headquarters. After a hasty meeting with his generals, Thieu ordered the ARVN to abandon the Central Highlands and regroup around Saigon. It was the most idiotic order given by any commander during the entire Vietnam War. Not in his wildest dreams did General Dung imagine that the enemy would do such a thing. It was a gift from heaven, and he grabbed it with both hands. The projected two-year campaign would be over in less than two months.

Thieu's order opened the floodgates of defeat. The escape route was to be a narrow dirt road winding between steep hills; there was no way the road could handle an army in full retreat. Worse, Thieu's commander in the Central Highlands was a coward surrounded by cowards. Instead of directing the retreat, he and his staff thought only of saving their own skins. They jumped into their helicopters and flew away, abandoning their troops.

Thus began the Convoy of Tears, the most tragic episode of this tragic war. A half million people—soldiers, their families, local villagers—jammed the road. Columns of military vehicles stretched as far as the eye could see. Farmers pulled carts loaded with pots, pans, bedding, and clothing. Women with children clinging to their black pajamas walked beside the carts. General Dung lost no time in ambushing the convoy, killing thousands of civilians. The ambush in turn triggered mass panic, leading to the deaths of many more thousands. Terrified people pushed and shoved against one another, desperate to escape. Survivors told of blood flowing down the road in tiny streams. "I saw old people and babies fall down on the road and tanks and trucks would go over them," a soldier recalled. "Nobody could control anything. No order. The troops were mixed with the dependents and civilians and were trying to take care of all the children and wives. You can't imagine it."[10] Fewer than one in four reached the coast. Most left behind died or fell into Communist hands.

General Dung swept forward, capturing one stronghold after another. The ARVN left vast supply dumps, fleeing in such haste that they failed to destroy valuable equipment. They abandoned the air base at Pleiku without a fight. On the runways, parked wingtip to wingtip, were hundreds of planes and helicopters; the ARVN just handed them to the invader, along with millions of gallons of fuel. Strangely enough, there was little fighting between the opposing armies. According to an American official on the scene, there was no war at all. South Vietnam had decided to quit. An entire society was crumbling before the eyes of an astonished conqueror.

Having seized the Central Highlands, General Dung broke through to the sea, thereby cutting South Vietnam in half. In the meantime, a second wave of attacks rolled across the Demilitarized Zone and the Cambodian border. This was the deathblow. On March 25, the NVA took Hue without firing

253

---

[10] Quoted in Jonathan Schell, *The Real War: The Classic Reporting on the Vietnam War*, p. 51.

a shot. Once again the Communist flag flew above the Citadel. Without pausing, the northerners sped southward along the coastal highway.

Communist troops were in high spirits. Passing a line of refugees, they laughed and asked where they thought they were going. "Wherever you run," they said, "we will be there soon anyway." That was the plain truth. Five days later, they captured Da Nang. Once thought to be impregnable, this symbol of American power easily fell to the invaders. In addition to billions of dollars worth of equipment, the Communists took 100,00 prisoners. They were not gentle with captives. To prevent escapes, they shot ARVN officers through both hands, then tied barbed wire through the wounds. Thousands of military men got away by shooting civilians or pushing them off outward-bound ships and planes.

The Communist drive continued, gaining speed by the hour. Famous places, places watered with American blood, were overrun one after another. Chu Chi, Chu Lai, Nha Trang, Da Lat, and Cam Ranh Bay fell in quick succession. By late April, only Saigon remained, and it was doomed.

Saigon in its final days was "cloud-cuckoo-land," a Vietnamese mythical place where people lived on dreams. Many Saigonese refused to admit that their way of life was finished. The city's discos did a profitable business. Bars and restaurants had never been so crowded. People gathered around dinner tables to discuss the coming miracle. No, the United States would not abandon its ally, they said, trying to convince themselves. At the last moment, when all seemed lost, the bugles would sound; just as in Hollywood cowboy movies. Swarms of Cobra gunships would hover over the enemy spearheads, spitting rockets and machine gun bullets. B-52s would blot out the sky with their awful bombs. U.S. Marines would storm ashore, eager for the fight.

Finally the reality of the situation could not be ignored.

Signs of impending disaster were everywhere. Foreign embassies began to pack up and leave. Rich and powerful South Vietnamese left aboard chartered airliners. On April 21, President Thieu resigned, but vowed to stay on and fight to the end. Lies. Five days later, he loaded fifteen tons of personal baggage aboard an American jet and fled the country. Rumor had it that he also took three tons of South Vietnamese gold. Perhaps he did. Today he lives comfortably in a large house outside London. Vice President Ky promised to lead the defense of the capital. More lies. Ky seized a helicopter and flew it to the deck of the carrier U.S.S. *Midway*. He is now a businessman in California.

Americans managed to rescue 120,000 South Vietnamese during the final days. By plane, helicopter, and boat, they were brought to a naval task force waiting in the South China Sea. In the early hours of April 30, the last Americans were taken out by helicopter from the roof of the U.S. Embassy. The last American casualties were two Marines killed at Tan Son Nhut Airport.

Communist troops burst into Saigon three hours later. Moving swiftly, they occupied key points in the city without opposition. North Vietnamese soldiers stood guard outside the banks. Radio Saigon began broadcasting Viet Cong slogans. NVA tanks smashed through the gate of the presidential palace and a soldier ran toward the flagpole. Hauling down the South Vietnamese colors, he replaced them with the flag of North Vietnam, a gold star on a red background. Later that day, Radio Hanoi announced that Saigon had ceased to exist. From then on it would be called Ho Chi Minh City. That was as it should be, now that Uncle Ho's work was finished. For the first time since the French landed at Da Nang in 1858, Vietnamese controlled every inch of Vietnamese soil.

Citizens of Ho Chi Minh City were surprised upon taking

a closer look at their "liberators." They had expected to see hardened jungle fighters, men larger than life. Instead, they saw scrawny farm boys, country bumpkins in the big city. Communist propaganda had told the soldiers that Saigon was poor, compared to Hanoi. In Hanoi, a portable radio was a major possession, owning a refrigerator or television the dream of a lifetime. Now they found themselves in a great sprawling bazaar. Peddlers crowded the streets, offering their wares. Shops were filled with watches, radios, cameras, refrigerators, televisions, and clothing. Unlike Hanoi, where everything was rationed, shopkeepers actually tried to talk them into buying. The troops did, indeed, buy—practical easy-to-carry things like clothing, watches, and dolls for their children.

Troops assigned to private homes never imagined such places could exist. Knowing nothing of modern conveniences, they were always being surprised. Beds. Ordinary people slept in beds, not on straw mats spread on the bare ground. Some things, however, were positively dangerous. A favorite Saigon story told how a soldier stepped into a shower and turned on the hot water. He leapt out, screaming, "*My nguy!*" ("American puppet!"), certain that he had been booby-trapped. Toilets held their own surprises. Although a bit too low, these gleaming containers of clean water could only be for washing vegetables, they thought. But after a careful scrubbing, there would be a roar and the vegetables vanished in a whirlpool. Toilets, too, were *My nguy.*

These surprises, however, were only the beginning. A victory parade was held in Ho Chi Minh City on May 7, the twenty-first anniversary of the French defeat at Dien Bien Phu. Hour after hour, the NVA marched past the reviewing stand. Troops carried enlarged pictures of Uncle Ho, along with banners reading NOTHING IS MORE PRECIOUS THAN INDEPENDENCE AND LIBERTY, LONG LIVE CHAIRMAN HO, and UNITY, UNITY, GREAT UNITY. But as the hours passed, NLF officials, who had led the movement in the South for years, grew restless. The Viet Cong was nowhere to be seen. Only at the end did a few guerrilla units appear under the flag of North Vietnam. When asked about the rest of the Viet Cong, General Dung said it had become part of the NVA. At that moment the officials knew they had been betrayed.

The NLF program, we recall, had spoken about democratic principles. Civil liberties were to be guaranteed, enemies forgiven, and Vietnam unified by peaceful means according to the wishes of the people. Yet these principles were merely a scrap of paper to Hanoi. They were a tool, just as the NLF itself was a tool, in the struggle for power. The Americans had always claimed that the conflict was a northern invasion, not a southern civil war. Finally, when it was too late, the NLF realized that it had been Hanoi's puppet all along. Having outlived its usefulness, the NLF was abolished at Hanoi's command. The North Vietnamese, backed by NVA bayonets, took over and ran South Vietnam as a conquered territory. Southerners who had fought for independence were filled with disgust. Truong Nhu Tang, who we met earlier, was bitter because "the lives so many gave to create a new nation are now no more than ashes cast aside."[11]

The conquerors made a mockery of the NLF's program. In place of democracy, South Vietnam fell under the dictatorship ruled from Hanoi. The government demanded that everyone think alike, act alike, and be alike in every way — that is, the Communist way. Nothing was safe from government interference. Political parties, except the Communist, were abolished. Freedom of the press, which had increased during the last years of President Thieu, vanished overnight.

257

---

[11] Truong Nhu Tang, *A Viet Cong Memoir*, p. 310.

Newspapers, radio, films, and music fell under tight government control. Bookstores were closed and police sent to search bookshelves in private homes. Any book that did not meet Communist approval was burned. And any person who did not look "proper" ran afoul of the Patriotic Youth, squads of teenagers with red armbands. Stationing themselves on street corners, they stopped anyone who offended their sense of morality. Men had to button their shirt collars. Women wearing lipstick had it smeared over their faces. High heels were torn off shoes. Miniskirts were condemned as "counterrevolutionary provocations."

Religion felt the heavy hand of Communist oppression. Government approval was required for all forms of religious activity: worship, gatherings, preaching, education, charities. Buddhists came to think of Ngo Dinh Diem as gentle alongside the Communist thugs who ruled their lives. Thousands of Buddhist schools, orphanages, day care centers, and newspapers were closed by government order. Buddhist property was seized and statues of Buddha were smashed to pieces. Monks were forbidden to travel or preach; those who disobeyed— and hundreds did—were arrested. Monks who had led the opposition to Ngo Dinh Diem found themselves behind bars.

As in the days of Diem, Buddhist monks and nuns gave their lives in protest. On November 2, 1975, twelve monks and nuns burned themselves to death in a temple. This time, of course, television cameras did not record the event. The Communists tried to cover it up, claiming that the leader was a sex criminal who murdered the others, set fire to the temple, and then killed himself.[12] But their comrades managed to get the truth to the outside world.

The secret police were everywhere. Nothing was too

---

[12] Ginetta Sagan and Stephen Denney, *Violations of Human Rights in the Socialist Republic of Vietnam, April 30, 1970–April 30, 1983*, pp. 10–12.

small, too insignificant, to escape their notice. Family gatherings, such as weddings and funerals, required a police permit and had to be attended by a policeman. Any meeting of more than three persons outside the family was viewed with suspicion. Those involved had to report on who attended, where they came from, and what was said. If the reports differed, all were arrested. Demonstrations, of course, were forbidden, unless sponsored by the government.

Every "crime" was serious, punishment swift and harsh. Having forbidden books, for example, could ruin your life. On June 25, 1981, a man named Bui Dinh Ha was tried in Ho Chi Minh City for lending "reactionary and decadent books." The judge sentenced him to prison for life at hard labor.[13] Humor carried a similar penalty. Thanh Viet, one of the South's favorite comedians, was jailed for "spreading counterrevolutionary slogans"—that is, telling unapproved jokes. Not even former Viet Cong were safe. Many were jailed, not for any crime, but because, as non-Communists, they might be disloyal. When their wives protested, they too were arrested and never seen again.

Everyone connected with the old order was considered untrustworthy and therefore to be eliminated. Rather than cause panic by arresting so many people at once, the Communists used a typical tyrant's lie. Everything that was to happen, they promised, was for the victim's own benefit. Soon after the fall of Saigon, former government officials, military officers, ARVN soldiers, policemen, schoolteachers, health workers, writers, journalists, and religious leaders were told to report for "reeducation." They would not be punished, the order said, but sent away for a few weeks to learn about their mistakes and study communism. No fewer than one million people reported for reeducation. Some of them are still "learning."

259

---

[13] *Ibid*, p. 21.

Upon reporting, they were sent to isolated camps under armed guard. These little corners of hell had barbed wire fences, floodlights, and watchtowers with machine gun posts. Inmates lived in long, low barracks of rough wood roofed with straw or tin. They slept on wooden shelves arranged in two levels, one above the other. A shelf held as many people as could fit on it. They lay on their backs, in filthy rags, without room to move or turn over.

Part of the camp day was indeed given to education: inmates memorized lectures on communism and gave them back word for word. Most of the time, however, was spent clearing mines by hand (illegal under international law), chopping down trees, digging wells, and building more camps. Payment was in food, and those who failed to do their allotted work starved to death. Conditions were so harsh that the toughest jailbirds broke down. Nguyen Van Tang, who had spent much of his life in French and South Vietnamese prisons, told a fellow inmate: "My dream is not to be released, it is not to see my family. My dream is that I could be back in a French prison thirty years ago."[14] Yet there were few escapes. The hostage system that had kept the Viet Cong from deserting now kept the inmates in line; if they weren't on their best behavior, they knew their wives and children would be arrested and "reeducated."

Vietnam after unification was an embittered, poverty-stricken land. Its Communist government had broken every promise it had ever made about democracy and civil liberties. Pham Xuan An, the former *Time* correspondent and North Vietnamese spy, is disillusioned by the fate of his country. In 1989, he told an American visitor: "All that talk of liberation twenty, thirty, forty years ago, all the plotting and all the

[14] Doan Van Toai, "A Lament for Vietnam," *The New York Times Magazine*, March 29, 1981.

bodies produced this impoverished, broken-down country."[15] No one had gained from the war, least of all the Vietnamese people.

The Communists' record in economics is a scandal. Private businesses—shops, banks, factories—were taken over by the state, causing shortages of vital goods. Peasants were forced to join state-run cooperatives, which bought their produce at the lowest prices; many killed their farm animals rather than sell them at giveaway prices. Each year thousands of desperate Vietnamese flee their homeland in small boats. Many have drowned. Many others have been killed by pirates who roam the South China Sea. Still the boat people keep coming, driven by the hope of a better life. Anything, they imagine, must be better than their own country. Matters have not been helped by the American-led boycott of trade and investment in Vietnam. Except for Communist officials and the army, no one is prosperous in today's Vietnam. The army, 1.2 million strong (as of 1989), is the world's fourth largest, after those of the Soviet Union, China, and the United States.

Indochina was not to enjoy peace after 1975. In the same week as the NVA took Saigon, the Khmer Rouge overthrew the Cambodian government. Led by a fanatic named Pol Pot, it committed genocide against its fellow countrymen. Cambodia, renamed Democratic Kampuchea, became the land of the "killing fields."

Pol Pot wanted to build the perfect Communist society. This meant returning to "Year Zero," turning back the clock and starting from scratch. On his orders, Cambodia's cities were emptied at gunpoint and their inhabitants herded into slave labor camps deep in the jungle. The Khmer Rouge made Viet Cong terrorists look like Sunday school boys.

261

---

[15] Safer, *Flashbacks*, p. 183.

Anyone with an education was considered corrupt and killed; if you wore eyeglasses, you were instantly shot, for that proved you could read. In less than three years, 2 million out of Cambodia's 7 million people were murdered, tortured, starved, or worked to death. Thousands of others died in a senseless war with Vietnam.

Cambodia and Vietnam are traditional enemies. In the days of the emperors, Vietnamese armies carved large chunks of territory out of eastern Cambodia; Saigon was originally the Cambodian fishing village of Prey Nokor. The Khmer Rouge, determined to regain those territories, raided Vietnamese border villages. Vietnamese living in Cambodia were massacred in droves; none were spared, even women and children. On December 25, 1978, Vietnam retaliated with a full-scale invasion. The Khmer Rouge was driven back to the jungle and a puppet government set up in Phnom Penh, the capital. In the years that followed, Cambodia became Vietnam's Vietnam—a war between a foreign army and bands of guerrillas.

The Cambodian invasion affected Vietnam's relations with China. As we have seen, Hanoi had received aid from both China and the Soviet Union during the Vietnam War. At the same time, however, the Communist giants began to quarrel between themselves. Once the war ended, Hanoi had to take sides. The choice was easy, given Vietnam's age-old fear of its northern neighbor. "When the danger from the south is averted," says an ancient proverb, "the threat from the north is twice as great." In return for aid, Vietnam gave the Soviets Cam Ranh Bay as a naval base.

The Chinese, angry at the Soviet-Vietnamese alliance, sent weapons to the Khmer Rouge. Hanoi, angry at this "betrayal," started persecuting Vietnamese of Chinese heritage. Chinese-owned businesses were seized by the government. Chinese were arrested, beaten, and driven across the border

The legacy of war, 1979. Top, Vietnamese "boat people" attempt the often fatal trip across the sea. Bottom, two young Khmer Rouge, no more than twelve years old, prepare to fight back against the Vietnamese. Pol Pot's regime and the Vietnamese invasion had so devastated Cambodia that children were often the only ones left to fight.

in large numbers. In February 1979, China decided "to teach Vietnam a lesson" and invaded its northern provinces. Vietnam's battle-tested forces held fast and the Chinese withdrew after three weeks of savage fighting. Suddenly the notion of a unified Communist enemy vanished in gun smoke, and with it the domino theory.

Vietnam had come full circle. Once again it was a united nation, fearing China and driven by its ambitions in Cambodia. As of today, no one can tell how the story will end.

These events were scarcely noticed in the United States. There was little press coverage of them, and none of the antiwar groups, so outspoken during the war, chose to get involved. The ordeal in Indochina was over and best forgotten, they felt.

Yet there were those who could not forget—would not forget. Among them was Ginetta Sagan, director of Humanitas, an international human rights organization based in California. Sagan began to gather information, much of it from boat people living in Thailand and other Southeast Asian countries. What she learned made her launch a one-woman crusade. Vietnam's human rights record was an outrage, the Cambodian holocaust a stain on humanity. Somehow Americans had to be made to think about these horrors, to demand that things be set right.

Sagan joined forces with Joan Baez, a popular folksinger. Baez was a pacifist, a friend of Dr. Martin Luther King, Jr., and a human rights activist. During the war, she had visited Hanoi, not to support the Communists, but to protest the cruelty of all wars. In 1979, the two women decided to gather signatures for a protest letter to Vietnam. The reaction of former leaders of the antiwar movement stunned Baez. Efforts were made to stop her. Callers phoned at all hours of the night to "reason" with her. Friends *ordered* her to get her name off the letter.

The letter, signed by seventy-eight prominent individuals, was printed in the *New York Times* of May 30, 1979. In it, the Vietnamese government was condemned for the reeducation camps and other human rights abuses. Overnight, Joan Baez became an outcast for speaking the truth. Former comrades in the antiwar movement called her "a CIA rat," accusing her of "betraying" the Vietnamese. Why they behaved as they did is a matter between themselves and their own consciences. Nevertheless, this incident was an eyeopener. If it proved anything, it was that the passions of the 1960s had still not cooled. America, deep down, was as divided as ever about Vietnam.

Veterans also carried the 1960s with them, only in a different way. Resentment over their homecoming lingered. They usually did not speak of it, but it was there, just below the surface.

What finally brought it into the open was the hostages taken at the U.S. Embassy in Tehran, Iran. In January 1981, the Iranians released fifty-two hostages after more than a year of captivity. The nation went wild with joy. The news media were filled with stories such as "Our Brave Captives" and "Welcome Home, Heroes." Reporters followed them, wanting to know every detail of their captivity. How did it feel to be locked up? Did they miss their families? What did they eat? New York gave them a ticker-tape parade down lower Broadway, the famed "Canyon of Heroes." Hostages received gold medals, automobiles, and lifetime baseball tickets.

Suddenly, veterans saw the contrast between the hostages' return and the silence and hostility that had greeted them. The dam penning in their feelings burst, releasing a flood of anger, pain, and frustration. At long last veterans broke their silence. They held up WHAT ABOUT AGENT ORANGE? and WHAT ABOUT US? signs during parades for the hostages. Not that they had anything against the hostages; they deserved recognition for what they had been through. But so did the veterans, the forgotten men.

A group of veterans decided to turn resentment to a good purpose. The American people *would not* be allowed to forget. They *would* remember, and honor, those who had done their duty in Vietnam. And from remembrance and honor would come healing and reconciliation.

The veterans planned to build a memorial to the dead in Washington. They collected money, explaining what they hoped to do and why it was so necessary. Whatever their feelings about the war, people from all walks of life supported the project. Senator George McGovern gave it his blessing, as did General Westmoreland. Congress donated the land, a site on the Mall between the Lincoln Memorial and the Washington Monument.

On November 11, 1982—Veterans Day—the Vietnam Veterans Memorial was dedicated and opened to the public. It is not the traditional war memorial decked with flags and statues of soldiers in heroic poses; there is a statue set to one side, but it shows only three ordinary grunts in combat dress. The memorial is a low wall built of panels of polished black granite rising from the earth for a distance of 492 feet. Into it are carved the names of the fallen, listed chronologically, beginning with the first casualties in 1959 and ending with the last in 1975. It is the only war memorial that involves the visitor in a personal way. When standing in front of it, you see your own image reflected in the names of the fallen.

The memorial has become a place of pilgrimage, almost a sacred shrine. Families take rubbings of the names, think a bit, cry a bit, and finally come to terms with the past. Veterans point to names and remind little children—their children— that, but for that soldier, their father would not be alive today. Others search and search, then walk away happy at

Lest we forget. On a rainy Veterans Day, a wheelchair-bound veteran breaks down before the Vietnam Memorial. Behind the wall is a flag made of more than fifty-eight thousand flowers, one for each American who died in the war.

not finding a name. Nor could I find the name of my former ninth grade pupil, the Green Beret corporal. He survived.

On my visit I did find something I have cherished ever since. It was an index card wedged into the space between two of the panels. A single sentence was typed on the card, and I copied it into my notebook: "In our sleep painful memories fall drop by drop upon the heart until, in our own despair, against our will, comes wisdom, through the awful grace of God." Only later did I learn that it was a quotation from Aeschylus, an ancient Greek writer of tragedies.

In Aeschylus' words lies the essence of our story. He understood that tragedy can bring wisdom, if only we heed its lessons. The Vietnam War was a tragedy for all concerned. Although its rights and wrongs will be debated for generations to come, its lessons are clear. Vietnam teaches us that war is a serious matter and should only be undertaken for the most serious reasons. Those reasons, simply put, are the security and well-being of the United States. It further teaches that, if we do fight, we must win, because there are no rewards for losers. It is wrong to send people into battle without giving them the nation's moral as well as material support.

The Vietnam tragedy offers yet another lesson—perhaps the most important one of all. It tells us something about ourselves as a people. America is a nation built upon law, not personal whim. The Constitution, the supreme law of the land, defines what is necessary for war. War must be the decision of the whole people, united behind its leaders. No leader, however well meaning, has the right to take us into war without our informed consent. Anything less is a betrayal of the principles upon which this nation was founded. If a war cannot be justified to the people who must fight it, then it should not be fought at all. That is justice. That is democracy. That is what America is all about.

SOME MORE BOOKS

The number of books on the Vietnam War is vast and growing steadily. Here are a few of the ones I found most helpful.

Baker, Mark. *Nam: The Vietnam War in the Words of the Men and Women Who Fought There.* New York: Berkley, 1983.

Beesley, Stanley W. *Vietnam: The Heartland Remembers.* New York: Berkley, 1989.

Blakey, Scott. *Prisoner of War: The Survival of Commander Richard A. Stratton.* Garden City, NY: Anchor Books, 1978.

Broughton, Jack A. *Thud Ridge.* New York: Bantam Books, 1985.

Caputo, Philip. *A Rumor of War.* New York: Holt, Rinehart and Winston, 1977.

Chanda, Nayan. *Brother Enemy: The War After the War.* New York: Collier Books, 1986. A history of Indochina after the fall of Saigon.

Chanoff, David, & Doan Van Toai. *Portrait of the Enemy.* New York: Random House, 1986.

——*The Vietnamese Gulag.* New York: Simon & Schuster, 1986.

Cortright, David. *Soldiers in Revolt: The American Military Today.* Garden City, NY: Doubleday, 1975.

Davidson, General Phillip B. *Vietnam at War: The History, 1946–1974.* Novato, CA: Presidio, 1988.

DeBenedetti, Charles. *An American Ordeal: The Antiwar Movement of the Vietnam Era.* Syracuse: Syracuse University Press, 1990.

Denton, Jeremiah A., Jr. *When Hell Was in Session.* New York: Reader's Digest, 1976.

Edelman, Bernard, ed. *Dear America: Letters Home from Vietnam.* New York: Norton, 1985.

Eschmann, Karl J. *Linebacker: The Untold Story of the Air Raids over North Vietnam.* New York: Ivy Books, 1989.

Fall, Bernard B. *Hell in a Very Small Place.* New York: Lippincott, 1967. This is the classic account of Dien Bien Phu and should not be missed.

Gibson, James William. *The Perfect War: Technowar in Vietnam.* Boston: Atlantic Monthly Press, 1986.

Goldman, Peter, and Tony Fuller. *Charlie Company: What Vietnam Did to Us.* New York: Morrow, 1983.

Greene, Bob. *Homecoming: When the Soldiers Returned from Vietnam.* New York: Putnam, 1989.

Halberstam, David. *Ho.* New York: Knopf, 1987.

Hammel, Eric. *Khe Sanh, Siege in the Clouds: An Oral History.* New York: Crown, 1989.

Herr, Michael. *Dispatches.* New York: Knopf, 1978.

Hersh, Seymour M. *My Lai 4: A Report on the Massacre and its Aftermath.* New York: Random House, 1970.

Herz, Martin M. *The Prestige Press and the Christmas Bombing, 1972.* Washington, D. C.: Ethics and Public Policy Center, 1980.

Ho Chi Minh. *Ho Chi Minh On Revolution: Selected Writings, 1920–1966.* Bernard Fall, ed. New York: Praeger, 1967.

Hubbell, John. G. *P.O.W.: A Definitive History of the American Prisoner-of-War Experience in Vietnam, 1964–1974.* New York: Reader's Digest, 1976. This is *the* book on the subject.

Karnow, Stanley. *Vietnam: A History.* New York: Viking, 1983.

Kearns, Doris. *Lyndon Johnson and the American Dream.* New York: Harper Collins, 1976.

Kovic, Ron. *Born on the Fourth of July.* New York: Pocket Books, 1977.

Lacouture, Jean. *Ho Chi Minh: A Political Biography.* New York: Random House, 1968.

Lewy, Guenter. *America in Vietnam.* New York: Oxford University Press, 1978.

Lowry, Timothy S. *And Brave Men, Too.* New York: Crown, 1985.

Maclear, Michael. *The Ten Thousand Day War: Vietnam, 1945–1975.* New York: St. Martin's Press, 1981.

McCoy, Alfred W. *The Politics of Heroin in Southeast Asia.* New York: Harper Collins, 1972.

McQuaid, Kim. *The Anxious Years: America in the Vietnam-Watergate Era.* New York: Basic Books, 1989.

Mangold, Tom, & John Penycate. *The Tunnels of Cu Chi.* New York: Random House, 1985.

Marshall, Kathryn. *In the Combat Zone: An Oral History of American Women in Vietnam, 1966–1975.* Boston: Little, Brown, 1987.

Mason, Robert. *Chickenhawk.* New York: Viking, 1983.

Maurer, Harry. *Strange Ground: Americans in Vietnam, 1945–1975: An Oral History.* New York: Holt, 1989. The best book of its kind; don't miss it.

Nolan, Keith William. *The Battle for Hue.* Novato, CA: Presidio Press, 1987.

O'Brien, Tim. *If I Die in the Combat Zone.* New York: Delacorte, 1973. A grunt's-eye view of the war.

O'Neill, Robert J. *General Giap: Politician and Strategist.* New York: Praeger, 1969.

Oberdorfer, Don. *Tet!* Garden City, NY: Doubleday, 1971.

Parmet, Herbert S. *Richard Nixon and His America.* Boston: Little, Brown, 1990.

Pike, Douglas. *Viet Cong: The Organization and Techniques of the National Liberation Front of South Vietnam.* Cambridge, MA: M.I.T. Press, 1966.

——*The Viet Cong Strategy of Terror.* Saigon: U.S. Embassy, 1970.

Pisor, Robert. *The End of the Line: The Siege of Khe Sanh.* New York: Norton, 1982.

Sack, John. *Lieutenant Calley: His Own Story.* New York: Viking, 1971.

Safer, Morley. *Flashbacks: On Returning to Vietnam.* New York: Random House, 1990.

Sagan, Ginetta, & Stephen Denney. *Violations of Human Rights in the Socialist Republic of Vietnam, April 30, 1970–April 30, 1983.* Atherton, CA: Aurora Foundation, 1983.

Santoli, Al. *Everything We Had: An Oral History of the Vietnam War by Thirty-Three American Soldiers Who Fought It.* New York: Random House, 1981.

——*To Bear Any Burden: The Vietnam War and Its Aftermath in the Words of Americans and Southeast Asians.* New York: Dutton, 1985.

Scholl-Latour, Peter. *Death in the Ricefields: An Eyewitness Account of Vietnam's Three Wars, 1945–1979.* New York: St. Martin's Press, 1979.

Stanton, Shelby L. *The Rise and Fall of an American Army: U.S. Ground Forces in Vietnam, 1965–1973.* Novato, CA: Presidio Pres, 1985.

Summers, Col. Harry G., Jr. *On Strategy: A Critical Analysis of the Vietnam War.* Novato, CA: Presidio Press, 1982.

——*Vietnam War Almanac.* New York: Facts-on-File, 1985. A basic work of reference.

Taylor, Clyde, ed. *Vietnam and Black America: An Anthology of Protest and Resistance.* Garden City, NY: Anchor Books, 1973.

Terry, Wallace. *Bloods: An Oral History of the Vietnam War by Black Veterans,* New York: Random House, 1984.

Thompson, James Clay. *Rolling Thunder.* Chapel Hill, NC: University of North Carolina Press, 1980.

Truong Nhu Tang. *A Viet Cong Memoir.* New York: Vintage, 1985.

Turley, William S. *The Second Indochina War.* New York: Mentor, 1986.

Unger, Irwin, & Debi Unger. *Turning Point: 1968.* New York: Scribner, 1988.

Van Dyke, Jon M. *North Vietnam's Strategy for Survival.* Palo Alto, CA: Pacific Books, 1972.

Viorst, Milton. *Fire in the Streets: America in the 1960s.* New York: Simon & Schuster, 1979.

Willenson, Kim. *The Bad War: An Oral History of the Vietnam War.* New York: New American Library, 1987.

Zaffiri, Samuel. *Hamburger Hill, May 11–20, 1969.* Novato, CA: Presidio Press, 1988.

Zaroulis, Nancy & Gerald Sullivan. *Who Spoke Up? American Protest Against the War in Vietnam, 1963–1975.* Garden City, N.Y.: Doubleday, 1984.

INDEX

275